Readers Love An

Love Comes Home

"…it was so well written; you don't want the story to end."
—Crystal's Many Reviewers

"Overall, this is another outstanding book by Andrew Grey. I smiled a lot. I got misty-eyed more than once. In the end, I fell in love with yet another group of outstanding characters."
—On Top Down Under Reviews

"In typical Andrew Grey fashion, we visit real people in real settings who have real life things happen to them."
—Top2Bottom Reviews

Inside Out

"I promise you don't want to miss this one."
—The Novel Approach

"I adore Andrew Grey and once again he impressed me by writing a great story."
—Gay List Book Reviews

"The chemistry is off the hook and the storyline is intriguing."
—MM Good Book Reviews

"Inside Out is funny, sexy and a must have for any fan of romance!"
—Guilty Indulgence Book Reviews

"This was a fun, sexy, and very sweet story with some seriously hot scenes. Go, Andrew!"
—Rainbow Book Reviews

Readers Love ANDREW GREY

A Daring Ride

"All the things we've come to love from Grey are there in the print. An emotional, engrossing, and sexy ride is what's in store with this latest work from one of the best authors in the genre."

—MM Good Book Reviews

"I quickly got sucked in by the story and the characters. There really is so much substance in the plot and the people… he doesn't need a lot of extra language to pull you in."

—Mrs. Condit & Friends Read Books

A Heart Without Borders

"I felt like I was right there with the characters, feeling the heat, the desperation and the total devastation right along with them. There is no doubt in my mind that this book will stay with me for a long time."

—The Novel Approach

"In true Andrew Grey fashion, this book delivers not only a romance but a powerful lesson on the courage, hope and optimism of people in a country devastated by disaster and poverty."

—Hearts on Fire Reviews

Stranded

"A great story of how time passes and people allow their relationship to settle into routine and they lose their appreciation for their partner. This doesn't mean that they are no longer deeply in love, sometimes they just need a reminder."

—Gay List Book Reviews

"*Stranded* is an amazing combination between an intense thriller-like stalker story, a sizzling romance, and a character study which, through tension and drama, brings out the worst and the best in both main characters."

—Rainbow Book Reviews

By ANDREW GREY

Accompanied by a Waltz
Copping a Sweetest Day Feel
Crossing Divides
Cruise for Christmas
Dominant Chord
Dutch Treat
A Heart Without Borders
In Search of a Story
Inside Out • Upside Down
A Lion in Tails
Mariah the Christmas Moose
North to the Future
One Good Deed
A Present in Swaddling Clothes
Shared Revelations
Simple Gifts
Snowbound in Nowhere
Stranded • Taken
Three Fates (Anthology)
To Have, Hold, and Let Go
Whipped Cream
Work Me Out (Anthology)

ART SERIES
Legal Artistry • Artistic Appeal • Artistic Pursuits • Legal Tender

BOTTLED UP STORIES
The Best Revenge • Bottled Up • Uncorked • An Unexpected Vintage

THE BULLRIDERS
A Wild Ride • A Daring Ride • A Courageous Ride

CHEMISTRY SERIES
Organic Chemistry • Biochemistry • Electrochemistry

FIRE SERIES
Redemption by Fire • Strengthened by Fire • Burnished by Fire • Heat Under Fire

Published by DREAMSPINNER PRESS
http://www.dreamspinnerpress.com

Published by DREAMSPINNER PRESS
http://www.dreamspinnerpress.com

LOVE COMES Around

ANDREW GREY

Dreamspinner Press

Published by
DREAMSPINNER PRESS

5032 Capital Circle SW, Suite 2, PMB# 279, Tallahassee, FL 32305-7886 USA
http://www.dreamspinnerpress.com/

Love Comes Around
© 2014 Andrew Grey.

Cover Art
© 2014 L.C. Chase.
www.lcchase.com
Cover content is for illustrative purposes only and any person depicted on the cover is a model.

ISBN: 978-1-63216-109-3
Digital ISBN: 978-1-63216-110-9
Library of Congress Control Number: 2014944173
First Edition September 2014

Printed in the United States of America
∞
This paper meets the requirements of
ANSI/NISO Z39.48-1992 (Permanence of Paper).

To Jane, Lynn, Julianne, Anne, Polly, Kat, Shannon, Rose, and all the other incredible people on Dreamspinner's editorial staff. You're all amazing, and I hope Love Comes Around to find you.

CHAPTER
One

CONNOR BOUNCED up the stairs of the Pleasanton Home for Children and pulled open the door. He knew that "home" was a more modern way of saying orphanage, and whenever he got a call to come here and make repairs, he always rushed over and made sure he had extra time to spend with the kids. Inside, he took a few steps into the hall, and the door thunked closed ominously behind him. That sound always struck him as having a note of finality about it, as if the door only worked one way and then there was no turning back.

"Connor O'Malley," the woman behind the counter said as she looked up from her computer. "They told me you'd be in today. The railing on the main staircase is loose, and we're afraid one of the kids might get hurt. This old place is held together with duct tape, super glue, and whatever magic you seem to be able to work."

"Hey, Maggie," he said with a smile. "I'll take a look and then go get what I need." He went toward the back and to the main staircase. The boys in particular loved to slide down the old thing. Connor had to admit it was a great banister for sliding, and if he were younger, he'd give it a try. He climbed the stairs, testing the banister as he went. He found the weak spot and searched for the source. Two spindles in a row had given up the ghost. He looked for more and found nothing else.

"How bad is it?" Maggie asked when he approached the desk.

"Just two spindles. I'll have to go back to the shop and fabricate them for you. I don't have anything to match. But I'll get some temporary replacements and have them in place within the hour." He smiled at her and she returned it. Then her phone rang. Connor headed toward the door, letting her answer it. He had things to get done and his to-do list kept getting longer. He got in his truck and drove to the hardware store, where he picked out two standard turned spindles he could use to shore up the banister. He also bought the wood he would need for the final ones he'd fabricate, along with the other items he needed for projects he had underway back at the shop.

He parked in front of the home and carried the supplies he needed inside. He waved at Maggie as he passed the desk and headed right to the stairs. It didn't take him long before he had the old spindles out and had placed the temporary ones. He'd use the ones he'd removed as the models for the new ones. Then he cleaned up everything and began carrying his tools back out to his truck. "Why is it so quiet?"

Maggie smiled. "We don't have many kids right now, thank God." She was a kind, sweet soul. Connor remembered her from high school. She was smart and always willing to help others, no matter what. Maybe that was why she was working here. "But it never stays that way."

The front doors opened and a man strode in, pushing a child in a wheelchair. "Hey, Jerry. Honey, did you have a good time?" she asked, directing her question to the boy in the chair.

"You bet," he answered brightly, his eyes huge. When he smiled, it was a little lopsided, and his teeth were extremely crooked, but Connor couldn't help but see the joy and sparkle in the kid's eyes.

"Why don't you go on down to your room, and I'll be in to see how you're doing in a few minutes. I need to talk with Mr. Harrington." Maggie smiled at him, and Jerry headed down the hall before turning around in his chair.

"Thank you, Mr. Harrington. I had a great time."

Connor watched as Jerry disappeared down the hall. Then he carried his tools out to the truck and stowed them in the back. He knew the man inside from somewhere, but he just couldn't place him. He pushed it out of his mind and went back inside for the rest of his things. He smiled at Maggie, who was still talking to the man in the perfectly pressed pants and shirt. He looked like something out of a magazine, with his hair done just so.

"It was so kind of you to take Jerry for a few weeks. He really needed some time away from here," Maggie said. "The chances of him being placed are so small...." Connor forced his legs to continue moving as anger welled inside him. How in the hell could someone take a kid like that for two weeks and just bring him back? What was he—a used car? No, he was a child. Connor picked up the spindles and the last of his things to carry back to his truck.

"I'll see you later, Maggie," he said when he saw she was still talking to Dan. That was it, Dan Harrington. Connor remembered him from school, but he hadn't seen him in years. He stopped and let his gaze roam over him for a few seconds. He remembered Dan as really smart in school, but very quiet. Dan had only been at Pleasanton High for a year. Sophomore year, if his memory served. Their junior year he hadn't come back. From the looks of him, he must be doing very well. Not that it mattered. Connor reminded himself of what he'd just seen and continued on his way out to his truck. He had a job to do, and it was to help make sure these kids were safe. Maggie returned his wave as Connor left the building; he needed to get back out into the sunshine and clean air. After taking a few huge breaths, he placed the old spindles in the back of the truck with a clang before hurrying around to the driver's side and taking off toward home and the work waiting for him—and there was plenty of it.

Connor drove out to the edge of town, where he lived, and around to the back of the house. He then parked outside his workshop. He got out and slammed the truck door behind him. Connor knew there was really no need for him to get upset. Maggie didn't seem angry or disappointed, and he could always tell with her. But that little scene with Jerry had touched a nerve in him, one he thought had healed a long time ago. Connor took a deep breath and tried to put that out of his mind. He walked around to the back of the truck and pulled down the tailgate with more force than was necessary.

His phone rang and he was tempted to ignore it. Connor pulled it out of his pocket, knowing that if he didn't, she'd only continue to call. "What's up, Maggie? There isn't something else you need, is there?"

"Nothing other than to know why you took off out of here like a bat out of hell. You usually stay and do things with the kids." She didn't say that they'd been asking, which Connor was grateful for.

"I have a lot of work out here that I need to get done." That wasn't a complete lie. He did have plenty of work, but nothing was pressing other than completing the banister work, and he'd get to that first. The rest were commissions and jobs he had time to finish.

"Please. I know you, remember? You always leave extra time when you're here, and when was the last time you didn't finish something early?" He heard mild scolding in her voice. "You spend hours in your shop, working way past when most folks are in bed. When was the last time you went out and had some fun?"

Connor thought for a few seconds. "I enjoy my work. It's fun for me," he countered.

"It's still work. You need to go out, find yourself someone, and start a family. There's more to life than just work."

She was probably right, but Connor was settled. He'd bought the property he had for many reasons, including the fact that it was set away from other people and he could work all he wanted without being disturbed. Besides, he wasn't interested in women and, well, he'd learned that it was best if he stuck to himself and did what he loved. No one got hurt that way, and some of his first lessons in life had been how not to get hurt. "Maybe, but it's what I love. There's nothing like working with your hands, taking wood, forming and shaping it with care in order to bring your vision to life."

"Okay, I understand. You want to be alone and you don't want others to bother you. That's fine. But I won't stop pestering you, and when you come in next time, I expect you to have a few minutes for a cup of coffee."

The tension in his back and arms began to release. "I certainly will, just the two of us." He added the last part because Maggie had a habit of saying they were going for coffee and then he'd end up with her and one of Maggie's girlfriends that she'd push his way. He wasn't interested in anyone, women especially. He didn't want to hurt her feelings—she was a good friend, if pushy—but he just wanted to live his life peacefully and without a million emotional complications.

"Fine, I get the message. But someday, Connor O'Malley, I am going to send just the right person your way and you are going to thank me for the rest of your life." He heard the smile in her tone.

"You can be as delusional as you want. I'm happy the way I am, and I don't intend to change." He sounded more gruff than he intended.

"Now who's delusional?" Maggie retorted.

"You're just blissfully happy because you finally got Ethan to ask you to marry him." He couldn't help smiling. Maggie and Ethan had been high school sweethearts. He'd moved away for college, but she'd never given up on him, and after she'd gone to school herself, he'd returned, and Maggie had pursued him with the tenacity of a mother grizzly. The story had been all over town, especially when it had a happy ending. Connor, on the other hand, had listened to her bemoan her fortunes in the romance department the entire time Ethan was gone, and even for a while after he returned. That had firmed up his belief that romantic entanglements only complicated things and were definitely something he didn't need.

"Yes, I am. We haven't set a firm date, but it will be about this time next year." She paused, and he heard her talking to someone else. "I have to go, but I'll see you when you come back to finish the repairs." She spoke in a soft tone generally reserved for Ethan or one of the children. "And for God's sake, don't work too hard." She hung up, and he shoved the phone back into his pocket, then unloaded the back of his truck into the workshop.

Connor turned on the lights and put everything away in its place. He set the old spindles on the side of the workbench and then unloaded the dowels of pristine wood he'd use to replace what had worn out. That was what he loved most—taking what was old and damaged to work on it and bring it back to life. He also designed and made custom furniture that he sold through a few furniture stores downstate. That part of the business paid for most of the other things he wanted to do. He had a number of pieces in various states of completion. Most of them were at the stage where they needed time for glue to dry or were ready for finish. So he decided to start work on the spindles right away and then finish up construction so all the finishing could be done at the same time.

Connor got to work. When he was in the zone, time always seemed to get away from him, and today was no exception. He planned how he was going to make the spindles and then measured the old ones, cut the dowels to length, set up the lathe for turning, and prepared the wood. When he was done with what he could do on each project, he moved on to the next one, slowly progressing through the process from raw wood to a finished project that he could be proud of.

After hours of thinking only about the task at hand, his stomach interrupted him. Connor looked at the clock above his workbench and grimaced. It was nearly ten at night, and he hadn't eaten since lunch. He set the projects aside, pleased with his progress, and went through the process of cleaning up. Then he turned out the lights and closed the shop door behind him before walking to the back door of the house.

It was silent once he shut the back door. No one greeted him. He'd thought of getting a dog, but the poor thing would starve for hours while he was working. Connor tended to forget everything, including to feed himself, let alone another creature. Connor turned on the light over his old kitchen table and opened the refrigerator. He pulled out the stuff for sandwiches and began making himself stacks of ham and salami on rye bread. Once he had his sandwiches made, he reached into the refrigerator for a can of beer, but decided on milk instead. He hadn't had any today, and if he didn't drink it up, it would spoil. After pouring a glass, he closed the refrigerator door and went into his living room.

For a man who made furniture into works of art, his own living room looked like something out of a grandmother's attic. Connor didn't even notice it any longer, but the pieces were mostly things he found at secondhand stores or things he'd gotten because he thought he might restore them someday to their original splendor. Instead, they remained in their tatty state and graced his living room. Not that it mattered to him. Connor sat down in his favorite chair and turned on the television. He set the plate and glass on the table next to him, and then watched and ate without paying much attention to either.

Like he did most nights, Connor took his dishes to the sink, rinsed them, and put them in the dishwasher, which he ran once or twice a week. After returning to his chair, he turned off the lights and sat in the dark watching whatever was on, and eventually he closed his eyes.

At some point, he woke up, looked at the old flip-number clock near his chair and groaned. He stood up and worked the crick out of his back from falling asleep in his chair again. Then he turned out the light and walked down the hallway to the bathroom. He cleaned up and got undressed, then threw his clothes in the full hamper. He told himself he had to do a load of laundry in the morning. Then he padded across the wood floor to his bedroom, pulled down the covers, and climbed in. He closed his eyes and expected to quickly fall to sleep. But he didn't.

Connor kept thinking back to what he'd seen and heard at the home earlier that day, and his anger rose once again. He had no reason to be angry, per se. It was just that to take a kid for two weeks and then return him like he was an unwanted toaster drove him crazy. He knew what it felt like to be passed around and not know where home was. He knew about a lot of the things those kids in the Pleasanton Home lived every day. Thankfully they had Maggie and Gert to look after them.

Gert Hansen was a middle-aged, grandmotherly type who, along with Maggie, was one of the kindest people he'd ever met. She could also stop a kid running down the hallway at full speed with only a look. Then there was Jerry. Just the thought of the boy's curled hands and legs, huge eyes, and crooked smile made Connor's eyes fill with tears. He'd thought of adopting from the home—he'd even considered taking Jerry—but he couldn't. Those kids deserved better than him. A real family. Not a single guy who…. Connor sat up and shook his head, trying to get all these thoughts out of his head. He wanted them to stop. All that was behind him, and he'd made a life for himself, such as it was. Yes, he was alone, but he didn't depend on anyone for anything, and no one depended on him.

Connor assuaged his rambling thoughts and what-ifs by promising himself that when he went back to make the repairs, he'd be sure to spend some extra time there, and he'd stop by the bakery and get a big box of cookies for all of them. He settled back on the mattress and took a deep cleansing breath. His mind quieted, and he closed his eyes once again.

A pair of shiny shoes flashed into his mind, followed by a set of legs in crisp pants. His view traveled to where the man leaned slightly forward, his butt filling the seat of his pants. Damn, that was a sight to see. He smiled and let his imagination run. It had been a while since he'd allowed himself the simple pleasure of fantasy, and it felt nice. His body tingled a little with excitement. The man turned around. Tight pants clasped his narrow hips, his hand worked at the opening, lowering the zipper just enough that Connor caught a glimpse of lightly olive-toned skin. He let his mind wander upward. The shirt that had been there was now gone, and Connor let his mind ghost over a pair of tight abs and the full chest that had once filled out the shirt. The man stroked over his chest, plucking his nipples lightly. Connor slid his own hand over his chest, making the same motion as his fantasy man. They liked the same things. He increased the pressure and pressed his head back against the pillow.

A smile formed on the full, thick lips of the man, and Connor wondered how they would feel kissing him. He slid his hand down to his cock, wrapped his fingers around it, and stroked lightly, just to get things warmed up. Then the rest of the face came into view and he groaned. What the hell was he doing fantasizing about Dan Harrington? Connor knew he needed an outlet for his repressed lust, but him?

He pulled his hand away and rolled onto his side, giving up for the night. What he needed was a good night's sleep and not to be thinking about Dan and Jerry and orphans. Because as soon as he did, he'd start thinking about his childhood, and he'd be damned if he wanted to go there. Jesus, most nights he slept well, but now he was all worked up.

He needed to keep his mind occupied with something else, so he threw back the covers and pulled on a pair of old sweat pants, a T-shirt that had seen better days, and an old pair of sneakers. He walked through the dark house, grabbed the flashlight beside the back door, and left the house.

Instead of walking to his workshop, he headed across the yard to the building next door. He used the flashlight to illuminate the lock on the building and set the combination. When it sprang open, he opened the door and went inside. He didn't bother switching on all the lights. Instead, he turned on the lamp he'd used the last time, grabbed his set of carving chisels and mallet, and got busy. Soon he had exactly what he wanted. His thoughts centered on his work.

Hours passed, and he made good progress on the curl he'd been trying to get right. It looked perfect, which made him smile. Once he was done, he stood up and admired his progress before turning out the light. After locking the building, Connor went back to the house to bed. This time he had dreams, but they were different, filled with happy music. He loved those dreams.

CHAPTER
Two

DAN SPENT his early morning in his office at his home, making phone calls. He had a few deals he wanted to close, and it wasn't going to get done otherwise. He was on his last call for the morning—a videoconference. "That's exactly what I want," he told the managers assembled in the conference phone on the other end of the video feed. "This deal must go off without a hitch, and you're the team that will make it happen." Everyone nodded at his firm words. "I have every confidence that you can get this deal done and the building rehabbed and ready for occupancy before the holidays or else I would have chosen a different team. Now make it happen, and, Carl, I expect a report on all progress on my desk first thing each Monday morning." He gave them a quick smile and disconnected the feed. That task was complete and he was happy with the result, so he stood up and brushed off his pants. There was nothing actually on them; he simply did it out of habit. He checked the clock and smiled.

A soft knock sounded on the door and then it opened.

"Morning, sweetheart," he said, and Lila came in the office. He walked around the desk and hugged her, careful to avoid her crutches. "Did you sleep well?" Lila often had trouble sleeping, and he was relieved when she nodded. "Good. I'm glad."

"Daddy, my legs didn't hurt last night," she said proudly. They both knew what a milestone that was for her. It was the first night that had happened, and Dan was thrilled.

"Did you do the exercises the doctor told you before bed and after you got up?" he asked.

She straightened proudly, blue eyes sparkling in a cherubic face framed in blonde hair. "Yes, Daddy. I remembered, and my legs don't hurt." She was excited for a few seconds, and then it dimmed. "Wilson made me breakfast," she said and made a face. "I hate oatmeal," she whispered and looked toward the door, probably to make sure he wasn't there.

"Then ask for something else. You know you can do that. Wilson will make you whatever you like. All you need to do is ask." He gently set her crutches aside and lifted her into his arms. She was light, and he hugged her tighter, swinging her in a circle, to squeals of delight. "You'll never have to worry about being scolded for asking for what you want." She'd been living with him for nine months, and he'd finalized the adoption six months earlier, but she was still reticent about asking for anything. "You're my little girl and I want you to be happy." He was determined not to spoil her too much. But she was such a quiet child, and Dan desperately hoped she would come out of her shell. Besides, he was a firm believer in giving his daughter whatever she needed and most of what she wanted. She was going to have the things he never did as a child.

"Okay, Daddy. I don't want oatmeal and I want waffles," she said.

"Good. All you have to do is ask Wilson, and tomorrow you'll have waffles." He hugged her and grinned. Her wants were so small. "I have to go somewhere this morning, but when I get back this afternoon, you and I can go swimming in the pool."

"Wilson too?" Lila asked.

"If he wants, yes. But you'll have to invite him." Dan knew that Wilson would demur unless Lila batted her eyelashes at him. It was part of the way he remained professional. "Go on and watch television for a little while if you want, and maybe I'll have a surprise for you when I come back."

Her face lit up, and he could tell she was dying to ask what the surprise was. He would have told her if she had asked, but she didn't. Dan kissed her on the cheek and set her gently on her feet, giving her back the metal crutches that attached to her arms. He hoped that eventually she wouldn't need them any longer. He wanted to take her by the hand, but that wasn't possible, so he followed her out of the office and made sure she got settled in the family room.

Then he grabbed his jacket, because the wind off Lake Superior could be brutal, and got ready to leave. "Wilson," he called softly into the kitchen. "I'll be back in a little while."

"Are you going to get him, sir?" Wilson asked.

"Yes," Dan answered with a smile.

"Excellent. I miss him. We all miss him," he said.

Dan couldn't help grinning like an idiot. He'd missed him too, and it was time to rectify his mistake.

"I'll have things ready here when you get back." Wilson smiled at him. Dan had found Wilson before he'd moved back to Pleasanton. It had been merely by chance. When he'd bought his home in Ann Arbor a few years earlier, Wilson had been the caretaker for the property. The house hadn't been lived in for years, but Wilson had cared for the property for the owners and done a wonderful job. Dan had agreed to keep him on, and they'd grown to like each other. Wilson was rather formal, and at first Dan hadn't been sure how he felt about having domestic help. But Wilson was efficient, and Dan simply liked him. He was good company and provided good conversation. Over time, Dan had come to rely on him for many things, and Wilson took good care of him so he could go about his business,

"Thank you," Dan said. "He can stay on the first floor bedroom to begin with, but I want him to have the run of the house. So we'll have to give some thought to how we do that."

Wilson nodded and grinned. "Just go get him, and I'll help you with whatever you need."

"Excellent. Lila is in the family room, and she has a request for breakfast tomorrow. I won't tell you what it is, but I can say it's not oatmeal."

"I don't know why she won't just ask," Wilson said. "You know—"

Dan held up his hand. "I know full well that you'd do anything for her. But it will take her more time. She's six years old and has seen more hardship than most kids ever do." He paused and then smiled. "We're going swimming this afternoon."

"I'll have everything ready," Wilson said with his usual efficiency.

"You might get an invitation as well," Dan said and watched the expression on Wilson's face. He nearly laughed out loud.

"Very good, sir," Wilson said formally, which was a sure sign he knew he was going to be outfoxed but had to put his best face on it. "Everything will be ready."

Dan thanked him and nodded. He left through the front door, jumped in his large Mercedes sedan, and took off down the circular drive. He grinned as he drove. Now that he'd made up his mind, the doubts and unsettled feelings he'd had for the past day were gone. This felt right, and his heart screamed at him to hurry up. He drove as quickly as he could to the Pleasanton Home for Children. A truck was just leaving ahead of him, and he snagged the spot right in front of the door.

He practically jogged up the stairs and inside. The desk was empty, but the sound of children filled the halls. "The bus will be here soon," he heard Maggie say, and soon kids were trooping down the stairs, with Maggie right behind them.

"Mr. Harrington, I wasn't expecting you," she said as she passed. "I'll be right back." She was smiling, and the kids didn't stop talking excitedly. The sound was cut off when the door closed, and Dan leaned against the old scarred desk and waited for her return. She came back through the door a few minutes later, blowing her bangs upward slightly.

"The kids aren't off to school, are they?" Dan asked as she approached him. "It's the middle of summer."

"No. Once a week the library sends a bus over and the kids spend part of the day there. They have reading programs for them and they serve lunch and give them a day out. The ladies there are really great, and the program is run by one of the teachers, so they're well supervised. It gives us a day free here to clean and make sure we can keep everything in order." She looked down at her desk and then back at him. "Let's get a cup of coffee. I'm dying for one, and you can tell me why you're here."

"I think we might need Gert for this one," Dan said, and Maggie's eyebrows lifted slightly.

"I hope nothing is wrong. Jerry has always been such a good boy." Her deep concern for him touched Dan deeply. She reached for the phone and spoke with Gert, then hung up. "She said to grab the pot and bring it to her office. I'll be right back."

Maggie walked down the hall and unlocked one of the doors. She came out with a pot of coffee and some mismatched coffee mugs and then motioned for him to follow her to an office just off the hallway.

"Mr. Harrington, it's good to see you again," Gertrude Hansen said when he entered the office.

"Please, call me Dan," he said to both of them as he shook her hand. Then he took the chair she indicated and accepted the cup of coffee from Maggie.

"What can we help you with?"

"I'd like to give Jerry a home," Dan began. "When I brought him back two days ago, it didn't feel right, and that feeling hasn't gone away for me or the rest of the people in my family. So I'd like to know what I'd need to do to adopt Jerry."

Gert set her cup on her desk, untouched. "You're serious."

"Very. He captured all our hearts when he was with us, and I never should have brought him back. Instead, I convinced myself that taking care of him long term would be hard given the needs of my daughter. I realize I was wrong."

Gert looked at Maggie and then back to him. "I really can't advise that. Mr. Harrington... Dan... Jerry is relatively easy to care for now, but it's going to become more and more difficult as time goes by. We've had to build contingency plans for his eventual care."

"And let me guess: those plans consist of an assisted-living home followed by nursing care," Dan said.

"Of a sort. Because of his age, they will be modified, but yes. That is what he will need, and unfortunately we're not talking decades, but most likely in a few years." Gert stood up and walked around her desk, then leaned on it. "You know that Jerry is terminal. His type of muscular dystrophy will eventually claim his life. Are you really willing to put yourself and your family through that?" She gazed down at him like a scolding grandmother.

"Actually, I am," Dan countered. "I'm well aware of Jerry's condition. I'm also aware of his sweet nature and kind heart. So I'll ask you again to please get the paperwork together."

"Dan...," Gert began gently.

He stood up. "No. I won't accept anything other than a yes. That little boy deserves a home and people who will care for him whether he has twenty years or two. I know you mean well, I really do, but Jerry is going to have a home, a real home. He will never have to go into assisted living or a nursing home. I have more than enough resources to hire whoever is required to care for him when the time comes. Hell, I have enough money to buy the entire damned hospital and pay the staff if I have to. This isn't about taking care of Jerry." Dan let his high-powered executive tone creep into his voice, the exact same one he'd used on the videoconference earlier. It rarely failed to get him what he wanted. "Jerry is already part of our family. I was just too wrapped up in other things to see it."

Gert nodded, glanced at Maggie, and smiled. "All right. As long as you know what you're getting into. We already have all the paperwork from your earlier adoption, and your home was already checked out for Lila's placement as well as the two weeks Jerry was already with you. But permanent placement of a child like Jerry will require additional work."

"Yes, I'm aware of that. I have a room for him on the first floor. It's the one he used when he was with us last time. We'll be looking at the possibility of installing an elevator or a stair lift in the house. A bathroom will be fitted for his needs on each floor. I've already added a ramp on the side door because it made it easier for Lila, and the backyard hardscaping was reworked in the spring to eliminate stairs and add gently sloping walks and paths in their place. I know what will need to be done."

Gert sighed. "You certainly have done your homework." She smiled. "And bless you. I had to ask the tough questions, but I'm so pleased Jerry will live in a good home." She turned to look out the window. "I wish they could all be placed like that. That would be my dream—that we could actually close our doors because we weren't needed any longer." She sighed again and turned back to him. "That, however, isn't likely to happen."

Dan sat and watched her. He knew she was right, and she didn't need him to confirm it for her. "Where is Jerry now? Did he go to the library with the others?"

"No. He stayed behind. He didn't want to go, so he's in the art room with Arlene."

"Does he do that often?" Dan asked. "Stay behind when the other kids go on outings?"

"Sometimes," Gert answered. "Mobility is an issue for him, as is using even some public restrooms. They aren't always equipped for what he needs, and he's getting old enough that he wants to be as self-sufficient as possible, especially when it comes to things like that."

"I understand. I had to help him a few times, but was careful to let him have his privacy," Dan said.

"Maggie, why don't you and Dan go explain things to Jerry. I think he's going to be as happy as you are. I'll take care of the paperwork for temporary custody, and then we can work with your attorney to complete the formal adoption the way we did last time."

"Thank you," Dan said. "I appreciate all your help." He got up to leave the office.

"It's us who should be thanking you. Children with disabilities are very difficult to place. Babies and small children are easy, older children much tougher, and disabled kids... nearly impossible. It takes a person with a huge heart to do what you're doing." Gert looked at him seriously. "I know Jerry will have a good life with you." The "however long or short" was left unsaid, but it hung in the air like fog on a cool summer morning.

Dan left the office and followed Maggie down the hall. She opened one of the doors, and Dan stepped into a room with scarred tables and art supplies everywhere. It looked as though there had been an explosion in a combination crayon, coloring book, and construction paper factory. The walls were covered with drawings, some mere scribbles, others carefully done. All were pretty to Dan. He had to admit he wouldn't have seen the beauty in scribbles of color on top of a coloring book page a year ago, but he understood now. One of the walls of his bedroom was covered with the framed drawings and pictures Lila had made for him. The one that held pride of place was the first one she'd written "For Daddy" on. He'd cried after she'd given him that.

He saw Jerry sitting in his chair at one of the tables, a crayon clutched in his curled hand, carefully and slowly filling in between the lines, his tongue sticking out slightly as he concentrated. Dan knew this was good therapy for him. It helped Jerry retain the motor skills he had. "Jerry," he said gently so he wouldn't startle him.

Jerry looked up, and Dan watched as the look of concentration shifted to a smile and then a huge grin. "Hi, Mr. Harrington," Jerry said. To Dan, the words were clear as a bell, but to others, they would sound slightly slurred. "Did you come to see me?"

"I'll leave you two alone. Just come to the desk when you're ready." Maggie motioned to Arlene, who followed her out of the room. The door closed behind them, and Dan walked over to where Jerry sat.

Dan sat in one of the undersized chairs next to Jerry. "I have a question for you, Jerry. Did you have a good time when you stayed with us?"

"Sure, the best!" Jerry said with innocent enthusiasm.

"Then I have something I want to ask you, but this is your decision. Do you understand?" Dan had had a very similar talk with Lila almost a year earlier, except she'd been younger. Jerry nodded. "I'd like you to come home to live with us permanently."

Jerry dropped the crayon and it rolled off the table onto the floor. "For real?" The disbelief in Jerry's voice damn near broke Dan's heart.

"Yes, for real. I want you to come home with me and be my son and Lila's big brother. Is that okay with you?"

Jerry eyed him with suspicion. "Only for two weeks like last time, right?"

Shit. He knew he'd really messed up. He had to make this right. "No. This time you'll stay forever. I'll adopt you and that will be your permanent home. No more coming back here, unless it's to visit Miss Maggie and Mrs. Gert or some of your friends."

"No matter what?" Jerry asked, and Dan leaned forward to hug the boy's frail body lightly.

"No matter what… forever." He managed to get the words out before his voice broke. Jerry might only be eight years old, but he knew how the world worked. His disbelief clearly showed that.

"But what about…." Jerry looked down at his chair. "I had to sleep away from everyone, alone."

"You'll use that same room until I can have some changes made to the house so you can get upstairs. Then you'll have a room near Lila and near me." Dan pulled out his phone and quickly added a reminder to find a carpenter as quickly as possible. He needed to get the changes made as soon as he could. "Will that be okay? Or if you want, I'll carry you up the stairs each night so you can be near us. It's up to you." He should have thought of that when Jerry had stayed with them before. It would have made Jerry feel more included. He really needed to pay closer attention to how things might look to his children.

Jerry smiled again, his lips higher on one side, but it was a gorgeously bright smile that Dan would never get tired of seeing. "This is for real," he said.

"Yes, it's for real. So if you want, we can pack your things, and I'll sign what Mrs. Gert needs me to sign, and we'll go on home and get you settled. I'm sure Wilson is home right now making your favorites, and this afternoon we're all going swimming." Jerry shook back and forth in his chair. When he'd first done it, Dan had thought something was wrong, but he now knew it was Jerry unable to contain his excitement. "Then let's go." Dan motioned for him to lead the way, and Jerry's chair hummed as it moved toward the door.

"I'm gonna be adopted," he said with joyful abandon as soon as he saw Maggie. She bent down and hugged him, both all smiles.

"You sure are," she said happily. "Now we need to get your things packed so you can be ready to go." She took Jerry to his room, and Dan watched him go with a smile on his face. Then he headed to Gert's office, where he signed the forms that gave him temporary custody of Jerry until a court approved the final adoption. By the time he was done, Jerry was coming down the hall toward him, a bag resting on his lap, with Maggie behind him, carrying another.

"Are you all set?" Dan asked.

"Yes," he said with his special smile. Then he turned to Maggie, and Dan saw him sadden. "But I'll miss you."

Maggie knelt down next to his chair. "Don't you worry, sweetheart. You can visit us anytime. But Dan is going to give you a good home, a real family, and all the love you could ever hope for. That's what you deserve, sweetheart. So don't be sad because you're leaving. It's what you were meant to do, just like I was meant to be here and help take care of you." She hugged him, and Dan saw tears running down her cheeks. She wiped them away quickly. "I'll see you very soon, I promise."

Dan said good-bye to her, and to his surprise Maggie stepped up to him and hugged him. "You have a special heart," she said tearfully into his ear.

Dan had never thought of himself that way, but he smiled and hugged her back, unsure of what he should do. These sorts of situations always made him uncomfortable. When he'd first adopted Lila, he'd learned the joy of a hug and now he did it often. And he intended to be the same way with Jerry. But with adults and people he didn't know very well, this was a strange sensation that he knew little about. He didn't have a lot of experience being touched in an affectionate way, at least not that he could remember. "Thank you, Maggie," he finally said. She backed away, to Dan's slight relief, and stepped back.

"I'll go get Jerry settled in the car," she said, and Dan followed her gaze to where Gert stood looking at them. He walked over and thanked her for everything.

"I was wondering," he said, looking up at the massive old staircase that led to the second floor. "I'm going to need someone to work at the house to make the changes Jerry is going to require. I noticed someone working here the other day. Does he do good work?"

"The best." Gert stepped into her office. "He's very talented. We can't really afford him, but he helps us out for the kids." Gert wrote down a name and phone number and handed it to him. "He's known for his handmade furniture, but he likes to keep his hand in other things. He's installed all kinds of specialized fittings for the kids in this old building."

"Thank you. That's just the kind of person I was hoping to find." Dan always hired the best and expected the best work. He looked at the name on the card and tilted his head slightly, wondering why it was familiar.

"He's about your age," Gert supplied, and Dan nodded. He must have been someone he'd known in school.

"Thanks again," Dan said and held out his hand. She shook it with a grin.

"Finding each child a home is one of the rewards of this job. It doesn't happen often enough, but it's one of the true joys." She released his hand, and Dan walked to the front door.

Jerry was already in the car, waiting for him.

"Is everything ready?" Dan asked brightly. He opened the trunk, and Maggie handed him the bags to load in with the chair. Once they were all set, Dan thanked her again, and he and Jerry headed home.

CHAPTER
Three

CONNOR WAS busy working in the finish room. This was the touchiest part of the entire furniture-making process. The color had to be just right to bring out the exact highlights in the wood he was trying for, and the topcoats had to have the exact sheen. Not too shiny, but enough that the finish felt and looked deep. He liked to see the history of the wood in the finish. Trees grew over decades, sometimes hundreds of years. They were witnesses to nature's history. The finish process needed to bring that out and let the tree's story be told. He was just finishing up a coat of French polish on a desk he'd made out of some old-growth mahogany he'd gotten his hands on purely by accident. The wood had been stored in a barn for decades, and it was a miracle it was usable. His phone had rung occasionally, but he'd ignored it and let it go to voice mail. This process took concentration. He usually left his phone in the house on days when he was working on finish, and he was beginning to wish he had done so today.

"Yes," he said after snatching up the phone when it rang for the fifth time. The line was quiet for a second. "This is Connor."

"Good, I have the right number. This is Dan Harrington, and I'm calling about some carpentry work I'm going to need at my home. You came highly recommended for the type of job I need."

He sounded pleasant enough on the phone, but Connor's mouth went sour as he thought of his bringing little Jerry back to the home. He thought about all the things he had to do. "At the moment I'm rather busy. Maybe I could get to what you need sometime this winter." This was a small town, and Connor had learned a long time ago that being rude or short with people got around town fast, but there were ways of turning down a job without actually saying no. The easiest one was to either delay it beyond what the customer was willing to accept or simply price it too high. And working for Dan Harrington, great butt or not, was not something he wanted to do. Connor had all the work he needed, and he could be fussy about the jobs and the people he worked for. He didn't need to have anything to do with a heartless bastard like that. He'd had enough of them in his life already, thank you very much.

"I was hoping for something sooner than that. The job is very important, and you were recommended as the best man for the job," Dan persisted, his tone becoming more firm.

Connor had dealt with people like this before. "I really can't help you at this time. I have more work than I can handle at the moment."

"Won't you even come out to look at the job?" Dan asked.

"Can I check my schedule and get back to you?" Connor asked. That always seemed to put people off. Everyone liked to think their time and schedule were more important than his.

"Of course," Dan said and gave him his number. Connor didn't write it down. He had no intention of calling, and he doubted Dan expected him to. The game was over as far as he was concerned. They said a few pleasantries, and Connor hung up, put the phone on the bench, and went back to his finish work.

His phone rang five minutes later, and if he'd actually gotten started again he wouldn't have answered it, but he'd decided to get some water and hadn't begun, so he picked up the phone and saw it was Maggie. "Hey. I'll have the permanent spindles out there in a couple days. They're almost done."

"Thanks, but that's not why I called. Gert recommended you for a job, and I just got a call from Dan Harrington for another recommendation because you turned him down and ignored his offer. Apparently Gert was highly complimentary, but you blew him off."

"But…," Connor began, and she interrupted him.

"Gert has done a lot for you over the years and this is how you repay her? By making her look bad?" Maggie could be forceful, even pushy, when it came to him, but she'd never spoken to him like this. "So I suggest you call him back and make up some excuse that something opened in your schedule and you found the time to go out and at least look at what he wants to have done. He deserves better than the treatment you gave him."

"I don't want to work with him, all right? And I'm very busy right now with projects that are getting backed up."

"Please." He could see her rolling her eyes in that way she had when she'd caught him in some sort of lie. "I know you always work way ahead and hate deadlines, so you avoid them like the plague. You could probably take a month off and still meet every commitment you've ever had, so don't try to feed me a line of crap, because I'm not buying it."

"When did you get so dang pushy? Or pushier...." Maggie had always managed to get what she wanted from him one way or another.

"It comes with the territory. If I'm not pushy, then these kids don't get what they need, and you would never get out of your hole and join the rest of the human race. So pull out whatever stick you have lodged up your butt and call Dan back."

Connor capitulated. "Okay."

"Excellent," she said happily. "Now, while we're solving problems... I have this friend who—"

"No way," Connor said quickly. "I'm not going on any blind dates, and you are not some sort of matchmaker. I agreed to call Dan back, and I'll go out and take a look at the job. Consider that a win and stop pushing. Okay? I'm happy as I am and don't have any intention of changing." He had to get the hell off the phone. "Now can I please go back to my work and have a little peace?"

"Of course," Maggie said. "For now." He heard her laughing as he hung up the phone.

He wanted to swear, but there was no use. He couldn't fight her, and if Gert had recommended him, then he needed to at least make a show of being interested. Connor pulled up the call history on his phone and pressed Dan's number.

"Hello," Dan said.

Connor heard splashing in the background—it sounded like some sort of pool party.

"This is Connor O'Malley. If you're still interested, I saw that I have a few hours late this afternoon. If you're still agreeable, I could come out and you could explain what you have in mind." Connor really didn't have any intention of taking the job, but he could be polite and do this for Gert. "I'm not sure how soon I could get to it, but I might be able to rearrange my schedule if it's required." Connor figured he could always price the job high enough that Dan would be a fool to accept it. Gert and Maggie seemed to like the guy, and that was fine. But Connor couldn't get the sight of Jerry going back to his room in the orphanage after Dan had brought him back out of his mind. He knew exactly what that kind of situation felt like, and no one should have to endure it. Especially not Jerry.

"That would be great. I'd really appreciate it. Gert said you were the best, and I'd like to have the best for this job." More splashing and laughter drifted through the line. "I need to get back to the party, but could you come by about five? Does that work?"

Connor agreed, and Dan gave him the address. After they disconnected, Connor ground his teeth. No wonder he took Jerry back. A kid would probably cramp his party lifestyle. He told himself it was none of his business what Dan Harrington did with his life. He'd go over, look at the job, price it really high, and probably never have to lay eyes on the man again. He set down the phone and looked at the project he'd been working on. He wasn't in the mood to work on finishing any longer, so he decided that was enough for the day, put everything away, and closed up the finish area. Then he went out to the building next door and unlocked it, leaving the door open for air. He turned on his work light, picked up his chisel and mallet, and got to work.

Connor had finished what he needed to by the time he had to leave to go to Dan's house. He put everything away and locked up the building before walking back toward the house. The weather was gorgeous and the sun was shining, but he hardly noticed. Inside, he washed up and made sure his clothes were clean and didn't smell of finish chemicals. In the end, he changed his shirt and made sure he looked presentable before heading out to his truck.

He glanced at the address while he was driving through town. Connor knew just where the house was, in the wealthier part of town on the bluff with a view of the lake.

The house was large, but not the biggest one in town. Connor had always loved it, with its stone exterior, classic Tudor beams, and angles that made it appear slightly castle-like. He pulled into the circular driveway and parked behind a Mercedes. He got out and slammed the truck door before walking up to the front and ringing the bell. Connor was surprised when a strange man opened the door.

"Can I help you?" he asked in a slight British accent.

"I'm here to see Mr. Harrington. I'm the carpenter."

"He's expecting you," the man said formally and stepped back so Connor could step inside. Well, if Dan wasn't hoity-toity, with a butler and everything.

"Connor," Dan said as he approached across the hall. "Thank you for coming. I really appreciate it." Dan turned to the other man. "Thanks,

Wilson." He left, and Dan extended his hand. "I have a huge project and I need someone who can do it right in an older home like this one."

"Daddy," a small voice said, followed by a squeal of joy. He turned and saw little Lila standing on her crutches. "My—" She stopped when she saw Connor. "Connor," she said and slowly moved toward him.

"I see you know my daughter, Lila," Dan said, and Connor turned back to him, feeling a bit like a fool. Maggie had told him Lila had been adopted, but he hadn't known who'd taken her. Dan lifted her into his arms, maneuvering carefully around her crutches, and smiled as he carried her over.

"You adopted her?" Connor asked.

"It was finalized about six months ago." Dan gave her a gentle hug and set her back down. "Why don't you go into the kitchen with your brother and ask Wilson to make you a snack. I'll be in as soon as I'm done here." The way he smiled at her was almost enough for Connor to forgive him for taking Jerry back... almost.

"What I need to do is either put in a stair lift or an elevator," Dan said. He began walking as he talked, and Connor followed him. "I'm open to doing both. There are two sets of stairs to the second level, and I don't want to change the main staircase because it will affect the character of the building. Also, it has that abrupt turn, which I doubt will provide for enough room to allow smooth operation. The stairs just off the kitchen are a straight shot and probably a better bet." Dan took him around, and Connor looked at the rooms they passed through, with their comfortable but expensive furniture and art on the walls that cost more than what he made in a year. "These are the stairs." Dan motioned, and Connor looked upward.

"I put in one stair lift a few years ago, and I would think this would be plenty wide, and being straight will make it perfect." Connor turned back to Dan. "You said something about an elevator as well."

"That's preferable, as far as I'm concerned. It will be much easier for long-term operation and help ensure that Jerry can get up and down stairs on his own," Dan explained. Connor stopped in his tracks. "Is something wrong?"

"No," Connor said quickly. "I thought Jerry was back at the home. I saw him a few days ago when you brought him in."

Dan smiled. "I realized this was his home." A weird look passed over Dan's face that Connor could not place for the life of him. It was an odd combination of happy sadness. "He's staying on the main floor for now, but I want him to have a room near the rest of us." Dan led him back through the rooms to the other side of the house. "There are two large closets on this side of the house and a closet upstairs as well. They're large, and as far as I can tell, this one"—Dan opened the door to show him an empty closet—"is below the one upstairs. I'm willing to lose both of them to install an elevator. Is this something you can help with?"

Connor was still surprised and he nodded absently for a second. "It shouldn't be too hard. Elevators are beyond my skill set, but I can certainly research it for you. As for preparing the areas and reworking joists and things, I can certainly do that."

"Gert said you were good, and I know zilch about construction. I'm looking for someone who can act as a general contractor and make sure the work is done without compromising the integrity of the house. This is a grand old place, and I want it to stay that way."

Connor wasn't sure what to say. His mind kept going back to the fact that Dan was doing all this for Jerry. He'd been upset with the guy for no reason and had nearly turned down a great job with interesting challenges because of it. "I don't know how I can give you an estimate until I have a chance to take a look inside the walls and things. I can look in the basement, but that will only tell me so much.

"I can say that the stair lift is going to be much easier to get and install. It will also not be permanent, so if you need to remove it, that can be done without a great deal of effort. If you ask me, I'd say it's your best bet. With houses like this, once you open them up and start things, one issue leads to another." Connor shone his light into the closet. "There will be wiring that will need to be rerouted, and while the sidewalls aren't load bearing, I bet they contain wires and piping that go to the second floor." He patted the hallway wall. "This is load bearing, and any changes to it, like widening the doorway, will present complications."

"Okay," Dan said with a smile. "You've convinced me. But will the lift be something Jerry will be able to operate himself? I want him to be as free and independent as possible. It also has to have some sort of battery backup so he's never stuck."

"I'll look into them, and there are a number of companies that make them. They are custom to a degree, because each staircase is different, but I'm more familiar with the stair lifts than I am elevator installation."

"Okay. Then let's go with that to start. Can you do some research and give me an estimate? I can pay you for your time."

Connor shook his head. "That isn't necessary. It won't take me long, and I should be able to get something back to you in a few days." He heard laughter drift in from the next room.

Connor turned toward the sound and smiled. Dan walked in that direction, and Connor followed. When he entered the kitchen, Lila was at the table popping a grape in her mouth, with a coloring book open in front of her. Jerry had his chair pulled up to the table, and he was bent over a similar book.

"Look who's here," Dan said.

Jerry looked up and smiled at him. "Mr. Connor," he said and grinned. "I'm being adopted."

"Mr. Harrington told me," Connor told him.

"Please, call me Dan." Dan turned to Connor. "Would you like something to drink, or a snack? I really appreciate you coming out right away. I'd like to get things so Jerry can have the run of the house as soon as possible." He opened the refrigerator door. "You're welcome to a beer. Wilson also has soda, milk, and every kind of juice known to man, but only in boxes."

"A Coke is fine," Connor answered and took the can when it was offered. Dan was nothing like what he'd expected. While not the warmest guy in the world, he seemed to light up around the kids, and contrary to what Connor had thought for the last two days, he did have a heart. It just wasn't on display.

"Can Mr. Connor stay for dinner?" Lila asked rather meekly after looking at each of them.

Dan turned toward her, and for a second Connor thought he was going to scold her. Then he grinned and hurried to her. He lifted her out of her chair and whirled her around the room. "Mr. Connor is welcome to stay for dinner if he'd like. Why don't you ask him nicely, and if he says yes, then go tell Wilson." Dan looked at him with a smile that Connor didn't understand in the least. There was definitely something he was missing. Dan set Lila on her feet and helped her retrieve her crutches.

"Mr. Connor, would you stay for dinner?" she asked sweetly. "Wilson said he was making chicken, and it's really good."

"I'd like that," Connor answered, looking at Dan, who nodded, still smiling.

"Yay," she said with childish enthusiasm and then turned to slowly make her way out of the room. "Wilson," he heard her say once she'd disappeared from sight. "I asked Mr. Connor to stay for dinner, and he said yes."

"Wonderful," Wilson said, and a few minutes later he returned to the kitchen, trailing Lila as she moved. Connor saw Wilson and Dan exchange knowing looks, and Connor wondered if Wilson and Dan were more than employer and employee.

Jerry had returned to his coloring, and Connor walked over to see what he was doing. The design he was filling in was simple, but he was using multiple colors to complete each space, developing an interesting effect as he worked. "That's beautiful, Jerry."

Jerry looked up and smiled. "Thank you," he said and went right back to work.

"Coloring is good therapy for his muscles and hands," Dan said as Lila sat back down at the table and leaned her crutches on her chair. "You two be good for Wilson. I have a few other things I'd like Mr. Connor to look at while he's here. Finish up your pictures and I'll put them on the refrigerator when I get back." Connor looked at the stainless steel refrigerator and wondered where Dan was going to put any more pictures; it was already covered.

Dan motioned him out of the kitchen and through to a huge living area that overlooked the lake. "I want to remove this built-in bookcase. It was installed in the fifties and doesn't go with anything in the house. I'd like to replace it with a bookshelf cabinet with diamond-paned glass doors, probably dark in color and very rich looking, encompassing the entire side of the room. This house is large, so the installations should reflect that. There's no rush on that—Jerry's stair lift comes first—but I've wanted to do this for a while."

"Why don't I have you come out to my workshop so you can see some examples of what I do?" Connor asked. He was a little shocked that an hour ago he'd wanted to get in and out of here, and now he was staying for dinner and talking to Dan about other projects. Dan nodded. "Is it okay if I ask a question?"

"Sure," Dan said a little tentatively.

"Why were you so excited when Lila asked me to dinner? It seemed like an over-the-top reaction, and...."

Dan smiled to his ears. "I adopted her six months ago, and over that entire time Wilson and I have had to guess at what she wanted. Lila wouldn't ask for anything... ever. She hates oatmeal, but ate it at least three times a week because she wouldn't say anything or ask for something else. She finally told me this morning. So her asking if you can stay to dinner is, as far as I can remember, only the second thing she's asked for since she came here, and the first thing she asked for without prompting."

"And she asked for me?" Connor said, more than a little surprised.

"Why not? You're someone she knows and obviously remembers fondly. Jerry knows you as well, from the smile and the way he bounced back and forth in his chair. I've already found out that's his happy bounce. Apparently when he gets excited, his system overwhelms what his body is capable of, and he rocks." Dan seemed pleased.

"He has talent," Connor said. "Did you see the way he was coloring something as simple as a flower? He filled it in with all different colors so they blended when the eye looked at them."

"Are you an artist as well as a carpenter?" Dan asked with an amused smile.

"Only with wood, but I have a friend. Well, I'm more of a friend of Patrick's. He works with wood as well, but his partner is Ken Brighton. He's a famous artist, and I bet he'd like to see what Jerry is doing." Connor was fairly sure of it. Eight-year-olds usually didn't combine color like that, even with crayons.

"I've heard of Ken Brighton. In fact, I have one of his works in the house. I bought it in a gallery in New York a few years ago. I didn't realize he lived in the area."

"He and Patrick live in town, just a few miles from here," Connor said. The kids' laughter caught his attention and obviously Dan's, as well, because he motioned toward the kitchen.

Dan turned to him as they walked. "Dang, I forgot to ask you about the bathrooms. I suppose it's too much to hope for that you do plumbing and tile as well."

"That I don't do. But I can hang bars and things like that if you need it. I did odd jobs around town until my woodworking business got going well enough that I could make a living at it." Now he was volunteering to take on even more.

"Dinner will be ready in half an hour," Wilson said.

Dan bundled the kids off toward the bathrooms to wash up, and Connor sat in one of the kitchen chairs, unsure what he was supposed to do. He drank the last of his soda and watched as Wilson cleaned up the table, carefully setting the pictures aside. "Do you need me to help?"

"No, sir," Wilson answered. "You're a guest and it wouldn't be proper." He busied himself around Connor, setting the kitchen table and then taking the most wonderful-smelling chicken out of the oven. Connor tried to remember the last time he'd eaten something that took more than five minutes for him to make and he couldn't... unless he went out, and then it was usually to the diner, where he ordered the same thing each time.

Dan and the kids came back in, with Jerry rolling in his chair and Lila slowly making her way on the crutches. "You seem to be getting around better," Connor told her. He remembered when she was first learning how to use the crutches. Before that, she had been in a chair like Jerry.

"I wanna walk, and my legs don't hurt now." She set the crutches near the counter and took a single step before beginning to crumple. Dan was right there to catch her and help her into the chair.

"Honey, that's so wonderful, but let me know the next time you're going to do that so I can make sure I can catch you," Dan said, gently stroking her hair.

"Are you mad?" Lila asked barely above a whisper.

"No. I'm thrilled that you were able to take a step without your crutches. I just don't want you to fall and get hurt." Dan hugged her. "How about tomorrow when we're in the pool, you practice walking. The water will help hold you up, and you can make your legs stronger."

Jerry looked up from where he'd been sitting quietly. "I'll never be able to walk."

"No," Dan said. "But you will be able to do other special things. You and I will work to find out what those are."

"And Wilson?" It sounded like "Wiltson," which Connor thought was cute.

"Yes, and Wilson." Dan made sure they were both settled. Connor took the place Dan indicated, and they waited while Wilson put the food on the table. Connor wasn't sure how dinner would be, but once they were settled, Wilson sat in the empty place and began serving the kids.

Lila and Jerry began eating right away, as fast as they could. Connor knew exactly where that came from. There were often limited seconds back at the children's home, and if you were still hungry, the first ones done got more.

"Slow down. There's plenty, and no one is going to take it away from you." Dan lightly touched Jerry on the back, and he slowed down. "I promise you will always get what you want to eat, so never worry about that." Dan seemed so great with the kids.

Connor started to eat, and after a few moments Dan did the same, but he seemed to have one eye on his plate and the other on the kids. He was a natural, or at least that was how it looked to Connor. He didn't have much experience in that department at all. Lila laughed at something Dan did, and soon Jerry was laughing as well.

"After dinner we need to make sure you're all settled and have everything you need," Dan told Jerry. "Wilson has already put your things away for you."

Jerry frowned and looked at everyone around the table. "What about my books?"

"I placed those on the table next to your bed. I thought you would want them," Wilson said, and Jerry nodded.

"After dinner we'll make sure you know where everything is. You've stayed in that room before and used the bathroom, so you should be comfortable, and as soon as we can, you'll be moved to a room upstairs. I promise," Dan said.

"Thank you, Mr. Dan," Jerry said, and Connor clearly understood the need to get the mobility changes completed to the house as quickly as possible.

"I stay just down the hall as well. So you won't be alone on the first floor," Wilson said and looked at Dan. It was obvious that both of them cared for Jerry a great deal, and once again Connor wondered what the relationship was between the two men.

There wasn't much conversation around the table after that. Mostly everyone ate. Lila seemed quiet, and Jerry concentrated on his food. Connor saw Dan look over at Jerry a few times, but didn't offer to help, which Connor thought admirable.

"Connor invited us over to his shop sometime so we can look at some of his work," Dan said. "With both of you being such good artists, I'm going to need more space to show off your work and I'm hoping he'll help me build it." The kids nodded and continued eating. Dan went back to his dinner, and Connor ate as well.

"When did Dan bring you back here?" Connor asked Jerry. He was used to silent meals, but it seemed a shame not to talk with everyone around. The quiet wasn't unpleasant; in fact, it felt natural, but Connor felt edgy for some reason, and he couldn't put his finger on it.

"Today. Mr. Dan came today and got me. He said I was going to be adopted and everything." Jerry turned to Dan, who nodded his reassurance.

"Mrs. Gert and I are already working on that." Dan looked so happy. "Why don't you finish your dinner? You've both had a big day, and before you go to bed, I'll tell you a story if you like." Both kids were excited about that.

Connor couldn't stop a smile as the image of Dan sitting on the edge of one of the kid's beds telling them a story about princes and princesses, with maybe a giant or ogre thrown in. When he looked up from his plate, he saw Dan staring at him with a soft expression. Connor didn't move and watched him for a second until the butterflies in his stomach started. Then he looked away. He hadn't known if Dan was gay, but he'd gotten that feeling, and that look helped confirm it for him. Not that it mattered.

"May I be excused?" Lila asked when she was done.

"Yes, you may. Go wash your hands and you can watch television for a while." Jerry left the table as well, and Dan watched him go, his chair humming softly. "I'm sorry we weren't more lively at dinner. They're still adjusting, and I think we are as well," Dan said. Wilson stood and began clearing the dishes. Connor got up and set his dish next to the ones Wilson had carried. Dan did the same. "I really need to get the kids ready for bed and make sure Jerry's settled properly."

"Of course," Connor said. "Thank you, Wilson. It was an amazing meal. The kids were right—you make the best chicken."

"Thank you," Wilson said, and Connor left the kitchen. The sound of the television in the other room drifted to his ears and he smiled when he heard the "Beep Beep" of an old Road Runner cartoon. It brought back memories of his early childhood.

Dan's phone buzzed in his pocket, and he stopped and pulled it out. "Excuse me, I'll be right back." He went into the next room.

Connor stood where he was and used the opportunity to take in the incredible surroundings. The central hall was amazingly grand, with its impressively massive staircase done in rich, dark wood. He walked over and gently rubbed it. Deep color like that only came from the finish being on the wood for a century or more. He wondered if he should go, but Dan had asked him to wait, so as long as it didn't take too long….

"That's not what I want," he heard Dan say firmly, almost snapping. "I need the entire property to be cohesive. That's what I told all of you this morning." The edge to his voice was cold. "I put you in charge because you asked me to. Now you need to deliver." And getting colder. "All right. I'll give you some leeway, but I want to see all the plans before you approve and begin anything."

He heard Dan's footsteps a few seconds later. Connor turned away from the staircase and nearly took a step backward. Dan's eyes were cold and firm. Connor didn't have to be the person who'd called to feel that chill. "I should be leaving. You have things to do." He did as well, and he needed to be gone.

Dan's expression softened almost instantly, and he didn't say anything for a few seconds. "I keep getting the feeling we've met somewhere before. Did we go to school together?" The puzzled look on Dan's face was kind of cute and a complete one-eighty from what Connor had heard on the phone.

"Yeah. I remember you from my sophomore year in high school. We had an English class and maybe biology together. After I saw you at the orphanage the other day, I remembered you."

"That's it. You always sat in the back and had long hair that flopped in your eyes. It used to drive Mr. Schaefer crazy on lab days," Dan said with a huge, bright smile. "He was such an old curmudgeon and had to have everything done just the way he wanted, and it was always the hard way."

Connor nodded. "That was me, and yeah, old man Schaefer was a piece of work. Hey, do you remember the time I brought in the live frog?" Dang, he liked it when Dan really smiled. It was warm and full. Heck, he liked a lot of things about the man, not least of which was the way his broad shoulders filled out his shirt. Dan was attractive; there were no two ways about that. But there was something under the surface that Connor couldn't put his finger on, and he wondered if he hadn't heard it when Dan was on the phone a few minutes earlier.

"I do. How did you get it to jump right in front of him when he was passing out the dead ones we were supposed to cut up? He must have jumped half a mile, and actually looked at the frog he was carrying to make sure it hadn't risen from the dead." Dan laughed, rich and full. But he stopped quickly, like it was foreign to him and he wasn't used to doing it or something. The reaction seemed strange. Connor, on the other hand, couldn't stop.

"That part was pure luck, and the god of frogs everywhere stepping in for a laugh. I swear!" Connor held up his hand. "I'd intended to put it in his desk drawer, but it got away just before class started and decided to make an appearance then." Connor settled down. "It was beautiful, though. We thought he was going to have a heart attack." Dan joined him again, and they laughed for a long time. Connor could still see the teacher turning red with anger as he tried to catch the leaping frog.

"Was that a political statement?" Dan gasped between laughs.

Connor shook his head. "It was just to be funny." Connor got hold of himself, and Dan did the same, their laughter ringing off the hallway walls before dying away. "I didn't know you very well then, just enough to say hey in the halls, if I remember."

"I was only in school here for the one year." Dan's expression saddened. "I missed it here after I left." Dan opened his mouth to say more, but didn't. He walked toward the front door. "I can't thank you enough for coming. You will help, won't you? Maggie and Gert said you did work at the home, so I figure you'll know what I need to do to make Jerry comfortable."

Connor walked to the door and reached to open it, then stopped with his hand on the knob. "Yes, I'll help." For some inexplicable reason, he wanted to both run away and stay. He wanted to run and not look back because of the way Dan had sounded when he laughed. He knew what that laugh meant, or what it could mean, and he was not ready for those kind of emotional complications. They'd brought him nothing but trouble. He had a quiet life doing what he wanted, but he'd be damned if, even now, he could truly take his eyes off Dan Harrington. Yes, he remembered him from high school. Dan Harrington had been his first crush when he'd realized he wasn't interested in girls. But of course he'd been too young to do anything about it. "I'll make a few calls and see how quickly we can do this for you. I have some contacts already, so I'll get back to you as soon as I can." Connor smiled and pulled the door open. "Good night." He stepped out into the cool evening air, the wind off Lake Superior adding a chill even in the heart of summer.

Connor descended the stairs and walked to his truck. He had to back up a ways before he could turn around and head out toward the street. He drove right home and parked. He needed time to think, so he went to the building next door and did what he always did when he needed to think— immersed himself in his pet project. He turned on his light and got started. He should have said that he was too busy. But he couldn't, not with Jerry involved. He could get the job done quicker and better than anyone else.

He knew he was being completely stupid. Yeah, Dan had looked at him a few times, and he'd gotten that fluttery feeling in his stomach that he got when he liked someone and he thought they might like him as well. But he'd learned to ignore it and move on. His life was good enough as it was. But he'd agreed, and though he'd had a crush on Dan Harrington, that was a lifetime ago. No, he was happy, or as happy as he was ever going to allow himself to be. He'd help Dan because helping him would help make sure those two sweet children wouldn't have to experience what he'd gone through. He set down his tools and wiped his eyes on the back of his hand. He hated thinking about his past and his childhood. There was so little good there. "Stop it," he snapped to himself, his voice echoing through the inside of the building. Then he put his chisel to the wood and began to work.

But he couldn't concentrate. He tried to form the intricate, flowing curls in the wood, but all he kept seeing was Dan Harrington's smile. It went all the way to his ears and eyes, just like Jerry's did. Dammit, why couldn't Dan have lived up to the low expectations he'd had that morning. Why did he have to be a nice guy? Connor didn't deserve a nice guy in his life; he didn't deserve anyone. That had been made crystal clear to him. He set down the chisel and tried not to conjure up the image of his father, but it came anyway. His father was gone, but his words rang in his ears just as loud and clear as they had when he was a kid. His mother hadn't said anything, hadn't argued.

Connor's hands were shaking, and he knew he could never work under these conditions, so he gave up, closed everything, and shut down the light before leaving the large space and locking the door. He walked across the yard as a chill wind blew. Connor looked up and saw the clouds obstructing the stars that had just begun to shine. The weather seemed to echo his mood. *Great.* He hurried toward the house and closed the door against the iciness in the air, but he couldn't shut out the chill in his heart.

Connor went into his living room and sat in his chair. He didn't do any of the things he usually did. The television remained off, and he sat in the dark without his beer or the sandwich he usually ate in this spot. Instead, he just thought. He'd let his world become so small and he hadn't even realized it. He spent his days in his shop because that was where he was happiest, or so he thought. Those few hours at Dan's stuck with him. Dan had apologized because there wasn't more conversation, but compared to the way Connor lived his life, dinner had been a party.

He still wondered about Dan and Wilson, not that it mattered. Dan Harrington would not be interested in him. Connor might have had a crush on him in school, and maybe now that he'd seen him again, some of those feelings had bubbled up. They must have come from the crazy part of his brain, because it meant nothing. That was a long time ago, and things changed—people grew up and moved on. Dan had everything, including the love of two amazing children. Those kids adored Dan; that was clear to him. Connor had been downright shocked when little Lila had asked him to dinner. What had he ever done to deserve those kinds of smiles? He couldn't remember anything significant. But whenever those two children looked at him, he wanted to hold them and tell them they were going to be all right.

His thoughts ran all over the place for a long time. He remembered childhood disappointments and Christmases with no tree or presents, followed by…. He pushed all that aside. He'd made his way alone and had built his life on his own. He'd determined that he would rely on himself and that he didn't need anyone. And some stupid idea he'd had almost ten years earlier was not going to change that. Nothing was. He could rely on himself and that was all. Nothing more.

Connor didn't turn on the lights; he knew the way well enough in the dark. In the bathroom, he stripped off the clothes he'd been working in and started the hot water. He turned on just enough light that he could see where he was going and then stepped under the spray.

The water felt good and helped settle his thoughts. Connor reached for the soap from the dish and began washing his arms. He kept his eyes closed and then snapped them open when he thought he felt the shower curtain move. Connor peered out. He was alone. He closed his eyes again and went back to washing. His mind was playing tricks on him.

Without thinking about it, Connor slipped back into an old fantasy, one he'd had many times, but hadn't used in a while. At first he thought about fighting it, but there was no harm in thinking, so he let it run. Dan was with him and he took the soap, smiling as it slipped out of Connor's hand and into Dan's. Connor kept his eyes closed and his own hands morphed into Dan's. He'd often played this game in the shower when he was younger. Dan had starred for a long time, but other men had as well. Now Dan was back, and Connor liked it.

Connor stroked his chest, and then it was Dan again, stroking him and knowing just how he liked to be touched. The hands wandered lower and Connor spread his legs a little farther apart, stroking his balls before gripping his cock and then stroking it just so. This was a fantasy, but he was really getting into it and he didn't want it to stop. Dan's strong arms closed around him, and Connor wanted his fantasy man to whisper how he'd always take care of him and that no one was ever going to hurt him again. Connor's legs began to shake and he gripped his cock tighter, stroking faster and wishing the warmth around him was more than mere hot water. He could almost feel warm breath on his neck, and the firm hands on his skin were no longer his. Connor's entire body sang with excited pleasure as he quickly built toward a body-shaking, mind-blowing release. He gasped and moaned loudly into the empty room as he came hard, gasping for breath.

Connor leaned back against the tile and breathed deeply, letting the smooth warmth flow through him. He was content and warm for the time being. But like all good things, he knew it wouldn't last. Sure enough, within a few minutes the high wore off. Connor opened his eyes and he was back in his bathroom, alone. The fantasy was over and its remnants were washing down the drain. Connor reached for the soap he'd dropped at some point. He washed up for real and rinsed before turning off the water and stepping into the cool bathroom. He shivered slightly as he reached for the towel and began drying himself.

One thing was certain this far north: summers were amazing, but if the wind was off the lake, the temperature could drop fast. In fact, Connor had sometimes needed to put on the heat in July because of the cold dampness that came with the lake wind. Once he was dry, he hung up the towel, turned out the bathroom lights, and stepped quickly to the bed. He warmed fast once he slipped under the covers. He sighed softly and rolled onto his side, trying to keep his mind from wandering. All he wanted to do was go to sleep and dream of nothing.

That didn't happen. He spent much of the night thinking of Dan, Lila, and Jerry. Truth be told, mostly Dan. At one point he woke with a start and thought of going to work to clear his mind, but he was tired, so he lay back down and went back to sleep.

CHAPTER
Four

DAN SAT on the edge of Jerry's bed, smiling. "Are you comfortable?" he asked Jerry after tucking him in. Jerry had been there for three days and seemed content.

"Yes," Jerry answered.

"You know you can tell me anything," Dan said. "You don't have to be shy or afraid of hurting my feelings. I want you to be happy."

Jerry shifted slightly and tried to sit up. Dan helped him and placed a pillow behind his back to support him.

"Are you sure you want to adopt me?" He grabbed the blankets in his curled hands, tugging lightly. "There are other kids who would be happy here and…." Jerry looked toward the door. "They wouldn't be so much trouble."

Dan knew what had brought this on and he'd expected it. Jerry had knocked a pedestal outside the living room with his chair and a vase had crashed to the floor. He'd been heartbroken and had actually started to cry. Dan had seen the same reaction from Lila the first time something like that had happened in the house. Dan had put away most of the expensive breakables until he could have the cabinet built in the living room, but had left a few things out. He'd be sure to put the rest away after the kids went to sleep. He wanted Lila—and now Jerry—to be comfortable in the house, not worried or walking on eggshells, so to speak.

"You aren't any trouble." Dan gently took Jerry's small hand. You are my son and that's all there is to it."

"You know I'm going to die," Jerry announced.

"We are all going to die someday. It's the way things work."

"No. The kind of MD I have is going to kill me. Most kids with it don't live past ten, and I'm already eight," Jerry reminded him, his eyes shiny and clear. Dan felt a lump form in his throat as he realized just how strong Jerry was. He hadn't known Jerry knew his prognosis, but it was probably best he did.

"I'm going to call a friend. His name's Peter Barry and he's a doctor. He and I went to college together, and I plan to invite him up here for a few days. We'll make an arrangement with the hospital here so he can take a look at you. That is, if it's okay with you."

"It won't change anything," Jerry said. Very little got past him. He might have his challenges, but his mind was sharp and he missed very little. "I'll still have what I have." Jerry tugged at the edge of the bedding.

"Yes, you will. But he's a specialist in muscular diseases, and maybe there are new treatments that will be able to help you." Dan had no intention of sparing any expense to make sure that Jerry and Lila had every opportunity possible. "But that's up to you. I'll do whatever you want."

"Will it hurt?"

"I don't know, but I'll be there with you the entire time, and no one will do anything unless they ask you first." Dan put up his hand. "I promise."

Jerry nodded, and Dan hugged him.

"I love you, Jerry," Dan whispered.

"I love you too, Dan, and I'm glad you picked me." Jerry smiled his crooked, happy smile.

"You sound like I had them line everyone up. There was no one else I was going to bring here to stay with me but you, and I'm sorry I took you back. I should have asked you to stay with us all along."

"It's okay," Jerry said, and he lowered his chin until it rested on his chest.

"No, it's not." Dan lightly touched his chin. "I want you to listen to me, okay? No matter what happens or what you do, I will not regret adopting you. You are part of our family and that isn't going to change. So you can stop worrying that if you do something wrong or if...." Dan searched for words.

"I get worse and can't do stuff," Jerry supplied.

"Yeah, I guess that's as good a way to say it as any. I will never send you back, and you will never stop being my son. I will carry you upstairs to your bedroom and anywhere you need to go. I will get you special chairs and anything else you need. You and Lila are worth more than the whole world to me."

Jerry nodded slightly. "Why don't you have a wife?"

That was a question he had not been expecting, and it threw him for a bit of a loop. He thought of his options. But he'd told himself before he'd adopted Lila that he would never lie to his kids. "I don't like girls that way," he answered carefully. "They're nice and I'm friends with some girls, but I don't want to marry one."

"Oh," Jerry said, watching him carefully. "That means we'll never have a mom."

"I'm sorry, but you won't. It will just be me. I hope that's good enough." Dan smiled and lightly tickled Jerry, who laughed and squirmed on the bed. Dan didn't tickle hard and stopped quickly, but hearing Jerry laugh was wonderful and it seemed to distract him from a topic he wasn't sure how to handle. "Go to sleep now, and if you need anything, Wilson is just down the hall. I'll leave your door open partway so he can hear you. He'll come and get me right away." Dan had to get the changes made to the house sooner rather than later. He'd thought of sleeping down here, but then he'd be away from Lila. "Connor is going to come over tomorrow and go over the changes he wants to make so you can move upstairs."

"This is okay," Jerry said.

"I know it is, and you're not a little kid. You're growing up, but I want you close, where I can hear if you need me." Dan smiled. "And I want you to be able to go anywhere in the house that you want to on your own, just like Lila and I do. This is your home too." And he wanted that to be the case in every sense of the word.

Dan helped Jerry settle down into the covers and kissed him on the forehead. "I'll see you in the morning." Dan lightly stroked Jerry's hair out of his eyes and then turned off the bedside light. A small nightlight burned in the corner of the room. Dan stood up, made sure Jerry's chair was right next to the bed, in case he needed it, and then moved quietly out of the room. He closed the door partway before walking down the hall to his office.

Lila had already been tucked in and had been asleep the last time he checked. The house was quiet, and he had work to get done. Dan settled behind his desk, turned on his computer, and spent the next few hours answering e-mail, reading progress reports, and setting up some video meetings for the following week. Running his business remotely was turning out to be more of a challenge than he thought it would be. But he wasn't going to leave, and if that meant a few longer nights, so be it. He really liked it here and felt at home. The kids seemed to be settling in well, and he had no intention of uprooting them. He might have to make a few trips in to the office, but he could do that to shake things up as long as he had his home and family to come home to. *His home and family.* Dan stopped and stared at the screen.

His phone vibrating on the desk brought him out of his happy thoughts. He snatched it up and answered it.

"I saw you online and wondered if there was anything you needed," his assistant, Trevor, said.

Dan looked at the clock. "What are you doing working at this hour?" He was trying to catch up because of the kids, but....

Trevor snorted, a sound Dan had never heard him make before. "I'm sorry, boss," Trevor said. "Everyone knows when you work. Haven't you noticed that you leave messages and you get the answers before morning?"

Dan paused like he was waking up from a dream. "Are you saying that everyone logs in at night in case I'm working?"

"That's pretty much it," Trevor said lightly. "Now, was there anything you needed?" he added in his usual efficient tone, the earlier pleasant tone gone, replaced by what Dan usually heard.

"I don't expect people to match my schedule," Dan told him.

Trevor said nothing. The line was quiet. "So there's nothing you need?"

"Trevor...," Dan growled a little in his business voice. "What's going on?"

"Nothing unusual," Trevor finally answered. "As I said, I saw you online and wondered if there was anything you needed. I'm just finishing up the reports for the team that you requested."

"Why are you doing their work?" Dan pressed, his anger rising.

"I'm not. They sent them and I'm making sure everything is complete before I pass it on to you. That's my job, right?"

"Okay, Trevor," Dan said. "What's going on? Tell me all of it."

"Well...," Trevor prevaricated.

"Just say the truth," Dan pressed.

"Since you've been working odd hours for the last few months, a lot of the guys have taken to checking their e-mail and messages late at night. No one wants to come in and have you think that…. Well, that they waited too long… or something."

"How long has this been going on?" Dan pressed.

"I don't know. I started checking a while ago. I'm your assistant and I thought it was important. I don't usually actually see you online, but I…. God, you're angry now."

"No, I'm not. It isn't necessary for you or anyone to be online in the evenings just to match my schedule. I'm impressed that you are, and I appreciate the extra effort, but it isn't necessary. And to answer your question, there is something you could do for me. I need the preliminary quarterly reports completed a week early, if possible. The original date from accounting won't give me time to look them over."

"All right," Trevor said, and Dan could hear him typing. Dan fell into the usual routine and dictated everything he needed for the next few days.

"I appreciate it," he ended with. "I'll talk to you tomorrow." Dan hung up and continued working for another few hours before turning off his computer and heading to the kitchen. Now the house was completely still. Wilson had popped his head in an hour earlier to say he was going to bed.

Dan checked on Jerry and then went upstairs, where he made sure Lila was asleep. Then he went into his room, took a shower, and got ready for bed.

DAN HAD gotten up early and was at work in his office when he heard Jerry's chair hum in the hallway outside. He'd dressed himself, and Dan called to him quietly as he passed. Jerry turned and pushed the door open farther with his chair.

"Did you sleep okay?"

"Yes," Jerry said.

Dan loved how he always had a ready smile. "I bet Wilson is getting breakfast ready in the kitchen. I'll finish up what I'm working on and join you and Lila." Dan smiled at him and waited until Jerry had backed out of the room before returning to work.

By the time he looked again, an hour had passed. Dan groaned and hurried out of the office to the kitchen. The kids were sitting at the table with frowns on their faces. "We waited, Daddy," Lila said, "but you didn't come." Dan looked at Wilson, who began making him up a plate.

"I'm sorry," he said to both of them. "I was working and didn't see how late it had gotten." He looked out the windows and groaned. The world was gray as far as he could see, and rain was hitting the large windows that looked out over the backyard. He'd been about to try to make it up to them with a promise of time in the pool that afternoon, but that was out. "What do you want to do?" Dan asked as Wilson brought him a plate, and two pairs of eyes stared at him like he was the Grinch.

"Daddy, I want to go swimming," Lila whined. "You promised I could walk on water."

Dan began to laugh. "*In* the water, honey, and you can, but it's raining. Why don't you two get your coloring books and crayons while I eat, and then afterwards we'll go in the family room to see how big a block tower we can make."

They seemed happy with that, and Wilson helped them set out the books and crayons. Dan ate while they drew and colored. He thanked his lucky stars they were both content with simple activities, though he knew that wouldn't last forever. "Have you ever colored with anything other than crayons?" Dan asked Jerry as he watched him create his latest masterpiece.

"No," Jerry answered.

"Then maybe we'll go to the art store soon and see what you'd like." He thought of Connor telling him that Jerry had talent. His phone rang and he smiled. *Speak of the devil....* He'd already made a note to call Connor today. "Hello," Dan answered.

"Hi, this is Connor. I finished an estimate for the work you wanted done. I was wondering if I could come by and review it with you? If you're happy with it, I can order what's needed and get the work started." Connor paused. "I guess I jumped the gun, but I already got the stuff so I can get started on the bars in the bathrooms for you. I figured the sooner I could get that done, the easier things would be for Jerry."

"That's great," Dan said. "Please come on over and we'll talk, and I appreciate the initiative. I really want to get Jerry settled." For some reason his heart beat a little faster at the thought of seeing Connor again. The guy was handsome; there was no doubt about that. Dan had been nearly a monk for well over a year, and while he knew he'd never do anything with anyone who worked for him, even around the house, his mind still couldn't help bringing up Connor's smile or the way Dan had caught him staring at him over the dinner table.

"Daddy, you aren't eating," Lila said. "I wanna play blocks."

"Okay, honey," he said and felt his cheeks warm, embarrassed that he'd been thinking about Connor when he should have been paying attention to the kids. He finished eating and then carried his dishes to the sink. "Let's go play blocks," Dan said. Lila stopped what she was doing and picked up her crutches from where she'd rested them against the table. Dan stopped himself from helping her get up. "I'll be right in," Dan told her, and she left the room. "You don't want to join us?" Dan asked Jerry as he knelt next to him.

"No, I can't play those things like other kids," Jerry said.

"Who told you that?"

"I always drop the blocks and knock things over. The other kids don't ask me to play like that anymore, and they...."

Dan hated the way Jerry had been made to feel. It hadn't been the same for him, but Dan understood that feeling of thinking you weren't good enough. "Well, here, dropped blocks don't matter, and knocking over the tower is half the fun. So come in with Lila and me." Dan stood up and placed his hand on Jerry's shoulder. "You're always wanted here." He turned away for a second, swallowed the lump in his throat, and took a deep breath. How much would he have given to have heard those words when he was younger? Dan had longed for them, but he'd never heard them—not once. The old longing that sprang up nearly overwhelmed him, but he pushed it back. He didn't want the kids, or anyone else, to see him like this. He'd learned to be strong a long time ago, so he pushed it aside.

"Okay," Jerry said. He carefully set down the crayon, and Dan concentrated on the here and now and followed him into the family room, where Lila was already settled on the floor, surrounded by large cardboard blocks.

"Mr. Connor just pulled up," Wilson said from the entrance to the room.

"Ask him to come in here, please," Dan said, and Wilson nodded. Dan turned to Jerry and quickly realized that joining Lila and him on the floor was not at all practical. "How about if Lila builds the bottom, and Jerry can build the middle. I'll build the top."

Jerry and Lila seemed happy. Lila began piling the large blocks on the floor near where Jerry sat. Once it was high enough, she put blocks on Jerry's lap, and he placed them on top. Dan turned as a throat cleared.

"I didn't mean to interrupt a construction project."

He stood and walked over to where Connor waited. "I'm sorry. We got started and I—"

"No need to apologize."

"Will you two be okay in here?" Dan asked. Neither of them answered; they were having too much fun.

"I'll keep an eye on them," Wilson said, and Dan thanked him quietly, leaving the room to let the kids play.

"I have an estimate for the stair lift. It may vary some based upon precise measurements, which I can take today. If you're okay with it, I can call the company, give them the exact information, and get the order placed. I prepped the company, and they said that if you want a rush, it's 10 percent more, but they can get it here by truck in less than a month."

Dan looked at the amount, but didn't really care. "Please go ahead and order whatever you need, and have them rush it." Laughter drifted in from the other room. He peered around the corner as the last blocks rolled to a stop after toppling.

"Let's build it again," Lila exclaimed gleefully, and Dan smiled and turned back to Connor. He hadn't realized Connor had moved closer as well, and he nearly stepped into him.

"I'm sorry," Connor said quickly and stepped back. Dan gasped in surprise, and as soon as he did, he got a nose full of musk and heat. Connor had obviously been working before he'd gotten there. It wasn't a bad scent. In fact, it went right through Dan and settled in his groin.

"It's all right," Dan stammered, and once again he saw Connor looking at him. He quickly turned away. "Let's go over everything in the kitchen, and then you can get started." Dan turned and led the way. He had to get his thoughts together. Connor was handsome, and he remembered him from school. Dan had watched Connor O'Malley when he thought no one was looking, and if he were honest, he'd been very attracted to him. But that didn't matter, not now. He wasn't worth Connor's notice, not really, at least not that way. That had been a while ago, and it wasn't important now. At least he highly doubted it would be important to Connor.

Dan pulled out one of the kitchen chairs and motioned for Connor to take a seat. "Would you like some coffee?"

"On a day like this? You bet. Sometimes I wonder if we get more than ten days of summer a year here," Connor remarked.

"Have you always lived here?" Dan asked as he opened the cupboard and pulled out two mugs. He lifted the coffeepot off the warmer and filled the mugs. "Would you like cream or sugar?"

"Black is good," Connor answered. "I've always been in the area. I was born in town and never really went very far." Dan set the mug in front of Connor, and he wrapped his hands around it like he was cold. "I never did much of anything. Not like you." Connor lifted the mug and sipped from it. "I'm sorry. I'm sure you're busy and have a lot of things to do. I shouldn't be taking up your time."

"You're not," Dan whispered.

"Like I said, I never went anywhere." Connor set down his mug and pulled a sheaf of lengthwise folded papers out of his back pocket. "This is what I have for the bathrooms. I checked ADA standards and recommendations. It will make it easier for him to use them. I thought we could start with the one he's using now and then do the one upstairs that he'll use eventually. We'll add grab bars, lower the vanity, and adapt the walk-in shower so he can roll right into it."

"That sounds perfect."

"Yes, and I thought if I replaced the showerheads with ones that have a hand attachment, it would help." Connor showed him what he had in mind. "They had one in stock at the hardware store, so I snatched it up. I figured I could have them order another one if you liked it. I can install that and the grab bars today."

"Sounds great," Dan said with a half smile. "Please go ahead and do what you can today, and do the rest whenever you can. That would be awesome."

"I also drew up these plans for the cabinet in the living room." Connor spread out the next piece of paper, and Dan looked at the rather detailed drawing. "I'll have to get measurements, and I can make adjustments where needed, but see if this is what you have in mind."

Dan pulled out the chair next to his and shifted closer so he could see the drawing better. When he settled, his shoulder bumped Connor's slightly. He also got another whiff of his heady scent, and when he glanced at Connor, he saw him gazing right back. Dan held stock still, looking into Connor's eyes for what seemed like an instant and a lifetime all at once. They were deeply beautiful, and Dan stifled a shiver at the pain that reflected back at him. Then it was gone, and Connor blinked and turned away. Dan didn't turn away at first, but continued looking at Connor, wondering if he'd seen what he thought he'd seen. "Sorry," Dan said and turned toward the drawing.

The cabinet was massive looking, with carved architectural details and diamond-paned glass doors. Connor had even carried the design lower into the wooden doors on the bottom. "It's perfect," Dan said as he continued looking and casting furtive glances at Connor. "Where will you get the carved pieces? These look so incredible."

"I'll make them. It's Tudor style, so I thought I'd see how the figures work, and they do. I thought I could make one male and the other female, and I could make them look like Lila and Jerry if you like."

Dan was floored. "You can do that?"

"Yes. My work is very well known, and I got my business started by restoring a number of pieces for some of the families in town, so, yeah, I'll be carving the pieces. I can make them look any way you like."

"Could we do four of them? Adding ones at the breaks in the center sections?"

"Sure. I'll need to tone down the designs in the doors so it doesn't get too busy, but, yeah, it's big enough that four figures would work," Connor said, and Dan smiled. "Is there anyone special you want them to look like?"

"No. Just put Lila and Jerry on the ones you originally designed. The other ones can have generic faces. That would be fine."

"I love the idea of this being the focal point for the entire room. Do you want to use the center section for a television?"

Dan shook his head. "I want this piece to be a part of the house. Something that will go on for as long as it's around. Do you know what I mean?"

Connor nodded. "I think I do. You want it to be timeless."

"Exactly. I bought this house because it had a history and because it feels like it's been here a long time and will be here for a long time to come. I'm just its caretaker, so in fifty years, when people are interacting with holographic images for entertainment and the television is a thing of the past, I want this piece to still be relevant."

Connor smiled brightly, and Dan loved that look on him. "I love the way you think. When I build a piece, I make it to last. After I'm gone, I want my pieces to be the antiques of the future, the ones people collect and keep because of the way they look and how they're made. I was thinking of using glass shelves, and we could install lights in the top that would work all the way down." Connor pointed toward the empty space in the center. "What would you like to do with the space that's empty in the center? I had expected to use a television, but I could put in more doors."

Dan shook his head. "Do you think you could carve some decorations that would round off the space at the corners? I could use that space for displaying a larger piece."

Connor pulled a pencil from behind his ear and began making notes for the changes. He added a simple design that worked perfectly. "I like that, and it will make the unit the true focal point." Connor was grinning as he finished up his work. "What I'll do once I'm done in the bathroom is measure the space and the staircase to be sure I have everything needed. There were some specific measurements the lift company requested, as well as the slope of the stairs. It seems strange, but they can really vary in steepness in these older homes."

"Okay," Dan said. "And thank you. That is going to be stunning." Dan finished his coffee and stood up. "I'm going to let you finish your work. I know your time is valuable, and I've probably taken up too much of it already." Dan lifted the coffeepot off the warmer. "Would you like a refill? You can take it with you." Dan refilled Connor's mug as well as his own and watched him leave the room, trying not to look like he was watching.

Connor was a fine-looking man from the back as well as the front. Dan heard Connor in the hallway and then went to his office to check his e-mail. He had plenty, and he delegated some of it to Trevor before firing off notes to the rest of his management staff. Once his in-box was clear, Dan went back into the family room.

The blocks were scattered everywhere. Lila and Jerry were watching television and laughing at the antics of some show on the Disney channel with a music-star father. He loved that sound. "Connor is here putting grab bars and a handheld shower in your bathroom for you," Dan told Jerry. "He's going to make some other changes too. He'll do the same thing upstairs, as well, once he has the downstairs bathroom done. And… he's going to measure the stairs right over there for a lift so you can get up and down on your own. Once that's done, we'll move you upstairs."

"Thank you," Jerry said brightly.

"It gets better, because this weekend we're going to go to the paint store so you can pick out the color you want for your room."

"I want blue with horses and airplanes," Jerry said.

"Okay." That was an interesting combination, and Dan thought about seeing if he could find a designer for the room, but quickly discarded that notion. He wanted to take the time to put together Jerry's room just like he had for Lila. Maybe he could ask Wilson. He seemed to be able to solve any problem around the house.

"Daddy," Lila whined. "I can't hear."

"Okay," Dan said and quietly left the room. He'd instructed her not to turn the television up too loud. "Call if you need anything."

"I will," she answered without looking away from the show. Jerry looked just as engrossed, and Dan figured he'd use the time to get some work done. He went back to his office, but couldn't concentrate. The occasional clink of metal on metal kept distracting him. What the hell was it about Connor that seemed to pull his concentration whenever he was around? He wished he knew so he could stop it. Yet, part of him liked it a lot, because he saw Connor looking back at him sometimes.

"Can I bring you anything?" Wilson asked, stopping in the doorway.

"No, thank you," Dan said, and Wilson continued on his way. Another clink was followed by a thunk, and Dan got up and wandered down to where Connor was working. He didn't want to disturb him, but he wondered what was causing so much noise. Of course he had no idea, but when he peered into the bathroom, he got an eyeful. Connor was lying on his back under the sink, muttering softly to himself. Dan lowered his gaze and stopped. Connor's shirt had ridden up, and a strip of honey-colored belly was peeking out. Connor shifted and the shirt rode up further, and his pants sank just a little more on his hips, just enough so Dan could see the top of his pelvic bone.

Connor was a rugged-looking man; there was no doubt about that. Dan watched him for a full minute before beginning to feel like some sort of pervert. But he simply couldn't tear his eyes away. The sight was too amazing. "Is there anything wrong?" Dan finally asked.

"I'm just having a little trouble turning off the water to this room," he gritted. "There it is," he added breathily. Connor stood up and turned on the sink and the tub. Nothing came out. "I didn't want to affect the other parts of the house, but I think I have it."

"Okay," Dan said. He didn't quite know what to do and figured getting out of Connor's way was best. He ended up going back to his office and forcing himself to concentrate. There was plenty he needed to finish, so he turned his attention back to his work and away from Connor working just a ways away.

Dan ended up closing his door and spent the next couple of hours immersed in his work. When he came out, he heard the sound of the television and laughter drift down the hall. He went to check on the kids and found them playing with the blocks again. The table in the room was covered with crayons and coloring pages, the television was on, and they were immersed in their own playtime. It was perfect. Dan watched them for a few minutes, leaving them alone. They were happy, and he didn't want to interrupt.

Dan walked into the kitchen and sat at the table, where he stared off into space.

"Are you all right?" Wilson asked.

Dan nodded and heard a chair scrape along the floor.

"You know, sir, I never pry into your business."

"You're a part of this family, Wilson." He'd always had a difficult time thinking of Wilson as just an employee. He helped with the children and cared for him. Wilson saw and heard just about everything that happened in the house and said nothing to anyone.

"Thank you," Wilson said. Dan looked up—Wilson appeared to be waiting for something.

"Please," Dan said and motioned with his hand. "Go ahead and say what's on your mind."

"It's nothing, really, and I know it's none of my business. In Britain, I would never say anything, but you have been good to me and you're wonderful with the children. They're your whole life, as they should be. I

was never blessed with children, but I believe that's how it should be."
Wilson fidgeted slightly, which was unlike him. "The last people I worked
for, before I came to work for you… they were flashy, good people, but
very attention getting. They left the care of their children to nannies and
the like."

"I would never do that," Dan said, wondering where Wilson was
going.

"I know that. You want to raise the children yourself, and that's very
admirable."

"Are they too much for you? Do they get in your way?" Dan had
been worried that bringing another child into the house would be more
than Wilson could handle and had thought about bringing in another
person, but he didn't want a large household staff if he could help it. He
was more than happy with his home and all the people in it.

"Heavens, no. They're dears, both of them. I'd be proud to call them
my children," Wilson said quickly. "What I want to say has nothing to do
with them. And as I said, I know it's not my place, so…." Wilson stood
up. "It isn't my place, and I…."

"Wilson, you've seen me at my best and my worst. I come to you for
advice, and you give it freely. I count on that. Now I'm coming to you
again. Please say what you want to say."

Wilson glanced around the room. "I just wanted to say that I'm so
pleased you brought Jerry home. He seems happy, and you did a very
good thing." Wilson turned and left the room. Dan knitted his eyebrows
together. He knew that was not at all what Wilson had actually wanted to
say. He thought about going after him and asking him to tell him the truth,
but he wasn't quite sure how to go about it. He was confident Wilson
would tell him at some point.

A surprised shout rang through the house, and Dan jumped up and
hurried in that direction. It must have been Connor, but he'd never heard
him sound like that. Dan stopped in the bathroom door and peered in.
Connor stood in the shower with water running down the front of him.

"What happened?" Dan asked, suppressing a snicker.

Connor shivered and turned toward him. "I forgot to drain the
shower line, like an idiot. As soon as I loosened the connection, there must
have been some residual pressure, and, well…."

Dan had thought that Connor was going to do the showerhead first, but it appeared he'd done the grab bars, because they gleamed in the shower and around the toilet. Jerry's fingers might be curled, but he was very good at maneuvering himself. Dan knew a day would come when Jerry wouldn't be able to do that any longer, but he was determined to help him remain as independent as he could for as long as Jerry was able. "I'll go get you a T-shirt you can use."

"Thanks, but—" Connor turned fully around, and Dan couldn't hold back his laughter this time. Poor Connor looked like he'd wet himself.

"It's no problem. You're a little smaller than me, but I can bring you something to change into. Give me a minute." Dan hurried up to his room and got a shirt and a pair of older sweatpants. He rarely wore them, but he figured they would probably fit Connor, and it wouldn't matter if he got them dirty or wet. He returned to the bathroom and stopped dead.

Connor had pulled his shirt off. His back was to Dan, so he got a good view of honey-warm skin and broad shoulders that tapered to a narrow waist. The strength on display was intoxicating, as was the raw male scent. Dan closed his eyes for a second and inhaled deeply. "Umm, I brought you these," Dan said and handed Connor the clothes when he turned around. He took them and began pulling on the shirt, but not before Dan got a good look at his nice chest with a slight dusting of brown hair that tapered on his flat belly to a line just below his navel.

Dan watched longer than he should have and then turned away. "I'll let you finish up what you were doing," he stammered and hurried away down the hall toward the family room. The kids were coloring now, Lila at the coffee table, and Jerry trying hard to use his lap. From his frustrated expression, he wasn't succeeding.

"Why don't you move to the table?" Dan asked.

"Because then we can't watch TV too," Lila told him in that way kids have when you say something that sounds dumb to them.

There was a tray that hooked onto Jerry's chair in his room. When Dan had asked him about it, Jerry had said he hated it because it looked like a baby tray and he wasn't a baby. Maybe he could find him a lap desk.

Dan had been on edge for most of the day, and his thoughts felt scattered. The kids were settled and happy. He could hear Wilson making lunch, and he had work he could be doing, but he couldn't settle. If it hadn't been raining, he'd have gone for a walk or spent some time outside, taking in the fresh air, but instead he wandered through the house, living room to dining room to kitchen, and then down the hallway. He knew he was prowling the place like a cat, and he always ended up near where Connor was working.

On one of these passes, he met Connor coming down the hallway.

"What do you think?" Connor asked as he led Dan down to the bathroom just outside Jerry's door.

Dan peered inside. Everything was cleaned up, the grab bars and new towel bars looked really good, and the showerhead was perfect. "Jerry should love that."

"I think so too. The only thing is that someone will need to get it down for him. When I do the one upstairs, I'll find something that will have both so you can leave the handheld lower for him," Connor explained. "The other modifications will take longer, but this should help for now."

"That's excellent. Thankfully the bathroom upstairs is larger, so while this one is functional for him, that one will be even easier." Dan smiled. "This is really good. Thank you. I'm going to get Jerry so he can see it." He hurried back to the family room and told Jerry he had something he wanted him to see. Jerry closed the book he was coloring in and placed the crayon back in the box. He stowed everything in the bag that hung on the side of his chair and then followed Dan down the hall, his chair humming softly.

"Hi, Mr. Connor," Jerry said when he approached the bathroom. Connor stepped back, and Jerry went inside and stopped. "Is this all for me?" he asked, and Dan approached the back of his chair, lightly touching Jerry's shoulders.

"Yes. Now it will be easier for you to take a shower and use the bathroom. There are also towel bars that are lower so you can hang up your towels and easily get to them. Connor's going to make some other changes too." Dan grinned at Jerry's excitement. "We'll try to make things as easy for you as possible." Jerry turned around and smiled. Dan wondered how many eight-year-old kids would get excited about changes to a bathroom, but Jerry certainly was. "Thank you, Mr. Connor," Jerry said.

"It was your dad's idea," Connor said, and Jerry turned to him.

"Thank you," Jerry told him and then turned back around once more. Dan backed away and slowly closed the door. He noticed that the knob had been replaced.

"I should have said something, but a levered door is much easier for Jerry to open, so I went ahead and changed it out. I'll give you the old knob so you can keep it with the house. I tried to find one that wouldn't look too out of place. I can get matching ones for Jerry's room too."

"That's perfect," Dan said, blown away by how thoughtful Connor had been. After a little while Dan heard the toilet flush and then the water ran. The door opened and Jerry came out. The bathroom had been christened, and Jerry seemed happy. He rode down the hallway back toward the family room and kitchen. "I think Wilson has lunch ready. You're welcome to join us."

"I packed some sandwiches and stuff," Connor said. "I can eat in my truck."

"You don't have to. If I know Wilson, he made plenty." Dan motioned and followed behind Connor. Both Lila and Jerry were already at the table. Wilson fixed their plates and then did the same for him and Connor. Dan looked at Wilson and didn't start eating until he joined them as well.

"What else do you have planned for today?" Dan asked Connor.

"Well, since the bathroom is done, I was going to get all the measurements I need and make a list of equipment for the bathroom upstairs. Then I was planning to get out of your hair," Connor answered. "I have some projects back in my shop that I need to finish."

"You could play blocks with us," Lila suggested.

Dan grinned into his plate. "I think Connor has other things to do. But you and Jerry can play blocks all you want," he said. What surprised him was that he wanted Connor to stay. It was nice having him in the house. As the thought entered his mind, Dan reminded himself that Connor was here to do a job. Yes, he was a really nice guy and Dan was growing to like him, but he wasn't part of their family, and no matter how fascinated Dan had become with him....

Dan looked around the table and saw the others staring at him, and he wondered if his thoughts had somehow become visible to the others. He realized they were looking because he'd stopped moving with a bite halfway to his mouth. Dan finished it and resumed eating, but his thoughts continued to race. He wondered what it would be like to have Connor in his life. The kids liked him, that was for sure, and he liked the thought.

Connor was attractive, at least Dan found him so, but there was no way a guy like Connor would be interested in him.

He'd always known there was something wrong with him, and Dan had spent years trying to figure it out. The answer always eluded him, but it was there nonetheless; he knew it. For some reason, he wasn't considered worthy of being loved—that had been demonstrated to him many times, especially by his parents. It was part of the reason he'd been so driven to build his business and why he did many of the things he did in his life, some things he wasn't even aware of, he was sure. Once he was successful, guys only seemed to want him for his money. So there was no way Connor would find him interesting.

He put those thoughts from his mind the way he'd done dozens of times before whenever he met a guy he might be interested in. Dan knew that wishing for something that wasn't going to happen was futile. "Eat the rest of your lunch," he said to Lila gently.

"But you keep stopping, Daddy," she said.

"I'm sorry, I was just thinking."

"You can't think and eat at the same time?" Connor asked, and Dan snapped his head in his direction with a scathing remark on the tip of his tongue. He'd been picked on enough in his life—he wasn't going to stand for it now and in his own home. But the remark died on his lips when he saw Connor grinning at him. "Even I can do that. I bet you can do that too, can't you?" Connor said to Jerry and Lila, who both began to giggle. They looked at him, and Dan realized they were waiting to take their cue from him. He smiled and then began to laugh. The kids followed suit, and soon they were all giggling and laughing.

"I guess I can run a big company, but not eat and think at the same time. I definitely shouldn't be chewing gum, then." The kids didn't pick up on it, but Connor seemed to, and he pointed his fork at him with a wink.

It felt good to laugh. He didn't do it often enough. They finished eating with Dan keeping his attention on lunch. They talked and chuckled. At the end of the meal, the kids began getting silly, and he gently put an end to their antics. Wilson took their plates because they were obviously done, and they both asked if they could be excused. Dan said they could, and they went into the family room.

"They're kids," Connor said.

It seemed like a strange thing to say, but Dan understood.

"When Lila first came to live here, I expected that because she was challenged, she'd be different from other kids. I learned that with some exceptions, like asking for things, she's just like any other child. She can misbehave, get silly, have a case of the giggles, or pout when she doesn't get her way," Dan said with a small smile. "I'll admit that sometimes I'm tempted to go easier on her because of the challenges, but I guess I learned that if I treat her like any other kid, then she'll act and... *be* like any other kid." It was hard for him to explain.

Connor was nodding, and Dan found his opinion mattered. Why, he wished he knew, but having his approval was reassuring.

"Mr. Jerry has more challenges than Miss Lila," Wilson said. He was usually quiet at meals.

Dan nodded his agreement. "True," he said quietly, and he felt a dark shadow pass over him.

"There's something else isn't there?" Wilson asked, and Dan nodded slowly. "If I may be so bold...."

"Of course. The type of MD that Jerry has is debilitating, as you've seen. It attacks the muscles, and eventually it will weaken his heart." A lump formed in his throat. He hated talking or thinking about it, and he had to forcibly keep his voice from breaking. "Most children don't live past ten or eleven. At least they haven't in the past."

A clink echoed through the kitchen and then Connor's fork tumbled to the floor. "Did you know that when you agreed to adopt him?" Connor asked.

"I didn't at the time I made the decision to get him, but I was told and it didn't matter. He's my son," Dan said, and Wilson nodded. "I knew it would be hard, but who could look into those earnest eyes and bright smile and not fall in love?"

Connor bent down to pick up his fork. Wilson took it from him, got up, and brought him another. There was no five-second rule in this house: if it hit the floor, Wilson was on it.

"Lots of people," Connor said. "There have been lots of people through that place and quite a few children placed, but none of them adopted Jerry or Lila." Connor took the fork that Wilson handed him and took a bite of his macaroni and cheese casserole before setting the fork down again. "I thought of adopting Jerry, but I don't have the room or the facilities to really care for him... and... well, I'm very happy you did. But...."

Dan had a pretty good idea of what was coming next.

"You know it will be hard when...." Connor stopped.

He didn't have to say the words. They'd been running through Dan's mind for days. "I figured I would make the most of the time I have with him and worry about the consequences when the time comes. If it's two years or twenty years."

"Does he know?" Wilson asked.

"Yes." Dan couldn't stop a chuckle that nearly got caught on the lump in his throat. "He told me. In fact, last night he asked if I was sure I wanted to adopt him because there were other children who would be easier to care for and would be around longer." Dan had nearly cried his eyes out. "What can you say to that?"

"You are going ahead with it, aren't you?" Wilson asked.

"Of course." The lump in his throat vanished as determination filled him. "He deserves a family as much as anyone—maybe more because he needs it more." Dan didn't go into how much he'd come to realize that he needed both Lila and Jerry too. They filled a place in his heart he hadn't known was empty until they'd come into his life. Laughter drifted in from the other room, and Dan grinned.

"There's no better sound anywhere, is there?" Connor observed.

"No, there isn't," Dan said as his phone rang. He pulled it out and excused himself, then headed down the hall to his office. He didn't get off the phone for an hour, and by the time he hung up, his temper was short. But he'd managed to hold it together through the call, and by the end of it, the office building deal he'd been working on for a month looked as though it would go through, which meant after escrow, he'd need to take a trip to inspect it with the team he'd already put together to build the detailed plans for its future.

Wilson knocked on the door to the office, then opened it and stepped inside. "Mr. Connor took the measurements he needed and left about fifteen minutes ago. He said to tell you that he would call when he had the supplies for the upstairs bath and when he had the details for the stair lift."

"Thank you," Dan said. "I'm sorry I missed him."

Wilson didn't leave right away. "If I may be so bold, I think he was sorry he missed you as well." Wilson then went back toward the kitchen. Dan stared after him and wondered if Wilson meant what Dan thought he meant. *No*, he said silently to himself. That just wasn't possible. He went to find the kids and spent the next hour with them in the family room. It had finally stopped raining and the sun looked like it might peek through the clouds.

"Can we go swimming?" Lila asked when it brightened further outside. Dan walked to one of the sets of sliding glass doors and opened it. The chilly air blew right inside, and he closed the door again.

"I'm afraid not today. But I promise as soon as it warms up again, you can go swimming." He hoped it was soon. "Would you like to do a puzzle? We can set up a table in here and work on one together."

"You'll do it with us?" Jerry asked with a toothy grin.

"Of course," Dan said, his anxiousness slipping away. "I'll see if Wilson can set up a table and get the puzzles." He left the room and wasn't surprised to see Wilson already heading for the basement.

"I have it, sir," Wilson said quietly. One thing was for sure in this house: unless the door was closed, there were few secrets. Sound traveled everywhere. It had taken Dan a while to get used to, and he had to remember to close his office door when he was working in case he raised his voice.

"Do you know where the puzzles are?" Dan asked.

Wilson stopped at the basement door. "In the left side of the cabinet in the family room." Wilson was extremely organized, patient, and he kept the entire house running with little help from the rest of them. He generally took Sundays off, often spending them in his room, where it was quiet. He didn't own a car, but Dan always made sure Wilson had access to one of his at all times.

"Thank you," he said, and Wilson descended the stairs while Dan returned to the family room.

Dan found the puzzles, and Wilson returned with the card table and set it up. For much of the rest of the afternoon, he and the kids worked large puzzles of Mickey Mouse, Goofy, and one of Dora the Explorer. Jerry had turned up his nose at that one, but Lila insisted. Dan had to take a few calls, but mostly it was a quiet day at home. Dan had what he'd always wanted: a family of his own, surrounded by people who loved him. And that family was of his creation. He'd built it and made it from the warmth and depths of his heart. Jerry's laugh and Lila's snickers when they teased each other were sounds that added warmth no matter how cold it was outside.

"You should get yourself a boyfriend," Jerry said out of the blue.

Dan snapped his head around, dropping the puzzle piece he'd been holding.

"You said that you didn't like girls." Jerry placed the piece he'd clutched in his hand and picked up another one by moving it to the edge of the table. That wasn't what Dan had said, but he realized Jerry had put one of the pieces of his life together just as easily as he placed the next piece of the balloon image they were currently working on.

"I like girls… but…."

Jerry looked up from the puzzle. "You don't want to marry one, right?"

"Right," Dan said, glancing at Lila, who didn't seem to be paying much attention. "I don't want to marry one, but I have friends that are girls."

Jerry snickered, and Lila lifted her gaze from the table and she began to laugh too. "Daddy likes boys," she said. "Then why don't you marry one?" She continued giggling, and Dan realized this conversation was out of control.

"Okay, you two," Dan said trying to keep things light so they didn't realize they'd upset him. He didn't think it appropriate to discuss his love life, or the complete lack thereof, with his eight-year-old son and six-year-old daughter. "If I decide to go on a date, I promise both of you I'll tell you. But until then don't worry about me and boyfriends, girlfriends, or getting married, okay? I have all I need right here." Dan hugged each of them and then, thankfully, the conversation turned to other weighty matters such as farts and burps, which came with demonstrations from both of them.

Dan laughed with them and let them have their fun. His mind was on what Jerry had said. Maybe he should go ahead and try to find a boyfriend. It might be nice to have someone in his life. The thought made him laugh. He was successful and had a lot of money. He was sure he could attract guys, but he didn't want someone who'd want him only for his money. And as far as he was concerned, that was the only reason anyone would date him, so he dismissed the notion and went back to playing with the kids.

CHAPTER
Five

CONNOR WORKED in his shop for the next week, trying to keep his mind from constantly wandering to Dan. He arranged to have the rest of the bathroom renovations completed. The vanities were lowered and the roll-in showers completed. The workers were particularly motivated by the promise of the large bonus Dan offered them to get the renovations done and done right within the week.

He hadn't been able to get over how Dan could have adopted Jerry knowing what he knew. Not that he thought it a bad thing in the least, it was just that Dan kept surprising him, and he'd never thought of himself as a guy who was easily surprised. He'd seen and been told some pretty harsh things in his life, so what people did to each other didn't faze him. Connor had been on the receiving end often enough to know that well. He'd spent the last two days finishing furniture and had pieces ready for delivery, which was excellent, because he could use a good payday. He wasn't hurting, by any means, but a steady income was a wonderful thing. He'd laid out all the pieces he'd need for the cabinet Dan wanted and had priced the lumber and materials as well as his anticipated labor. The total cost had made even his eyes widen when he'd added it up, but when he'd called and told Dan, he'd simply said to go ahead with it.

He'd been able to find some incredible walnut that would be perfect for the piece. He'd even found the pieces he needed to complete the carvings. That had added to the price considerably, but Dan had simply reiterated that it would make the piece seem more substantial and a part of the original building. Connor was waiting for a lumber delivery, so when he heard a truck pull into the drive, he expected it to be the lumber he'd found and arranged to have shipped.

"I got some sort of lift thing," the driver said when Connor met him at the truck. He handed Connor the paperwork, but Connor shook his head.

"You delivered it to the wrong address. This is the billing address, but here is where it needs to be delivered," Connor told him and pointed out the mistake on the invoice. The driver immediately began to grumble as Connor handed him back the documentation. "It isn't far, and I can show you the way." He knew Dan would be anxious to get the lift installed, and Connor was eager to see the kids. At least that was what he kept repeating to himself, but it was Dan he kept thinking about whenever his mind was idle, and Dan who seemed to have wormed his way permanently into his dreams and fantasies. Not that Connor intended to do anything about it. The only possible outcome he could see was heartache, and he'd had enough of that to last forever.

"That's good of ya," the driver said.

"Give me a few minutes to close things up and I'll lead the way." Connor walked back to the shop and turned everything off before returning to where the driver waited.

"That looks cool," he said, pointing toward the building on the far side of the property. "Don't see many octagonal barns."

"Nope, you don't," Connor agreed. It wasn't a barn, but he didn't go into that. The description was close enough, and he didn't talk to people about what was inside. The last thing he wanted was people nosing around his business, and folks tended to talk and do just that. "Shall we go?" Connor walked to his truck and got in, then pulled out and waited for the driver to follow him.

Connor called Dan's house on the way. Wilson answered the phone, and Connor told him what was happening. "Just have the driver park near the garage, and I'll have the doors up," Wilson said. "He can unload there."

Connor wanted to ask if Dan was at home, but Wilson had already disconnected, and it wasn't any of his business anyway. He'd been hired to do a job. Connor placed his phone on the seat and made sure the truck was still behind him as he drove toward town and guided the driver to Dan's home. Connor pulled into the empty drive and parked out of the way. Wilson met them and motioned for the truck to go around to the side of the house.

Connor helped the driver unload the larger and heavier pieces from the truck and made sure everything was accounted for. Wilson signed for the shipment and thanked the driver, who got back into his truck and, after a light toot of the horn, pulled down the drive. "Please tell Dan I'll be over in a few days to start the installation," Connor told Wilson as he got ready to head back to his truck.

"You can tell him yourself if you like. He's around back with the kids." Wilson motioned toward the back of the house, and Connor left the garage and walked along the side yard. Sounds of laughter and splashing reached his ears before he turned the corner and saw Dan, Lila, and Jerry in the pool. At first he wasn't sure he wanted to interrupt, but then Dan climbed the stairs with Jerry in his arms. He set him in his chair and straightened up. Connor moved forward like steel drawn to a magnet.

Dan was gorgeous—tall, broad shouldered, with a smooth chest, cut with lines that said Dan had worked very hard in his life—and Connor had to force his gaze away. He'd sort of expected a businessman's desk-induced paunch, but none of that was visible anywhere as far as he could see, and Dan's bathing suit hugged his hips just right to show off his trim shape.

"Mr. Connor," Jerry yelled as he waved. "Did you come over to go swimming with us?"

He approached the pool and saw Lily in the water. "Look at me, I'm walking," she said excitedly. There was a floaty toy around her waist to help keep her up, but she was indeed using her legs to move around the pool.

"What brings you by?" Dan asked as he picked up a towel and wrapped Jerry in it before getting one for himself.

"The lift pieces were delivered today. They came to my place instead, so I escorted them over. They're in the garage, and I'll be over to start the installation in a few days. I have some things I need to finish first. I hope that's okay?"

"Of course," Dan told him with a smile. "Since you're here, would you like something to drink? There's lemonade, or I can arrange for a beer if you want one."

"Lemonade would be nice, thank you," Connor said. Damn, he kept trying to find something to look at other than Dan, but he was continually failing. He sat down, and Dan turned and poured him a glass, giving Connor a good look at the way his suit clung to his backside. He stopped a groan and turned to where Lila was still playing.

"Are you ready to get out?" Dan asked her. Lila shook her head and continued moving. "She's very determined and asks every day if she can get in the water. Ever since she realized it would help her walk, I can't keep her out." Dan tugged Jerry's chair closer and lightly rubbed his arms before getting a second towel and putting it over him. "We can't stay out here much longer. Jerry is getting cold, and you'll turn into a prune," Dan directed toward his daughter.

"Okay," Lila agreed and turned to make another trip back across the pool. Connor watched her. He needed something to do other than stare at Dan.

"Hold on to the side of the pool," Dan told her, and Lila nodded.

Connor watched Dan make sure Jerry was encased in towels. When Connor turned back, all he saw was the toy floating on the water. Without thinking, he leaped into the pool and grabbed Lila, pulled her to the surface, and got her head above water. She sputtered and coughed once before looking at him and starting to cry.

Dan was shaking when he pulled her from Connor's arms and held her close to him. "It's all right, you're safe."

"I wanted to walk without the…." She began to cry again.

"I know and it's all right now," Dan soothed, but Connor heard the fear in Dan's voice as he climbed out of the pool. "I should have been there with you."

"I'm not a baby. I just wanted to walk and I slipped," she said. It took Connor a second to realize that she was more upset about not walking than she was that she'd nearly drowned. Thankfully, Dan didn't mention it, even though the worry was clearly written on his expression. "I took off the ring because I wanted to walk and—" The rest was cut off by tears. Dan held her, and Connor saw tears running down Dan's cheeks.

"It's all right. You will walk, I know it," Dan said, comforting her. "But you can't push yourself. If you get hurt, it will take longer for you to walk." Dan was still shaking, and Connor wasn't sure what to do. Without really thinking about it, he placed a hand on his shoulder just to let him know he was there.

"Oh, God," Dan said, turning around. "You're soaked."

Connor realized his clothes were stuck to him and he began to shiver a little. The water had been warm, but the air was cooler and he was drenched to the skin. He pulled his soggy wallet out of his back pocket and patted his legs. Connor remembered that he'd left his phone in his truck, thank goodness.

"Wilson," Dan called at the top of his voice. One of the glass doors opened and Wilson hurried out. "Please take Jerry inside to his room so he can get dressed. I'm going to get Lila inside and up to her room. Once Jerry is inside, could you get Connor some dry clothes from my room?"

"What happened?"

Dan turned to Wilson. "He just saved Lila's life." Connor could tell Dan was near tears.

"I'm all right," Connor said. "Just take care of the kids. I can get myself home."

"No," Dan said earnestly. "I want you to stay." He seemed so flustered. "Please."

Connor wasn't sure what to do, but he followed Wilson and Jerry inside. As Connor toed off his wet shoes by the door, Wilson said, "Go upstairs. His is the last room on the left. It has its own bathroom. I'll bring you some clothes you can put on." Connor followed the directions as Dan carried Lila up the stairs right behind him.

He went into the bedroom and through to the bathroom, where he began stripping off his clothes. He placed the soggy mess in the bathtub. A soft knock sounded on the door and it opened slightly. Clothes were placed on the granite vanity top and then the door closed again.

"When you're done, I'll put your clothes in the dryer," Wilson said through the door.

"Thank you," Connor replied and stripped off the last of his wet clothes and used one of the towels to dry himself before pulling on the sweats and T-shirt. He hoped he remembered to return these. He still had the other ones he'd borrowed the last time he'd been here.

When he was dressed, Connor gathered his clothes in a towel, opened the door, and padded barefoot out of the bathroom. He couldn't help stopping to take a better look at Dan's bedroom. He hadn't known what to expect, but he was shocked to find the walls covered with crayon drawings and finger paintings. They were beautiful. The bed was plain, but huge, with a solid green spread. The room wasn't big on warmth as far as he could see, but it screamed how much Dan loved his children. As he looked around, he saw some of Jerry's masterpieces already framed.

"Are you all set?" Dan asked as he came in the room.

"Yes, thank you." He looked toward the bathroom. "Wilson said he would dry my clothes for me."

"Yes. He also has your wallet. It's on the counter in the kitchen. He laid things out to dry for you."

Connor headed toward the door. He felt like an intruder in this room. It was too personal and showed him things he wasn't sure Dan meant for him, or anyone, to see. Dan's heart was on display in that room. "Thank you," he said nervously. "I should get going. I'll be sure to bring back the clothes I borrowed." Connor stepped around Dan and out into the hallway.

"Please don't," Dan whispered. "Please don't go." Connor stopped. "I need to get dressed first, but I'll meet you in the family room if you'll stay."

Connor didn't know what Dan had in mind, but his heart raced at Dan's request. He nodded and took one final look at Dan in only his bathing suit before turning and heading toward the stairs. He met Wilson in the kitchen and handed him the bundle of clothes.

"I'll get them in the dryer as soon as I can. They shouldn't take too long to dry. Your wallet, on the other hand, is a soggy mess."

Connor figured as much. "I appreciate you doing what you can."

"Please go in and sit down. I have some water on for tea. I figure that will help warm you both."

"Where are the kids?"

"I believe Miss Lila is lying down and Mr. Jerry is in his room. I hope he lies down as well. We all had quite a scare." Wilson turned toward the stove, and Connor went through to the family room, where he sat in one of the large leather chairs near the windows to catch the warmth of the sun.

"I have to thank you again," Dan began as he walked into the room about ten minutes later. "I don't know what to say. I should have been watching her closer and—"

"It wasn't your fault. You looked away for a few seconds, and she took off the ring."

"I still should have been watching her," Dan insisted, obviously feeling guilty.

"Sometimes things happen. I'm just glad I was here to help her." Connor shifted toward the edge of the seat. "Both kids are incredibly special. They aren't what you expect when you simply look at them and don't get to know them."

Dan nodded. "But I could have lost her and it would have been my fault."

"But you didn't. She's fine and in her room. Jerry is fine too."

Dan sat down, but he didn't look comfortable, like he wouldn't allow himself to be at ease at all. "Sometimes I wonder if I did the right thing... with both kids. I think I was being selfish."

Connor jumped out of his seat. "What you did for those kids was the most unselfish thing I've ever seen anyone do. Those two wonderful kids wouldn't have a home without you. Jerry has been at the home at least since he was five, maybe longer. Maggie told me once that they had pretty much given up on anyone adopting him and they were making plans for the eventual care they knew he would need."

"But Lila almost drowned today. What if I'm not good enough to take care of them?" The pain in Dan's voice made Connor wonder who had hurt him so badly.

"It was an accident, and if I hadn't jumped in, you would have within seconds. Does she blame you?"

Dan shook his head. "I don't think she fully understands what happened. She keeps concentrating on the fact that she wants to walk."

"Then maybe she's blaming herself too," Connor suggested. "I understand being scared. All I could think of when I pulled her out of the water was that I needed to get her back to you. She was only under the water for a few seconds at most. She got a little water in her mouth and that was all."

Dan lapsed into silence. "Maybe I should have the pool removed?"

"Why? That pool will help Lila walk. You can get her a life vest instead of the floaty ring. And the next time you go swimming, make sure you aren't alone, that there's a second adult to watch Lila if you're helping Jerry. That's all you need to do." Connor's heart ached for Dan. He knew he'd feel the same if the situation were reversed, but he didn't blame Dan.

Dan was miserable. After a few minutes, Wilson entered the room with a tray. He set it on the table in front of them and silently left the room. Dan didn't move, so Connor poured two cups of the aromatic tea and handed Dan one of the cups. "What if I've taken on too much?"

"You haven't," Connor said. He sipped from his cup and then set it on the tray. He stood and took a few steps to Dan's chair. "You have the biggest heart of anyone I have ever met." Connor swallowed hard, and when Dan lifted his gaze and met him, he leaned in closer.

Connor expected Dan to turn away, but he didn't move at all. Connor closed his eyes and lightly touched his lips to Dan's. A jolt of energy surged through him, and Connor backed away in surprise. He hadn't been expecting that kind of intense reaction. He had to know, so he leaned forward again, lightly touching the back of Dan's head. The reaction wasn't as sharp, but it was intense. Dan felt so right. It was almost like he'd have missed something very special if he hadn't kissed him. "Wow," Connor said, half under his breath.

"You can say that again." Dan smiled. "I used to wonder what that would feel like when I was in school."

"What it felt like to kiss a guy?" Connor asked.

Dan shook his head slowly. "No, what it would feel like to kiss you." Dan blushed and looked away. Connor continued to watch him, and eventually Dan met his gaze again. "I used to watch you when we were in high school. I had a crush on you like you wouldn't believe."

Connor stepped back slightly in surprise. "Are you kidding? I used to watch you all the time. You were smart and really cute." Now it was his turn to blush. "I didn't have any idea."

"Neither did I," Dan said softly. "Not that it would have mattered. We were so young, and it wasn't like we would have really known what to do anyway. Then I left that following year, and...." He sighed softly. "I really could have used a friend back then."

"Yeah, me too," Connor agreed and waited, but it seemed that neither of them wanted to talk about it. Connor knew he didn't. So instead he kissed Dan again.

He shivered when Dan cupped the back of his head and deepened the kiss. Dan sucked lightly on Connor's lower lip, and Connor heard a soft moan. It took him a second to realize it had come from him. Dan shifted and tugged him closer. Connor placed a hand on the arm of Dan's chair to keep his balance and continued kissing him. He could hardly believe this was happening. He was kissing Dan Harrington. The little piece of his teenage self still inside rejoiced at having his fantasy fulfilled. When Connor pulled back, Dan's eyes were wide and his smile outshone the sun streaming in the windows.

"I never thought I'd get to do that," Connor said. "Can I share a secret with you? I used to dream about you all the time. I remember in school you had long hair that curled upward, and I used to wonder what it would be like to feel it and…." Connor stopped. He wasn't going to tell Dan that he'd been the star in his teenage hormone-driven fantasies. That was way too embarrassing. Dan chuckled softly, and Connor had an idea they were thinking the same thing.

"We were kids and we had hope that our lives would turn out for the better," Dan whispered.

"And yours did. Look at everything you have—your work, the house, the kids. You have a life most people would kill for," Connor commented. "And from what I heard around town"—by that he meant Maggie, but he wasn't going to rat her out—"you did everything yourself."

"Yeah, I guess," Dan mumbled.

"So don't be so hard on yourself. No one is perfect and everyone makes mistakes. Lila is fine."

Dan nodded and stood up. "I should go check on Jerry." He was met by Wilson entering the room.

"Mr. Jerry is in the kitchen at the table," Wilson told Dan. "I had him stay in there so you could talk." The way Wilson looked at them told Connor he knew the kind of talking they'd been up to for the last few minutes. Connor picked up his cup and then sipped his tea while Dan left the room. He heard soft voices coming from the kitchen, and then Dan returned.

"Is he okay?" Connor asked.

"Yes. He's drawing at the table. He wanted to go see Lila, but I told him she was sleeping and that they could play later in the afternoon." Dan took his seat and picked up his cup. They drank their tea in silence, but Connor noticed that Dan kept looking over at him. He was doing the same, and soon they both broke into a fit of laughter.

"You know, we're adults now. We don't have to play these games any longer."

"I guess I've gone without companionship of the carnal sort for so long that I don't know how things work anymore." Dan grinned and hooted. "I mean, I know how things work. I'm not dead… but not what's expected."

Connor took another sip of his tea. "I'm not interested in something that's only of the 'carnal nature.' I want more, I think. I've had relationships, if you could call them that, that never went past the bedroom, and I gave them up. It isn't worth it."

Dan tilted his head slightly. "Those are the only kind I've had." He sipped from his cup and placed it on the tray. "Why did you give them up?"

Connor held his saucer and the cup rattled slightly. He steadied it with his other hand. "Because I think I was always looking for something that wasn't there and was never going to be there. I figured it was better to take care of things myself than to keep getting hurt over and over." Connor set down the cup and sighed. "I understand if all you want from me is a quick thing, but I can't do that."

Dan sat back in the chair. "I didn't mean it the way it sounded. It's all I've ever had, and I'm not familiar with anything more."

"Why?"

"Because no one ever wanted more than that," Dan answered, and the pain that Connor had seen a glimpse of so many times now lay bare in Dan's eyes. For what seemed like the millionth time, he wondered what or who had hurt Dan so badly. He was no stranger to pain, but this was deeper, scarred-for-life kind of pain.

"Well, maybe I do," Connor said bravely. His insides were turning cartwheels and part of him wanted to run the hell out of there and never look back. But he knew Dan had a good heart, and maybe someone like that wouldn't hurt him. Maybe he'd have a chance with Dan if he was willing to take a chance himself. He sure as hell hoped so, because this was as close as he'd gotten in years to putting himself out there.

"Daddy," Lila called as she came into the room, using her crutches, a study in misery.

"Hi, honey." Dan put out his arms, and she came right to him. He carefully lifted her onto his lap, and she snuggled in as Dan leaned her crutches against his chair. "Did you sleep?"

She nodded. "I'm sorry, Daddy," she whispered.

"I'm sorry too. But I know you'll be able to walk someday, and we won't stop trying if that's what you want to do. But you gotta promise me you won't rush so you get hurt. I can take a lot of things, but not you getting hurt."

"Or Jerry," Lila added.

"Yes, or Jerry. I don't want either of the two of you to ever be hurt," Dan told her, and Lila snuggled closer to him. Connor picked up his cup and finished the tea. Then he excused himself and walked into the kitchen, where Jerry was still coloring, concentrating with his tongue between his teeth.

"Excuse me, Wilson, do you know if my clothes are dry?" Connor asked Wilson, who nodded. Connor followed him to the laundry room, where Wilson removed them from the dryer. Once he'd left, Connor changed his clothes in the small room, leaving the ones he'd borrowed in a small pile on the washer. Then he once again found Wilson and picked up his still wet wallet from the kitchen counter. "I'll be back in a few days to install the lift," Connor told Wilson.

"What should I tell Dan if he asks?" Wilson asked him.

"Just say I had some work I had to get done," Connor answered. He put on his still wet shoes and left the house quietly.

He felt like an intruder, and Dan didn't need him hanging around. Connor hadn't wanted to leave, but Lila needed Dan, and so did Jerry. His time was valuable, and there wasn't time for him. Dan could have anyone he wanted, and while it was nice that Dan had had a crush on him too, back in the day, it didn't mean anything now. At least Connor didn't see how it could.

He got into his truck and drove home. He didn't stop in his house or his workshop. He needed quiet and time to think, so he walked across the yard and unlocked the door to the octagonal shed and slipped inside. He turned on his work lights and stared at what he'd been working on. Then he picked up the piece of sandpaper and got to work smoothing the carved surfaces he'd been creating. It was a long, slow process that could take hours, but eventually the exact form and smoothness he needed took shape. By the time he was done, he was pleased, and the doubts and insecurities that had come to the surface while he was at Dan's had been put back into their boxes. He felt calm and settled.

Connor turned off the lights and stepped out into a dark world. He hadn't realized just how long he'd been working or that he was ravenously hungry. He locked the door and walked across the familiar yard to the house. He went inside and made himself his usual dinner—with an extra sandwich because he'd missed lunch—settled in front of the television, and fell asleep as soon as he was done eating.

CHAPTER
Six

"WHY DID Mr. Connor leave without saying good-bye?" Lila asked when Dan put her to bed that same night.

"I think he had some work he needed to do," Dan answered. He was nearly as confused as she was and didn't understand why Connor had left. "He said that he would be back in a few days to put in the lift for Jerry's chair."

"So I'll see him again?"

"Of course you will," Dan reassured her. But he wasn't completely convinced any of them would be seeing much of Connor. Dan had no doubt Connor would do what he'd said he would, but as the projects got ticked off the list, they would all see less of him. "But Mr. Connor has things he needs to do."

"You like Mr. Connor, don't you, Daddy?" Lila asked.

"Yes. Mr. Connor is a nice man."

"Jerry says you like Mr. Connor for real. Like, you want him to be your boyfriend." Lila snuggled under the light covers. "Do you want Mr. Connor to be your boyfriend? 'Cause if you do, you should ask him. I bet he'll say yes."

"You think so, huh?" Dan teased, tickling her lightly, and giggles filled the lavender and pink bedroom. He didn't tickle her for very long. "Well, I don't know what I want or what Connor wants, but asking him isn't as easy as you make it sound, honey."

She rolled over until she was facing him. "Daddy, you said all I have to do is ask if I want something."

"I know, honey, but this isn't as simple as asking Wilson to make you waffles for breakfast. There's a lot more to this." Dan knew that asking Connor was only going to get him a "no." Sure, Connor had kissed him a few times, but then he couldn't get out of the house fast enough, so obviously Dan had been right all along. He wasn't what Connor wanted, and it helped confirm the notion that no one was going to want him and he needed to build his own family—one where he knew the people loved him, and that was Lila and Jerry. They loved him with no questions asked, and that was all he needed. He could get along just fine with his business and the kids. He didn't need anything else. "Why don't you close your eyes and go to sleep?" Dan leaned over her bed and gently kissed her forehead. "I love you, sweetheart."

"I love you too, Daddy," Lila said and settled on the bed. Dan turned out the light and partially closed her bedroom door. Then he walked down the hall and stairs. Jerry was in his room, still in his chair at a small table in the corner.

"Do you think this is good?" Jerry asked. He lifted a piece of paper, and Dan took it and looked at the image. Dan had bought Jerry some colored pencils for him to experiment with, and Dan nearly took a step back as his own face stared out at him from the page.

"This is wonderful," Dan said, staring at the drawing. He remembered that Connor knew Ken Brighton. Dan had bought one of his paintings a year earlier, but he didn't know the artist personally. When he saw Connor again, he'd ask him if he would introduce them. Jerry's talent needed to be nurtured, and Dan knew nothing about art other than what he liked. "You're very talented." Dan knelt next to him. "You have a real gift."

"It's just a drawing," Jerry said dismissively.

"It's a very good drawing, and I really love it."

"I'm going to make one for Mr. Connor too, see?" Jerry said and motioned toward another sheet of paper. The bold outlines of Connor's face were plain to see. Few of the details and none of the shading had been done, but it was most definitely Connor.

"That's wonderful too," Dan said. "Now put your pencils away for tonight and let's get you ready for bed. Did you brush your teeth and did you get your shower?" He didn't really need to ask, since he could see that Jerry was in the same clothes he'd been wearing since they'd gone swimming. "Do you want some help?"

"I can do it," Jerry said.

"Okay. Then go get your shower, and I'll come back in to tuck you in and say good night." Dan left the bedroom and stopped in Jerry's bath to set the showerhead down where he could reach it when he rolled his chair into the shower. Then he went to his office, keeping the door open. He worked on e-mail and other things while he listened to the water run. This was becoming a part of his regular routine. He wanted Jerry to be as independent as possible, but he also needed to be close by in case Jerry required help.

He tried to concentrate on work and returned a few e-mails, but he spent most of the time wondering why Connor had left the way he had. Dan had been hoping they could talk some more. He knew it would have to be once he'd gotten the kids settled, but he'd been hoping Connor would stay. He seemed to like him, if the kiss had been for real and not some pity thing. Dan gasped at the notion, and then his anger began to rise. If Connor thought Dan needed his pity, he was sorely mistaken. With his ire raised, he attacked his work with a passion, just like he always had in the past. And once he had Jerry tucked in bed, Dan returned to his office and went straight back to work.

At one point Wilson told him he was heading to bed. Dan nodded and thanked him before returning to work. He spent hours catching up on things that he'd let sit for a while, until his plate was empty. Then he yawned and checked the clock. It was after two, and he knew he needed to get to bed because the kids would be full of energy in the morning.

Dan stood up and worked the crick out of his back. Then he walked quietly down the hall and checked on Jerry, who was sound asleep. He stared at him for a few minutes, watching as he slept, his roiling emotions calming. Dan then turned and, as quietly as possible, walked up the stairs. He checked on Lila, who had kicked off her covers, something she would never have done a few months earlier. Her little legs were getting stronger, and Dan smiled wearily. He gently covered her back up and then went to his own room. He closed the door and went into his bathroom to clean up. Dan thought about showering, but he was too tired, so after brushing his teeth, he undressed and got ready for bed. After turning out the lights, he opened his door so he could hear if Lila needed him and then climbed into bed.

Even though he was exhausted, he tossed and turned for a while and kept thinking of Connor. The man had him so confused. Their kiss had been electric—Dan swore his hair had stood on end—but then Connor had left. Dan knew that was what he should have expected, because it was what always happened when he began to care for someone. "Screw it," he said out loud and rolled over again, punched the pillow, and closed his eyes. He needed to rest and forget about it. Eventually he fell asleep.

Dan felt like crap when he woke up. His mouth tasted like he'd been drinking. He brushed his teeth, shaved, and took a quick shower before dressing. He felt better, but still not 100 percent, when he was done. Served him right for staying up so late. Then Dan went downstairs and found both kids and Wilson in the kitchen. He sat at the table with his eyes closed and tried to wake himself up.

"Here you go," Wilson said and placed a huge mug of coffee in front of him.

"Thanks," Dan said and sipped the nectar of the gods.

"Can we go swimming today?" Lila asked. At least she seemed to have gotten over what had happened, even if Dan hadn't.

"Not today," Dan answered looking outside. "It isn't sunny and warm. But we will when it gets nice again. If the weather isn't better soon, we'll go to the therapy pool in town. I have a meeting this morning and another one early this afternoon. So both of you mind Wilson, and I'll be out to see you once I'm done."

"I wanna play with you Daddy," Lila whined softly, and Dan stood up and lifted her into his arms.

"I want to play with you and Jerry too. But I have work I have to do. So be a good girl for me, and when I'm done with my meetings, I'll take both of you for ice cream."

"Wilson too?" Lila asked, settling in his embrace with her arms around his neck and her head on his shoulder.

"Yes, Wilson can come too if he wants."

"Can Connor come?" she asked.

"I don't think so. He's busy," Dan answered, and the anger and frustration from the night before resurfaced. He hugged her and slowly rocked back and forth. Jerry watched them for a few moments and then returned to his breakfast. "Why don't you finish your breakfast," Dan said gently and set Lila in her chair. "How about after ice cream you can both find a book and I'll read to you?"

That brought a smile to her face and Jerry's as well. Dan sat back down and finished his coffee, talking with both kids until he had to go to his office for his conference call.

Which didn't go well. He was short with his employees and he knew it. As soon as he hung up, he began swearing under his breath. He knew he could be demanding and he wanted what he wanted, but he wasn't a grouch and he rarely lost his temper. But he had today, and it upset him. He picked up his phone and called Trevor. "Please schedule a meeting with the same team for next week," he said as soon as Trevor answered.

"I understand you weren't happy," Trevor said, and Dan could already hear him typing. "I have it set for next Friday at the same time. Is that good?"

"Yes, thank you," Dan said and then spent some time going over everything and reviewing his schedule for the following week with Trevor. He was going to have to make a trip into the office to spend some face-to-face time with his managers. He had good people, but since adding Lila and now Jerry to his family, he'd taken a step back from the business and he needed to change that. He wasn't sure how he would be able to juggle everything, but he'd figure out a way. Both the business and the kids were important to him, and he wasn't willing to sacrifice either.

"John McMillan came by yesterday and said he had a potential deal he wanted to talk to you about. He asked for a meeting in two weeks."

That got Dan's attention. He was disappointed that he'd missed him and glad he'd asked for a meeting. McMillan could be touchy and tended to do things his own way. "That's good. I'll plan to be in the office for most of that week. Put that as early in the week as you can." He could bring the kids down with him, and he'd call Peter to see if he could see Jerry while they were in town instead of asking him to travel up to them. That could work. The whole family could spend the week in Ann Arbor, and he could take the kids to see the sights when he was done working.

"Excellent. Do you want me to let everyone know you'll be here? Or should it be a surprise thing?" He could almost hear Trevor smiling.

"Let them know. I want everyone to be prepared. But warn them that dog and pony shows aren't going to get them anywhere." They always tried to show him their best and hoped he wouldn't see the rest. "Be sure to emphasize that I want accurate appraisals of all current projects, the good with the bad. Disclosure of what isn't working and a plan to fix it is going to go a lot farther than sugarcoating what's wrong."

"I'll be sure to do that," Trevor told him, still typing away.

"Good," Dan said and then paused as he thought through some things. "Is there anything you need me to do for you? I know you've been taking on some extra burdens since I moved up here, and I want to make sure it isn't overwhelming."

"No," Trevor said lightly. "I'm good."

"Okay. Is it possible to move that meeting I have this afternoon to this morning?" Dan asked.

"Let me check," Trevor said. "I don't think so. Everyone is booked solid."

"All right." Dan had hoped to consolidate some of his schedule. "Don't bother, then. We'll have it at one. Call me a few minutes beforehand." Trevor said he would, and they disconnected. He worked the rest of the morning until he heard an argument reach his ears. Dan sighed and got up. He needed a break anyway.

In the kitchen he found colored pencils all over the floor, Jerry sulking, and Lila with her head on the table, crying. "She took my pencils and threw them on the floor," Jerry said indignantly, the slur in his voice more pronounced now that he was upset.

"I just wanted to draw too," Lila whimpered.

"Did you throw the colored pencils on the floor?" Dan asked her, and she nodded.

"He was being mean. I don't want him for a brother anymore. You can take him back where he came from!" she spat out loudly and then reached for her crutches, which clattered onto the floor. Lila continued to cry, and Jerry backed his wheelchair away from the table and rolled toward his room, his chin reaching his chest.

Dan wanted to split himself in half. "Those were Jerry's pencils. I got them for him. Did you ask if you could use them?" Dan asked her as calmly as he could. He could feel the pressure from work and the argument beginning to build behind his eyes. His head felt like it was going to explode.

Lila shook her head.

"Maybe if you'd have asked, he would have said yes," Dan told her. "And another thing…." He lifted her up and pulled her onto his lap. "Jerry is just as much a member of this family as you and me and Wilson, so we don't say mean things like that to each other."

"But he…." She sniffled.

"You hurt Jerry, badly, and he went to his room." Dan touched her chin and she lifted her head. "What do we say to people when we hurt them?"

"Sorry," she said.

"That's right. But you need to say that to Jerry," Dan said and then set her down. He picked up her crutches and handed them to her. Then he watched her leave. As soon as she left the room, Wilson stepped to the table. "Don't pick them up for her. She'll do it when she gets back."

"Certainly," Wilson said and straightened up.

"I know you didn't intend to help with two kids when you agreed to continue working for me, and I was wondering...." Dan shifted in his chair. "You do a lot for all of us and it's appreciated, so I'm going to give you a raise effective immediately, and I'd like you to try to find someone to come in a few days a week to help you around the house."

"You want to hire someone else? Am I not doing enough?" The indignation was unexpected.

Dan chuckled. "I trust you to help with the kids, and if you're willing to do that, then I think you'll need someone to help with the other chores. It isn't necessary, of course, but...."

"No. I understand," Wilson said with a small smile. "I love both those kids. They're wonderful. I never had children of my own and...." It was the first time Dan had seen Wilson this emotional. "I'll see if I can get someone to come in who can help with the laundry and some of the other domestic chores."

"I've thought about a nanny," Dan said.

Wilson's eyes widened and he shook his head. "Those kids need you, not a stranger. They both had plenty of strangers when they were in foster care or at the orphanage. I'll help you any way I can. They deserve what's best for them, and if I may be so bold, I believe that's you."

"Thank you," Dan whispered, some of the stress slipping away. "Go ahead and find someone you believe will fit into the household."

"Do you want to talk to them?" Wilson asked.

"Once you've made a decision, yes," Dan said, and then he left the room and walked down the hall toward Jerry's room. He heard talking, and when he peered into the partially open doorway, he saw Lila hugging Jerry.

"I'm really sorry. Please don't go," she said.

"But I don't belong here. You can't possibly understand."

Dan pushed open the door. "Lila, go back to the kitchen and pick up the pencils from the floor. Wilson will probably help you if you ask him." She looked at him and then at Jerry. "It's all right," he soothed. He could tell she was worried about Jerry. She gathered her crutches and left the room. Dan stroked her silky hair and whispered that she should tell Wilson what they wanted for lunch. When she was gone, he closed the door.

"Jerry, I think it's you who doesn't understand," Dan began gently.

Jerry was at one of his drawers, pulling out clothes and stuffing them into one of the reusable grocery bags he'd brought with him. "I understand plenty," Jerry said. "It's you who doesn't. I don't belong anywhere." The tears started coming, and Dan stood up and gently turned Jerry's chair.

"I understand very well. See, I was just like you in a lot of ways." Dan leaned down so he could be close to Jerry. "Put your arms around my neck." At first he didn't think Jerry would do it, but then he felt him slide his little arms around his neck. Dan carefully scooped Jerry into his arms and carried him to the bed, where he sat down and settled Jerry on his lap. "I grew up thinking no one wanted me too. But I'll tell you something—I want you here, and so does Lila. She was just angry." Jerry rested his head on his shoulder, and Dan felt him heave his breaths. "We all do. You are part of this family, and we love you." Dan held Jerry so close. "You're as dear to me as Lila is."

"But she's been here longer, so you must love her more than me." Jerry's voice was soft.

Dan's eyes filled with tears. "I've loved her for longer, but not more." He gently stroked Jerry's short hair. "You'd break my heart if you left." He knew how it felt to be the one no one wanted, and he would not let that happen to Jerry. "I want you, and so does Lila." Dan whispered. "Sometimes people say things when they're angry that they don't mean." Jerry nodded and held him tighter. "Are you hungry?"

Jerry nodded.

"Then let's go have some lunch." He looked at the clock beside Jerry's bed and realized he had ten minutes before his next meeting. He got to his feet and gently placed Jerry back in his chair. He squirmed slightly once he got seated. "Are you comfortable?" Jerry shrugged, and Dan made a note to see about getting him a new chair. He might be outgrowing the one he had. There were so many things he needed to do. Jerry settled, and Dan waited for him to leave the room and then followed him down the hall to the kitchen.

Dan got the kids settled, and Wilson began lunch while Dan went to his office for his next call. Thankfully it went much better than the one that morning. The project was running smoothly, and he made a note to keep an eye on that team. "Is there anything you need me to do for you?" he asked at the end of the call.

"Just your continued support," the team leader told him with a smile that shone through the video conference.

"Then we'll meet in two weeks, when I'm in the office. Keep up the good work," Dan said and signed off the call. He closed the video window on his large monitor and opened his e-mail, groaning at the eight or nine messages that had come in while he was on the phone. Wilson came in with a sandwich, and Dan thanked him. His phone rang and he picked it up right away, then spent the next hour on the phone with Trevor, giving him instructions and clearing out his messages while taking quick seconds to eat.

By the time he was done, Dan was exhausted, but his desk was clear for the moment. He had reports he needed to read over the weekend, but he could do that then. He left the office and found Lila and Jerry in the family room with Wilson in one of the comfortable chairs, feet up, reading a book. He knew the second Wilson saw him because he pushed away the ottoman and began getting up. "Please relax," Dan said to Wilson. "I'm going to take the kids for ice cream. You're welcome to come with us if you like, or you can have a few hours alone." Wilson sat back down, and Dan got Jerry and Lila bundled into the new van with a lift and they headed to town to Lila's favorite ice cream stand. Once he'd parked the car, Dan got them out and settled at one of the tables under an umbrella. He found out what they wanted and went to the counter to place their orders. He waited, and when the counter girl passed his tray through the opening, Jerry's sundae had the wrong topping and nuts, and Lila's ice cream was already melting. Only his was right, and by the time he had the kids' orders remade, his had melted and needed to be redone. Dan did his best to keep his temper, but it was damned close to the surface.

He carried the tray to the table and helped both kids with their treats before sitting down. They chattered back and forth as they ate. Dan did his best to concentrate, but he was running on empty at the moment. "Why don't you see what kinds of shapes you can see in the clouds?" Dan suggested, and that occupied them for a little while and gave him a chance to catch his breath and eat.

"Hey, there's Mr. Connor," Lila said and called out. Dan looked up and saw Connor across the street, heading into the hardware store. "Why didn't he wave?" Lila asked once he'd disappeared.

"I don't think he heard you," Dan said. But he got the impression that Connor had, and his anger rose again. Connor might have rejected him, but Dan wouldn't let him hurt the kids. Dan picked up the dishes once Lila and Jerry were done and threw them away. He kept an eye on the hardware store, but didn't see Connor come out again. "Are you ready to go?"

"It's sunny now, can we go swimming?"

"It's not warm enough, honey," Dan said. The wind was off the lake, and while it was sunny, he was glad he'd put the kids in sweatshirts. It took him a few minutes to get everyone in the van, and then he drove back toward the house, gripping the wheel. "Why not me?"

"What, Daddy?" Lila asked.

"Nothing," Dan said and continued mumbling. He saw the kids looking at each other in the rearview mirror, but he continued driving. He pulled into the drive and got the two of them inside. They wanted to play blocks.

"I'll watch them," Wilson offered, and Dan headed to his office under a full head of steam. He spent a little time on the Internet, looking up what he needed.

"I'll be back in a while," Dan told Wilson and grabbed his keys. "Call if you need anything." Wilson nodded and Dan left the house, got in his Mercedes, and headed out of town.

It took him ten minutes to get to Connor's place. He probably should have thought this through better, since he'd just seen him in town. Thankfully, Connor's truck was there, and Dan pulled to a stop behind it. He got out and looked around. He'd had a shitty day and he figured it couldn't get any worse, so he might as well find out what was going on rather than sitting at home wondering.

Dan had always kept his business in one box and his emotional life in another. He'd decided to use some of the take-charge attitude from his business life to figure things out with Connor. But now that he was here, he was second-guessing his decision as the old doubts surfaced once again.

"Dan? What are you doing here?" Connor asked as he came out of the shed toward the end of the driveway.

"I came to see you," Dan said and strode to where Connor stood. "Why did you leave yesterday?"

"You were with the kids and you didn't need me around," Connor answered. "Is this about me kissing you?"

"Yeah, I guess it is," Dan answered forcefully. "Did you mean it, or was that some pity thing?" God, he was so going to regret this. He was starting to think he should just turn around before he made a worse fool of himself.

"No," Connor said in a whisper. "It wasn't pity." The look in Connor's eyes stopped Dan cold. The anger and confusion he'd built up all day and night slipped away as he saw all the doubts and insecurities he felt reflected back at him. "Shit...." Connor swore, almost under his breath. "I'm crappy at stuff like this."

"Stuff like what?" Dan asked with more force than he intended. "Kissing and then leaving?"

"Maybe you should go," Connor said.

Dan turned to leave, but stopped and strode to where Connor stood. He cupped Connor's cheeks in his hands and kissed him with everything he had... and Connor kissed him back. Dan released Connor's cheeks, wrapped his arms around him, and pulled him close. He didn't want to let him go. They kissed until Dan was totally breathless. He backed away slightly to gasp for air without letting Connor go.

"I'm not very good at this," Connor whispered.

"Good at what? Kissing?" Dan smiled. "I can tell you you're dang good at that."

"No. I'm not good at being with other people," Connor explained. "I usually end up getting hurt."

Dan scoffed and felt Connor tense. "You aren't the only one." Connor stilled and stared at him. "What, you think you're the only one with issues? It took getting good and angry for me to come over here."

"Wait," Connor said and stepped back. "You run a company that you started yourself. You have to have all the confidence in the world. You can't tell me that I intimidate you. Please."

Dan began to laugh and tugged Connor closer. "I can rule a boardroom, but put me in a club with a bunch of guys, and I'm a total wallflower. Wait... so you really do like me, and what happened yesterday wasn't...."

"No, what happened yesterday was because I've liked you since I was almost sixteen years old. But then you started talking about hookups, and I didn't want that, and before I could ask, you had to deal with the kids, so I figured I should leave and not bother you."

Dan couldn't believe it. "We're quite a pair, aren't we?"

"I guess," Connor whispered. "So you came over here to ream me out?"

"I guess, yeah," Dan said. "I've been hurt so much I guess I figured what was once more, and I'd built up a good head of steam that boiled over when we saw you go into the hardware store and you didn't wave back at Lila."

"That was her? I thought I might have heard someone, but I didn't see anyone and figured it was my imagination." Connor shook his head, and Dan pulled him close once again. It felt amazing to hold him in his arms, and Dan didn't want to let him go, but there was only so long he could stand here like this. "Dan... um, this is nice, but I need to get back to my workshop. I was in the middle of something." Connor looked back toward the workshop.

Dan released him and stepped back, disappointed.

"I have a few things to finish up and then I can be free. I could come over to start installing the lift," Connor offered.

"Why don't you come over when you're done, but join us for dinner instead?" Dan smiled and waited for Connor's reaction. Yeah, Connor had responded to him, and he'd said he liked him, but as soon as Dan released Connor, his confidence slipped away, and his belly began to jump and churn.

"That would be nice," Connor said and then smiled. "What time should I be there?"

"About six," Dan answered tentatively.

"Okay," Connor agreed, and Dan hurried up to him. He kissed him quickly and then rushed back to his car. When he'd come out here he hadn't had any sort of plan other than telling Connor off and maybe trying to settle some of his confusion. Dan had never dreamed of this outcome, not in a million years. His feet barely touched the ground as he reached his car and got inside. He started the engine, still smiling, and waved before backing out of the drive and making the return trip home.

Dan pulled into the garage and realized he didn't remember making the trip. He'd driven on autopilot, his mind on cloud nine. Connor liked him and they'd kissed, like, blown-his-socks-off kissed. He pulled into the garage, turned off the engine, and sat without moving. His excitement had overwhelmed everything else, but now caution wound its way back in.

Dan gripped the wheel and willed all of that away. He was taking a chance this time, and even though it made him nervous, what he'd seen in Connor's eyes told him maybe Connor would understand.

He sat in the car long enough that the windows began to fog. Dan took a deep breath and released it to calm his nerves. Then he opened the door and got out before closing it with a solid thunk that reverberated through the enclosed space.

"Daddy," Lila called as soon as he stepped into the house. He tensed, wondering if this was the beginning of another incident like earlier in the day. "Look what we made," she said, and Dan blew out his breath. He walked into the kitchen. Lila sat at the table, seated next to Jerry, with the fought-over colored pencils between them.

"See, isn't it better when you share?" he said to both of them, and he got glares of incomprehension.

"We drawed you pictures," she explained and handed him her drawing. She was getting to the point where simple shapes were recognizable, but other things were tough to figure out most of the time.

"Drew," Dan corrected gently and then bent down to look at her drawing.

"It's a horsey," she said, and Dan nodded.

"It's very pretty," Dan told her and kissed her on the head.

"There was a *Lone Ranger* rerun on television," Wilson explained. "They both watched it, enthralled, and then wanted to draw."

Jerry showed him his horse drawing. It was beautiful. He'd been using a picture from an old encyclopedia as a model, and the drawing was incredibly lifelike. "That's great," Dan said and bent down, hugging Jerry lightly. "You have real talent." Jerry smiled and then went back to his drawing. Dan watched him for a few minutes as he made small, exact movements to complete his drawing. Jerry looked up at him and smiled his unique smile, and it warmed Dan's heart.

"Me too?' Lila asked, and Dan walked over to where she sat and lifted her into his arms.

"I'm so lucky to have such amazing kids," Dan told them both. Lila squealed with delight, and he held her for a few moments before placing her back in her chair.

When he looked up again, Jerry was staring at him. "Someday, do you think I might be able to ride a horse?"

The question stopped Dan in his tracks. "I don't know," he answered honestly. "Where did that come from?"

"We saw it on television and the Lone Ranger looked like he was having fun." Jerry returned to his drawing. "I know I can't ride a horse… ever." His speech was very slurred, and Dan knew it was from disappointment.

Dan knelt down next to him. "I wish I could tell you that you can do everything everyone else can do, but we both know that isn't always possible. But how about if I look into seeing if you can ride a horse?"

"Me too?" Lila declared.

"Yes, you too," Dan agreed. He'd heard of places that did therapy riding, and maybe Jerry would be able to ride. He somehow doubted it, given the way that Jerry's legs tended to curl; he might not be able to balance on a horse. Dan would find a way, though. If it was possible, Jerry would ride a horse. "Is something wrong?" Dan asked Jerry when he saw him rubbing his hands together.

"It hurts a little," Jerry said, indicating his right hand. Then he shrugged and went back to his drawing as though nothing was wrong. Dan wondered how much pain Jerry simply lived with on a daily basis. If he had it all the time, he wouldn't know anything different and would think it was normal. Jerry had to be one of the toughest kids ever.

Dan stood where he was, watched them for a few minutes, and then caught Wilson's eye. He walked down the hall toward his office, and Wilson followed shortly behind him. "Connor is going to be joining us for dinner tonight," Dan told him.

"Very good," Wilson said with a smile, and before Dan could ask him what that was for, he'd already turned away. "I'll make something special."

Dan sat at his desk and brought up his file of contacts. After finding Peter's number, he made the call. "Peter, it's Dan Harrington," he said when the call connected and he heard a familiar raspy voice. Peter always sounded like he'd smoked a pack of cigarettes a day since birth, but he was an avid health nut, even in school, and would never have allowed something like cigarette smoke to touch his lungs.

"Danny," he said energetically, "how's the business mogul? We haven't talked in a while." Peter always sounded like he was in a hurry.

"It has been a while." Dan couldn't keep the smile off his face. "I'm calling because I need your expertise."

"What's wrong? I can fit you in whenever you need," Peter said in a rush, and Dan figured he was pulling up his schedule.

"It's not me. It's my son."

Peter went silent.

"You there?" Dan asked.

"You have a kid?" Peter asked.

"Two, actually. Lila is six and Jerry is eight. He's been with me for less than a month and he has MD. At the home they said his condition was terminal, but I want a second opinion. I'm hoping you can squeeze us in sometime in the next few weeks. He's a great kid and I'm in the process of adopting him."

"Wait," Peter said sharply. "You knew Jerry was terminal and you agreed to adopt him anyway?" He whistled. "I always knew you had the biggest heart of anyone I've ever met, but you really kept it hidden under the driven exterior. It took nine years, but now I have proof." Peter chuckled. "So, is there a man in your life? I didn't think so," Peter said when Dan didn't answer. He was one of the few people that Dan had ever shared his story with.

"Not at the moment, but maybe. There's someone here I like, but it's so new it may not be real."

"Come on, Danny. You never opened up to anyone. It took two years before you even hinted at what you went through as a kid. But don't you think it's time you left that behind and opened up to someone special?"

"We can't all be as happy as you and Sharon," Dan quipped.

"Danny, she and I are separated." Peter sounded heartbroken. "She wasn't prepared to deal with the reality of being a doctor's wife."

"Are you going to divorce?"

"I hope not. We're still talking and haven't made any decisions. She's an amazing woman, and I can't see my life without her."

"I'm sorry," Dan said honestly.

"I am too. I still love her, and I think she still loves me. It's just the hours and demands that she can't get used to. Not that I can blame her. I get calls at all hours, and half the time we went to bed together, she woke up alone."

"In business, everything is about priorities. So make her a priority," Dan suggested. "Sometimes all people want is time, and for the record, I saw the way she looked at you a year ago. That kind of love doesn't go away."

Peter scoffed lightly. "When did you become such an expert on love?"

"Those who can, do. Those who can't, teach."

Peter laughed loudly. "Or at least give advice," he added. "So this guy you're sort of seeing…."

"Yeah…," Dan said.

"Is he a good guy? One you think you can trust?"

"I'd like to think so." Dan's cheeks warmed. "I had a crush on him when I was sixteen." *God, that sounded so stupid.*

"Then take a chance," Peter told him. "Tell him about yourself. You never left that behind, but maybe if you talk to someone and are honest with him, he'll understand. It's nothing to be ashamed of." Peter paused. "And if this guy is the one for you, then he'll feel the same way I do."

"It isn't how he feels that's important. I just can't get hurt anymore."

"I know what you're doing. I went to medical school, remember, and I planned to be a psychiatrist for a while. You can't let the fear of getting hurt stop you from living your life and having someone to share it. You deserve that. You always have. Now that I've said my piece and probably pissed you off, I can't wait to see you and meet the kids. I'll make an appointment for Jerry and arrange for the tests at the medical center, and let you know when to come down. Nothing invasive or painful, I can promise that."

"Jerry will be pleased with that. He already asked me if it would hurt." Dan settled back in his desk chair. It felt good to be talking to an old friend. He'd missed that since moving here a year ago, but he loved the town and he had memories here. "By the way, I don't know for sure, because he rarely says anything, but Jerry may be in pain."

"That's possible. With MD, his muscles will deteriorate until they can't perform their functions any longer. But they don't necessarily do it at the same rate, so the stronger ones try to compensate for the weaker ones, and that can cause discomfort. When you bring him down we'll do a full workup. There are a number of drug therapies that can slow the progress of the disease and some that can reverse the effects, at least temporarily."

Dan's heart dropped a little. He'd been hoping for a miracle.

"This isn't magic, and MD isn't something you catch like the flu and wait out. It's something that we can treat and work with, but it is progressive.

You knew that. I can't be any more specific than that, and I've already told you more than I would tell a normal patient without an exam."

"I understand. Let me know when you'd like to see him, and I'll bring both kids by to meet you." Dan tried to keep the disappointment out of his voice. "I know you'll do everything possible."

"I will, of course, but the best thing for kids like Jerry is to give them the best life possible in the time they have. They have to live for today. And I know you'll do that." They talked for a few minutes more, and Dan invited him to come up for a visit and told him to bring Sharon as well.

"Playing matchmaker?" Peter asked.

"Just giving you the chance to take my advice," Dan said, and Peter said he'd think about it. After hanging up, Dan walked back into the kitchen, where Wilson was cooking and the kids were sitting at the table eating mac and cheese.

"Wilson is going to take us to the movies," Lila said with a grin.

"He is?"

"Yeah," Jerry echoed.

"There's a screening of *Cars* at the theater downtown, and I thought the kids would like to see it. And you can have a quiet dinner." Wilson turned back to the stove. Dan thought he might have been smiling. "We'll have a great time, and I can spend some time with the kids doing something fun."

"Thank you," he said. He hadn't planned on this evening being a date, but apparently Wilson had a different idea, and the kids seemed so excited, he wouldn't want to disappoint them.

"I'll have everything ready for you, so all you'll need to do is serve," Wilson said and then looked him over. "You have time to freshen up if you wish."

He was about to grumble, but the kids were looking at him, and when he looked down at himself, he realized he probably was a little rumpled. So he went upstairs to his room and shaved again before changing his clothes and making sure he looked "presentable," as Wilson would put it. When he was done, he rejoined the rest of the family. The kids finished eating and Wilson sent them to wash up before they got ready to leave. When they had left the room, Wilson explained that the dining room table was set and that dinner was in the oven. "Just serve the food at six thirty. I have places for each of them marked on the table, and I'll take care of the dishes when we get home."

"Are you handling me?" Dan asked with a little amusement.

"No, but I will if you don't start doing some things for yourself," Wilson warned. "Now, please have a pleasant evening." After Wilson finished in the kitchen, Dan made sure he had money for the evening's expenses and the keys to the van. He helped Wilson bundle the kids into the van and waved good-bye to them as Wilson backed out of the garage. He went back inside and realized he had nothing to do until he heard the front bell ring.

He was so nervous he actually fumbled with the door before opening it. What if Connor had just come over for dinner and Dan had read everything wrong? Dan opened the door and saw Connor smiling at him in a pair of nice pants and button-down shirt rather than the jeans and work shirts he'd seen him in previously. "Please come in."

Connor stepped inside, and Dan closed the door.

"Where are the kids?" Connor asked, looking around.

"Wilson took them to the movies," Dan explained. "When I invited you over, that wasn't part of the plan, honest. I figured we'd have a nice dinner with the kids and then maybe we could talk or something. But apparently I have a busybody for a house manager, and he decided that we needed to be alone for the evening. He took the kids out to the movies and made dinner. If that's too weird, we can just eat and talk like I planned. It doesn't have to be any more than that." Jesus Christ, he was rambling on like a nervous schoolboy.

"So you're saying this turned into a date night without you realizing it?" Connor was chuckling, and Dan nodded then joined him.

"That seems to be what happened." He shook his head.

"I think I'm okay with that as long as we take things slow," Connor said.

"I understand." He wasn't the king of rushing into things anyway. "Then please come in and have a seat. Wilson put out a bottle of wine that will go with dinner. I'll open it and get us some glasses." Dan motioned Connor toward the living room and got some glasses from the kitchen. He opened the wine and poured before returning.

Connor stood at the windows overlooking the lake. The waning sunshine sparkled on the water, making it look bluer than its usual gray.

Lake Superior, while incredibly deep, was big enough to make its own weather, and that usually meant clouds, wind, and lots of gray water, but not this evening. The water sparkled with what Dan wanted to interpret as hope.

"Connor," he said softly, so he didn't startle him, and then he handed him a glass when he turned around.

"This is an amazing view. What's between you and the water? It seems a ways away."

"Just some more land. I bought the house because the property was deep enough that should the lake decide to encroach, there would be plenty of distance. I'd hate to have the pool fall into the lake."

"One did that just a few years ago. The house was closer to Marquette, though. The lake took the land. In the fall they had a pool, but come spring when they returned for the season, it was gone without a trace. The lake had completely washed it away. Unfortunately, the house went a few years later too." Connor sipped from his glass.

"For the last few years the lake has been depositing sand, so I guess I've been lucky," Dan said, standing close enough to Connor that he could smell his cologne. "I also have a service that comes out in January and shores up the bank with old Christmas trees. They spike them in and the limbs catch the sand and hold it. It seems to work, because by spring I could barely see any of the trees. They'd been completely covered." Dan chuckled. "Not exactly the kind of conversation I expected."

"I guess not, but I'm not very good at talking about myself."

"God, same here," Dan said and lifted his glass. Connor clinked it, and they stood quietly watching the lake.

"Why'd you move back here? Your business is downstate, I understand." Connor turned away from the window.

"I had good memories here," Dan answered and motioned Connor toward one of the chairs. "Do you remember Mrs. Schaude from sophomore English?" Connor nodded. "Well, she contacted me about a year ago and asked if I could come up and speak to her classes."

"She was so demanding," Connor said.

"Yeah," Dan agreed. "But she was the one. That teacher who took me aside after class one day and told me that I was smart and I could do anything I set my mind to, and no one could ever take away my education and what I learned was mine to keep. After that I worked as hard in school as I could." Dan took a gulp from his glass. "She changed my life and I don't think she ever knew it. So when she asked me to come to her class, I couldn't say no. Once I got here, it felt like home. No place had felt like that in a long time, so I bought the house, figuring I could spend summers here. I commuted back and forth for that first summer, and then last fall I met Lila and my life changed forever. Now I spend most of the year here." He gulped some more of the wine.

"I always wondered why you were here for only a year."

Peter's advice rang in his ear. "I moved around a lot when I was a teenager. My parents should never have had kids. Dad bailed and Mom spent years swearing at him and wishing she'd done something other than have a kid. She didn't want me; I knew that well. I was fourteen when she left me with my aunt and uncle, then took off. They didn't want me either, but after Mom didn't come back and when they found out that she had died in California somewhere, I was passed to other relatives and eventually to foster parents who lived here in Pleasanton. They kept me for a year, and I thought they might keep me until I was eighteen, but my foster father got ill and I was sent to another foster home. By then I felt no one really wanted me and all I could rely on was myself." Dan expected pity from Connor, but he said nothing and downed his wine. "I did well in school and was able to go to college on grants, scholarships, and night jobs."

"My God," Connor said softly. "You were a throwaway too."

"Yeah, I guess I was. I just thought of myself as not capable of being loved. My own parents didn't want me, and my other relatives certainly didn't. Most of the foster parents cared, but they had their own lives."

"Is that why you adopted Lila and Jerry?"

"I guess. They're throwaways, like me. Their parents didn't want to make the effort to care for them."

"Did you intend to adopt when you went to the home?" Connor asked.

"God, no. I figured I'd stop by and see what they needed. Give a donation and try to make a difference." Dan finished his wine and set his glass on the table. "I walked in and met Maggie. As I was talking to her, a little girl on crutches came in and made her way over to me. She looked up at me, and before I knew it she was in my arms with her arms around my neck and I was a complete goner. That was all it took. I visited her every day and brought her home a week later. She was mine. I hadn't even realized how empty my heart was until the first time she called me Daddy."

A timer went off in the kitchen, and Dan checked his watch. He blinked a few times and stood up, relieved at the interruption. "I believe dinner is ready."

He was not comfortable talking about himself at all. If people knew things about him, then that knowledge could be used to hurt him. He'd learned that lesson very well when he'd met Billy Knowles. He'd heard they had a lot in common and had opened up to him, hoping he'd understand and maybe they could be friends. Dan had spent his entire junior year in high school listening to taunts about the fact that he was a foster kid. It seemed that Billy's parents were dead and he lived with his aunt and uncle. Even though they were both orphans, Billy was popular and he soon made sure everyone knew no one had wanted Dan. He now knew that Billy was probably covering for his own insecurities, but that changed nothing. He kept much of himself quiet after that and shared little with anyone.

Dan motioned for Connor to come with him and guided him toward the dining room. At one point he touched his back lightly, half expecting Connor to pull away, but he didn't. "I'll be right back," Dan said after he'd refilled Connor's wine glass, and then he hurried to the kitchen. He opened the oven door and put on the oven mitts Wilson had placed on the counter for him. The room instantly filled with the scent of roast beef and potatoes. He took out the meat first and set it on the stove. Then he pulled out the potatoes and carrots and carried them into the dining room. He set them in the places indicated by Wilson's small notes, picking up the papers as he went. He pulled the cucumber salad out of the refrigerator and took it to the table. Then he took another bottle of wine to the table before transferring the roast to the platter and carrying it to the table as well.

It was a feast—that was the only word for it. The entire room filled with the rich scent of beef and herbs. Dan carved the meat, and since Connor liked his well done, he gave him the end of the roast before taking a medium-rare piece for himself.

"This is wonderful," Connor said after eating his first piece of meat.

"Wilson takes good care of us," Dan said.

Connor raised his glass, looking at him closely. "I know what you told me was very difficult for you, because I have a similar story, and I'm guessing you don't tell people about it anymore than I go around telling my story to everyone."

"I never heard the term throwaway until you said it, but that was how I felt," Dan admitted.

Connor nodded. "I don't trust many people, and even those I do, I don't let get close." That sounded exactly the way Dan felt. "I haven't spoken to anyone about this in years."

They clinked glasses, and Dan sipped his wine, some of the hesitation slipping away. Peter had said he should take a chance, and maybe this was a good thing.

"I was sixteen," Connor began and looked down at his plate. Dan passed him the salad, and he put some on his plate. The movement seemed to be a chance for him to gather his thoughts.

"If you don't want to talk about this now, that's okay," Dan offered. "I think I've added enough depression to the evening for both of us." He took a bite and smiled. "I'll listen anytime you want to talk, but I don't want to force you." He felt better than he expected just telling someone who might understand.

"It's just hard," Connor said.

"What happened to me drove everything in my life."

"How so?" Connor asked.

"After my teacher, Mrs. Schaude, took me aside, I decided if I wanted to do anything I had to do it myself. So I worked hard, and in my junior year of college I bought a trailer outside of Ann Arbor that I rented to three law students. They paid me enough that I could cover the mortgage and have a little leftover. I bought the one next door, and by the time I graduated, I had a nice regular income. I continued buying properties, worked on them myself, and soon I was managing them full time. The business grew from there, and it grew fast."

"That's amazing. You must have been driven."

"I was. I had to do it all myself. Eventually I hired some of the men I went to business school with. We were friends and I knew I could trust them." Dan laughed. "That was hard as hell, but they proved themselves."

"Do you still own those properties?"

Dan shook his head. "My first really big deal was to sell them all as a lot to a management company at a big profit, and that financed my first deal for an office and apartment building. The rest is history." Dan smiled and began eating slowly. He'd talked about himself more in the last hour than he had in the past five years combined. But he felt okay about it.

Something about Connor told him it was all right. "So what do you do for fun?" he asked, changing the subject.

"In the winter I love to ski," Connor said. "Cross country, that is. It's a matter of necessity and sport where I live, because most of the time the snow is deep and the road isn't plowed, so the only way out is on top of it." Dan had noticed Connor's legs and wondered where the strength came from. "In the summer I like to walk on the beach or visit my friend Patrick. He works with wood as well, and sometimes we help each other with large projects. His partner is the artist I told you about. I should introduce you."

They ate and talked about lighter topics. Connor told him about his progress on the cabinet and the other pieces he was working on, and Dan told Connor about the deals and projects he had in the works. "I have to go to the office in a few weeks to check on the progress of everything," he said, thinking out loud. "If you like, invite Patrick and Ken over here for lunch next weekend. I'm sure the kids would like to meet them too, and that way Ken could take a look at Jerry's work."

"You really are a control freak, aren't you?" Connor said and then smiled.

"I always like things on my home turf. It's the businessman in me, I guess." Dan knew it was a lot more than that, but that was what he was willing to own up to. He glanced at Connor and knew he saw right through him.

"I'll call Ken after dinner. He's a great guy, though I know Patrick better because of the woodworking thing. Although when I tell them about the heated pool, I think I can convince them. Their daughter Hanna would never forgive them if they turned down an invitation like that. She's a little older than Jerry and a great girl."

"That would be wonderful. It would be nice for Jerry and Lila to have some friends. They don't get out as much as they should, and that's my fault."

"I tend to stay close to home and what's familiar myself," Connor said, and they both nodded and finished their dinner.

"Wilson made dessert, but I thought we might have it a little while later. I'm stuffed," Dan said.

"Yeah, me too," Connor admitted. "Let me help you carry this into the kitchen."

They cleared the table, and Dan put the leftover food away. He stacked the dishes in the sink and made sure the dining room wasn't a mess before turning out the lights. He thought about going back into the living room, but the sun was still shining. "Would you like to take a walk?" Dan grabbed a jacket and got one for Connor as well, and they walked out through the landscaped yard toward the dark-stained wooden steps that led to the beach.

"Your yard is wonderful," Connor said as he looked around. "I really like how they used mostly native plants and grasses."

"I didn't want something that would take a lot of special care, so I took what was here and had a landscaper use native plants to finish it. I figured they would be heartier in this environment." With the lake, the weather and wind made the environment around the house harsher than it otherwise would be. "Are you up for a stroll?" He motioned down the stairs, and Connor began the descent. Dan followed.

"Did you put these in? They look new."

"The previous owners rebuilt them just before I bought the house," Dan explained. "It looks like I may need to have them adjusted soon. The sand is already threatening to cover them in places." They made it to the beach, the waves crashing on the shore. The sky was mostly clear, and the few clouds began to turn red with the setting sun as they started walking.

"I used to go swimming in the lake each summer when I was a kid," Connor said. "My parents used to bring me down to the beach. I'd play in the water, and Dad and Mom would spend time with their friends. I thought it was normal, but I know now they were real hippie types and spent most of the afternoon talking, drinking, and getting high. I was just a kid, so I had my fun while they had theirs."

Dan stifled a gasp. "How old were you?"

"About Jerry's age, I would guess. I made sandcastles and played at the edge of the water while they smoked away the grocery and rent money." Connor began to walk faster, and Dan picked up speed to keep up. Then Connor stopped, picked up a piece of driftwood, and hurled it into the water. "I could have been sucked away by a wave and they wouldn't have cared or even noticed." He picked up a stone and hurled it into the water, followed by another. "I was just a kid, and they were too selfish to give a damn." Dan stayed close, but let Connor rage away. He'd done something similar a number of times. "I was eight fucking years old!"

Dan put his hand on Connor's arm and squeezed lightly just to remind him that he was here and that Connor wasn't alone. "Did they do that often?"

"I don't know. At the time I thought it was normal. They raised me and did their thing, as they called it, until I was sixteen, and then...." Connor pulled away and lifted a huge rock, hurling it into the water with a huge splash. "The fuckers got some bad weed or worse and died. Just like that, they were gone. The people I'd known all my life, their friends, the ones they thought of as family, disappeared like a fart in a gale, and I was alone." Connor began to shake, and Dan wasn't sure what to do. Words weren't going to do anything at all, so he stepped forward and did what he'd done earlier in the day—he held him. Connor struggled, but Dan continued to hold him

"It's all right."

"How in the hell can you say that? You went through the same kind of shit I did and you aren't all right."

"No, I'm not. I don't know if I ever will be, and maybe the same goes for you. But we have to let this shit go." Dan closed his eyes, stood still, and just held Connor, sighing when Connor returned the gesture. "It's eating us alive." He lightly petted down Connor's back, sliding his hand under his jacket, but over his shirt, making small circles.

"I was their kid, but they were more interested in drugs than me. Most of the time they were good and fun, but as I got older I realized that when they got with their friends and had their parties, they were out of it for days. Many times I ate whatever I could find until Mom came back to herself, felt guilty, and started trying to make up for it. She and Dad always went back to that crap, though, and then they were gone. The drugs were more important than me, and then I was less important than pond scum once they were gone. The county put me in foster care, but I didn't know how to behave in any sort of organized or disciplined situation outside of school. They had rules, but all I did was rebel. I met Gert when I was seventeen, and she helped me understand that I needed to finish school. She helped me get a place of my own when I turned eighteen and saw to it that I didn't starve until I could get a job."

"I know. You didn't know anything, and now you were on your own, trying to figure out how things worked before everyone hurt you."

Connor nodded. "You got that right. I went to work to feed myself and keep a roof over my head. Gert got me a job at the lumberyard, and they had a workshop the old owner used to use. I asked if I could use it because I figured I could make a few things to sell. They put them in the store and sold them all. I started working more in the shop, making things, and I got better. And I started making some money because they were good people and didn't take a percentage. All I had to do was buy the wood and supplies."

"See? Someone cared," Dan whispered.

"Yeah, they did, until they went bankrupt a few years later because one of the employees embezzled so much they couldn't keep going. Then I was out of a job and just as scared as I had been when I lost my parents. Well, almost. I sat down in my room and came up with a plan. I arranged to buy the woodworking equipment from the lumberyard and got a small place where I started making furniture. I got a few customers and they told others. Soon, like you, with a lot of hard work, I had a business. And eventually it grew, so now I can take the jobs I want and I get top prices for my work." Connor smiled slightly. "I was able to buy the house a little over a year ago. I had to do a lot of work on the inside, and I still have some things I want to do, but it's mine and it's home."

Dan understood the need for permanence. When he'd gone to college and moved into the dorm, it was the first place he'd lived that had felt like his. He'd become upset when he was told he'd have to move to a different place at the end of the school year, and summers were hell, because when most kids went home, he had to find a different place to live. But after the first year, he got the routine down. But it wasn't until he got his first place of his own that he really felt settled.

"Let's head back toward the house, okay?" Dan asked, and Connor nodded, still holding him. "This wasn't what I had in mind when I suggested taking a walk."

"I didn't mean to mess it up," Connor said flatly and stepped away.

"You didn't at all." Dan waited and extended his hand. Connor took it, intertwining their fingers. "I always wanted to walk along here with someone special," Dan said, and they started walking back toward the steps. The sun was setting quickly, and Dan wished he'd brought a flashlight. Looking ahead, he calculated that they should make it back to the steps before it got dark.

"You think I'm special?" Connor asked with disbelief ringing in his voice.

"Yeah, you're special... to me." Dan swallowed hard at the admission. Maybe it was having the kids in his life, but he'd gotten a little more comfortable about talking about his feelings, at least in private situations. "I don't talk about this stuff with most people and I have never held anyone or held hands on the beach." He squeezed Connor's fingers lightly. "I've been with guys when I was in college and stuff, but that was just sex. I've never had a real boyfriend."

"Me neither. Wouldn't let anyone close enough for them to stay around very long." Connor chuckled. "Not that there are a boatload of choices up here. Mostly I spent my time figuring out how I was going to live and support myself."

"Yeah," Dan sighed. He knew that feeling well. "No matter how well you do, you're still afraid it could all be taken away." He couldn't believe how much he enjoyed talking to someone who understood. "Those first few years I lived really frugally, and continued even after I started doing well, just because I was afraid to spend anything. I locked everything away and held on to it tight in case anything happened." The sun sank lower and lower, and Dan saw the steps getting larger ahead of them. If it got too dark, they could walk past without even seeing them.

"I did too. I think that's why I was able to buy the house. But I still keep thinking it could all disappear," Connor whispered. They reached the bottom of the stairs as the lights came on at the top of the hill. He'd forgotten about that and felt a little stupid. It wasn't likely he would miss his property. They stopped, and Dan turned to Connor, leaned in, and waited a few seconds before kissing him. He kept expecting Connor to pull away, and when he didn't, Dan kissed him harder, holding him tightly and then clutching him like a lifeline. Connor was doing the same to him. He'd held so much of himself inside for so long that now that he'd let it out, he needed to know it was okay, and Connor seemed to react the same way.

"I'm sorry I made such a fool of myself," Connor said when they broke the kiss, turning to look out at the water.

"You didn't," Dan said as the wind came up, quickly growing steadier and stronger. "Thank you for trusting me enough to tell me. I know what it meant, because it was the same for me." Connor turned back to him, and Dan kissed him again. "I've liked you since high school," Dan began, and then he brushed Connor's windblown hair out of his eyes. "And I've thought it would have been nice to have a friend then, but I wouldn't have trusted anyone enough to get close, and I don't think you would have either." Dan pulled him close, wondering where he was going with his thought and then realizing it didn't matter. "I'm glad you're here now."

"Me too," Connor whispered as the wind whipped around their ears.

Dan didn't want to break away, but they needed to get up the stairs. This wind meant a squall was coming in, and they needed to beat the weather. He released Connor and motioned for him to go first. Dan followed right behind, holding on to the rail. The wind whipped around them, blowing sand and carrying droplets from the lake. When they reached the top, Dan led the way across the yard, making sure everything was battened down before pulling open one of the sliding doors and then following Connor inside, closing the door quickly to shut out the wind. The billowing curtains settled back into place, and Dan led Connor to the kitchen. He figured they could use something to warm them, so he poured them each a glass of wine and ushered Connor into the living room. Dan flipped on the gas fireplace and closed the curtains to give the room a warmer feel, and then he settled next to him on the sofa.

Connor moved closer, and Dan put his arms around him and held him tight. "This feels a little strange to me," Connor said. "I've never done this with a client before."

"Well, I've never held anyone who was doing work for me before. But is that a real issue here?" Dan asked, and Connor shook his head. "I wouldn't expect you to do something for free or anything. This is too new to mess up with convoluted stuff like that." He sipped from his glass and then set it on the coffee table. Connor did the same, and then Dan leaned in and kissed Connor, who kissed him right back.

The energy between them was unlike anything Dan's limited experience had prepared him for. Connor tasted of the wine, but better, because it was Connor. Dan pulled Connor to him and they leaned back, resting against the cushions. His body and mind screamed for him to go faster. Something primal from deep inside told him to make Connor his. But it was too soon, and he'd promised he'd take it slow. In the past, whenever he was in a situation like this, it would quickly escalate to where they would fall into bed, and after some energetic acrobatics, they would part. He didn't want that this time, so Dan gentled the kiss, slowing down and taking the time to savor the curve of Connor's upper lip and the way his lower lip jutted out slightly when Dan began to pull away. And the little sounds he made, especially when Dan took a second to breathe, small whimpers that were as exciting and heart pounding as screams of passion, because they were for him.

Connor pulled away, and Dan stilled, wondering if he'd made a mistake. Connor reached for his wine and took a gulp before setting the glass down again. "Do you have any idea how unsettling this is for me?" Connor asked and then released a deep breath. "I want to believe this is real, but it's almost too much. It's perfect, too perfect for me. Nothing in my life has ever seemed this easy."

"This isn't easy. Not for me. I want to do what I've always done, but I won't with you. You're worth more than that and worth getting to know." Dan leaned close, lightly sniffing Connor's neck and blowing his breath over his skin. Connor shivered and his head fell back in a silent plea for more. Dan moved closer, lightly touching his lips to Connor's skin. He kissed and then sucked lightly, savoring the deep, salty flavor mixed with the scent of the water that seemed to have permeated Connor's skin and clothes. Connor groaned, soft and deep, a sound of sheer contentment.

"Is that what you do with other guys? Get them so wound up they can't see straight?" Connor commented, and Dan stopped. "Because you're going to make me forget myself."

"Not tonight," Dan said as much for his benefit as Connor's. He moved away and settled on the sofa, holding Connor's hand. Dan desperately needed a few minutes to breathe and let himself cool down. His pants were damn tight and his heart was pounding. He shifted to get a little more comfortable, hoping his excitement wasn't too visible. He reached for his glass and handed Connor his as well. They sipped their wine and listened as the wind whistled outside the windows with occasional tings as grains of sand landed against them, followed by drops of water that grew in intensity.

"The lake isn't very happy now," Connor observed.

"No. It amazed me the first few months I lived here, how quickly storms could blow up and how fast they fell as well."

"The lake does what it wants. The fall and winter are the worst, though. The wind can blow and howl for days. When that happens, I usually spend hours in my shop working, because the energy of the storms seems to energize me. I build and build on days like that."

"Do you ever have trouble putting the finish on pieces? I heard it was hard to do when it was humid."

"It is. I have a special room I use for it with ventilation, and when it's humid I use dehumidifiers to dry out the air. The same in the workshop—in the summer I run dehumidifiers, and in the winter I run humidifiers to try to keep moisture in the air. It keeps the wood from warping and becoming hard to deal with."

Dan got up and retrieved the bottle of wine from the kitchen. He returned and refilled their glasses.

"I shouldn't have any more," Connor said. "I won't be able to drive."

"Since this is the end of the second bottle, I think you're probably past that point now," Dan observed.

"So was that your plan? To get me toasted so you could have your way with me?" Connor said with a grin. Dan sat back down, and Connor leaned against him. "This is really nice."

"It is," Dan agreed. They grew quiet and just sat together, watching the fire. Dan didn't feel uncomfortable in the least about the quiet. It was nice. He checked his watch after a few minutes and began to get concerned.

"When are Wilson and the kids supposed to get back?" Connor asked, most likely following his gaze. It was after nine and Dan would have expected them to have been home by now. "Maybe Wilson stopped off to get them a snack?"

Dan was reaching for his phone when he thought he heard the garage door. He continued listening and then the back door opened.

"Daddy," Lila called through the house.

Dan sighed as the quiet slipped away. "Did you have a good time?" he asked as he stood up and walked out of the living room. Lila came toward him, all smiles.

"It was so much fun. The movie went zoom zoom and the car people were so funny." He picked her up when she got close. "Wilson had to pull off the road and we sat while the rain went all over us." She gestured, and Dan took her crutches from her before she whacked him. "Jerry was scared but I wasn't."

"It isn't nice to tattle," Dan said. "You get scared too sometimes."

"I know," she admitted shyly.

Dan set her down. "Why don't you go upstairs and get ready for bed."

"But Jerry...."

"He'll be getting ready for bed too. Now scoot and say hello to Mr. Connor on your way. He's in the living room." He handed her the crutches, and she made her way toward the living room while Dan went to see if Wilson and Jerry needed help. They were coming inside as he reached the kitchen, wearing the same kind of smiles Lila had worn.

"It was great," Jerry said. "I wanna drive a race car."

"Okay. I'll see what I can do. But for now, you need to say hello to Mr. Connor and then get ready for bed." Dan bent down and gave Jerry a hug, and then he moved down the hall. "I'll be in to say good night in a few minutes," he called after Jerry, and then he turned to Wilson.

"They were very good. Both of them sat still through the entire film. We did have a bit of a bathroom issue, but we got that sorted as well."

"What kind of issue?"

"There was a line before we went in, and Mr. Jerry needed to go, and… well, let's just say I got very pushy." The glint in Wilson's eye told Dan everything he needed to know.

"I'm glad you stood up for him," Dan said.

"Of course," Wilson told him and then turned away and opened the dishwasher.

"I don't think Connor should go home in this weather." Dan knew Wilson would not go to bed until everything was clean, so he left him to it. He found the kids talking to Connor about the movie. He reminded them it was bedtime, and they said good night and headed toward their rooms.

Dan sat and talked with Connor for a few minutes before excusing himself so he could tuck them in. "I'll make up the guest room for Connor in a few minutes," Wilson told him when he met him in the hall. Dan thanked him and spent the next few minutes talking to each of the kids and seeing that they were snug in their beds and happy.

"Wilson's making a guest room up for you," Dan told Connor once he joined him again in the living room. "The weather is really bad, and we've both had more wine than is safe."

"You're probably right," Connor agreed, but he sounded tentative.

"Will everything be okay at home during the storm?" Dan asked.

"I hope so," Connor said softly. "Everything was built to last. That's one of the things I like about it, and there isn't much I can do in a storm like this if something happens, besides ride it out." Connor shrugged.

"It's warm here and you're safe. That's what counts. If you tried to drive...."

"I know I shouldn't," Connor said. "It's just that it's been a long time since I slept anyplace but home. I don't travel much, and if I do, it isn't very far. I'd hazard a guess that when you go on your business trip, you'll have traveled farther than I have since I was a kid. Mom and Dad used to like to travel. They even had one of those stereotypical VW vans. I remember it as being a rust bucket, but we went all kinds of places in it."

"So you have good memories of your folks?" Dan asked, and Connor nodded.

"I do, I guess. I wished they'd cared about me enough to live differently so they would have stayed around, but...." Connor sighed. "There were good things, but they seem to get overshadowed by the mountain of shit that got piled on later."

Dan could understand that. He had some good memories from when he was a kid, though mostly they had faded and continued to fade over the years. "Would you like another glass of wine?"

Connor shook his head slightly. "Just some water, I think."

Just as Dan got up, Wilson came into the room carrying a tray. "I thought you might like some herbal tea," he explained and set down the tray. Dan was about to invite him to stay, but Wilson hightailed it out of the room before he could ask. Dan poured them each a cup and handed one to Connor.

"I guess someone else has gotten the idea we've had enough to drink."

"Does he always do that?" Connor asked. "It seems like he listens in or something."

"He may, but if he does, he never says anything." Dan sipped from the cup and was glad for something warm as the wind whistled outside. It made the room seem colder than it was. "Wilson once told me that to be good at his job, he needed to anticipate what I wanted before I knew I needed it."

Connor rolled his eyes. "What the hell does that mean?"

"I think he was saying that anticipation was a good part of his job. Yes, he watches what goes on and listens, though I doubt he skulks around the house. He observes so he can have things prepared for me. It took a while for me to get used to, but now he's a part of the family and not just because of what he does for us. He really is family to me in a lot of ways."

Connor nodded and drank some more of the tea. It tasted good. The wine had been warming, but the tea truly built a nice ember from within. "What do you usually do once the kids are in bed?"

Dan laughed. "Most nights I go into my office and work until I can't stay awake. Then I go to bed. That's been my life, either work or the kids. I rarely go out, and it's even rarer that I have people over." He didn't have a lot of friends. He'd lived in town and knew some people by sight, but mostly he was a stranger. It had almost always been that way.

"Do you talk to any of your relatives?" Connor asked. "I don't see any of mine and haven't talked to any of the people my folks knew, unless you count the one who stopped by to chat and hit me up for money." Bitterness rolled off Connor's words.

"God, same here. I heard from the same relatives who passed me on to others and then into foster care. They all reminded me how they'd helped after my mom passed. Lord, you'd have thought they raised me instead of making sure I knew none of them wanted me. Now I've got 'loving relatives.' Good for nothing. They wanted money, and one actually asked me for a job."

"What did you say?"

"I told Uncle Maury I needed a gardener, and that he could mow my lawn, weed my flower beds, and rake my leaves." Dan grinned. "He looked completely aghast and said he had experience managing money, and I told him if he'd managed his, he wouldn't need a job. Needless to say, I never heard from that lowlife—or any of the rest of them—after that."

"Well, I've lived here most of my life, and I know just about everyone in town in some way or another. Most people are nice to me. The kids in town think I'm the strange guy who lives in the country with a huge shed full of torture equipment."

"Come on…," Dan teased.

"I actually heard some of the kids talking once when I was in the hardware store. They were whispering so loud they might as well have been yelling."

"What did you do?"

"I snuck up behind them and yelled, 'Boo.' They screamed like schoolgirls and raced out of the place. I thought they were going to wet themselves." Connor began to laugh, and Dan nearly doubled over.

"You don't have torture devices in your shed, do you?" Dan teased.

"Actually it's a sex dungeon," Connor answered, and he tried to keep a straight face but failed. "Truthfully, it's where I keep my pet project. Maybe I'll show it to you sometime."

"You aren't going to tell me?" Dan asked.

"Nope. Some things should be a surprise," Connor said.

"Dad," Dan heard from down the hall and Dan stopped stock-still.

"Is that Jerry?"

"Yeah," Dan said and stood up. "He's never called me that before." He couldn't help smiling. He'd never tried to tell the kids what they should call him. That was up to them. If they wanted to call him Dan, he was comfortable with that. He'd noticed that Jerry hadn't called him anything much. A few times he'd called him Mr. Harrington, and then a few times Dan, but this was the first "Dad." He hurried down the hall and peeked into Jerry's room.

"I had a bad dream," Jerry said, and Dan came in and sat on the edge of his bed. "I was riding a horse like the Lone Ranger did, and I was doing really good, and then my legs curled up, and I was me, and then I fell off." Jerry sniffled, and Dan simply hugged him. "I'll never be able to ride a horse or do anything normal kids do, like the ones at the movies. They ran around and had a good time. Even Lila had fun with them, but no one came by me. They just kept playing."

Dammit. "You'll always be different, but that's not bad. It's just different. You can do things that none of those kids can do. See, none of those kids can draw or color the way you do."

"That isn't anything," Jerry sighed.

"Yes, it is. You're an artist, and I'm going to prove it to you if I can, okay?" Dan asked, and Jerry nodded. "Everyone has talents. We just have to find them. That's what one of my teachers told me, and she said that it was a teacher's and a parent's job to help their kids find them. And I know what one of yours is, even if you don't." He hugged Jerry tight. "Now you go back to sleep and don't worry about horses or the Lone Ranger. You're Jerry Harrington and that's good enough for me." He kissed him on the forehead and quietly left the room. Dan passed Connor in the hallway on his way into the bathroom.

Dan went back into the living room and finished his tea, waiting for Connor.

When Connor came back into the room, he said, "I overheard and I hope it's okay. I called Ken while you were with Jerry. He said they would love to come and meet you. I told them the address, and they asked what they should bring."

"They did?"

"Ken and Patrick are quite social. Patrick wasn't always that way, though. He can't talk because he got hurt about five years ago. He used to sing opera, but an accident injured his throat. So it's harder for him, but he's pretty good at letting people know what he wants or means. If not, then Ken and Hanna can help." Connor sat next to him on the sofa once again, and they talked and talked.

Dan found it surprising how easy it was for him to open up. They shared stories back and forth, Dan about his toughest deal and Connor about his pickiest customer. They laughed and even joked a little with each other.

Then Connor yawned, and Dan did the same right after him. The wine must have been catching up with both of them. Dan stood and extended his hand to Connor, who took it, and Dan led him through the house and up the stairs to the guest room. Dan showed Connor where the bathroom was as well as fresh towels, and then they stood outside Connor's door. Dan said good night, but didn't move. Connor did the exact same thing.

Dan stepped closer and Connor did the same. Then he pulled them together, and Connor's body melded with his. It felt so right and so perfect… and there was a bed so nearby. Dan's wine-hazed mind pushed him to press the advance, and he kissed Connor, tasting him, while Dan's heart beat loudly enough he swore they could both hear it. He stepped back and guided Connor down the hall, kissing and holding him tight until they were in his bedroom. Dan kicked the door closed and then guided Connor to the bed.

They tumbled onto it, giggling as they bounced. Connor fumbled with the buttons on his shirt, and Dan did the same, followed by Connor's pants, which he couldn't seem to figure out how to get over his shoes. Eventually, through trial and error, their clothes hit the floor, and Dan settled them on the mattress with a huge sigh. Then he tugged Connor to him, soaking up his warmth as he closed his eyes.

CHAPTER
Seven

CONNOR BENT down and tightened the last bolt on the lift. All that was left was for him to try it out. It had been more complicated and exacting than the other one he'd installed, but it was in, and he'd tested it out with his weight. Now he just needed to make sure everything worked with Jerry's chair. Over the past week, he'd been at the house quite a bit to complete the installation and prepare for the removal of the existing built-in cabinet. Every time he saw Dan, he'd wanted to ask him about that night. Connor couldn't remember a thing about what happened after they ended up in bed together, and Dan hadn't said anything about it. At one point during the night when Connor woke up, Dan was holding him tightly. He wasn't sure whether Dan had meant for them to fall asleep together. They'd been naked, but Connor couldn't remember if they'd had sex or not. His mind was a complete blank. He'd thought to ask Dan a number of times, but he hadn't, and Dan had never brought it up. Come to think of it, Dan seemed to have been making himself scarce. Connor finished the last adjustments and tried out the lift one more time before deciding it was time to stop acting like a scared little kid and find Dan.

He was in his office. Connor knocked on the doorframe and stepped inside. "The lift is ready," he said. "I was wondering if Jerry could try it out."

"Of course," Dan said and stood up. Connor figured it was now or never. "Did I do something wrong?"

Dan paused. "No, I was going to ask you the same thing. You've been avoiding me all week, and after our date when we ended up in bed together, I thought maybe you thought things had moved too fast or maybe I'd...." Connor could always tell when Dan was nervous, at least with him, because he tended to run on at the mouth.

"Did anything happen? I don't remember. I'm not used to drinking, and I think we had more than we should have."

"I don't remember anything other than me falling on the bed and holding you. I don't drink much either, and, boy, I was nervous, so I think I overindulged and…." Dan smiled and then began to laugh. "We really need to learn to talk about stuff."

"I thought you were ashamed of what happened," Connor said. That had hurt a lot, and he'd spent many late hours working well into the night.

"I thought I might have gone too far. You didn't say anything about it, and I was…." Dan shook his head slowly. "If all I did was hold you all night, then it was one of the best nights of my life, and I'm sorry I don't remember it."

"I thought you—" Connor began. All kinds of things had run though his mind. That they'd been intimate, and it had been such a disappointment that Dan was staying away. That they hadn't done anything, and Dan was angry. "We really need to talk about stuff."

"Yeah," Dan said with a smile. "God… I spent a week wondering if I'd been a complete ass." They both began to laugh. Connor felt better, but kind of dumb, and he expected Dan felt the same way.

"So, I have the lift ready for Jerry to try out," Connor said after clearing his throat a little.

"Excellent, let's get him. I know Wilson has been moving his things upstairs for the past few days, so he'll be thrilled to be in his new room." Dan walked toward him, and Connor stepped aside. To his surprise, Dan took his hand. It seemed so high school, but nice at the same time.

Jerry met them in the hall. "Is it done?" he asked with a grin.

"Let's go try it out," Dan said enthusiastically, and they followed Jerry to the back stairs, just off the family room. Dan seemed reluctant to let go of his hand, but he did, and Connor showed Jerry how it worked.

"This button raises and lowers the platform, and the lever here runs the lift." He bent down and showed Jerry how to lock his chair in place. "I have it set so it won't work unless you're locked in. That way you can't roll off and get hurt." Connor stepped back and let Jerry try. He helped him through the process, and soon Jerry was on his way up the stairs, grinning and rocking back and forth the entire time. Dan met him at the top, and Connor joined them as Jerry was led down the hall to his brand-new room.

"Wilson is still bringing up the last of your things, and he'll show you where everything is," Dan said from outside the closed door. He opened the door, and when Jerry went inside, he didn't say a word. Then he let out a squeal of delight. Connor peered inside. "You said you wanted blue with horses and airplanes. I'm not a designer and I wanted to do this myself, so I went with horses." The walls were a light blue and there were pictures of horses on the walls and a huge stuffed horse stood in the corner. Dan must have bought the largest one they had.

"It's the best room ever," Jerry exclaimed as he rolled up to a table with the figure of a horse standing in the middle. "Is it really mine?"

"Yes. This is your room. Mine is right across the hall, and Lila's is right next door. All your art supplies are in the baskets on the shelves, and we made sure everything in here was at a height where you can reach it. I also thought that when we're in Ann Arbor in a week, we'll go to a store that sells model planes and you can pick some out that we can hang from the ceiling." Dan bent down, hugged Jerry tight, and Connor heard him whisper to Jerry that he loved him.

Connor turned away, stepped out of the room, and leaned against the wall. He tried to remember his own parents acting that way and saying those words to him, just once. And he couldn't, not even on Christmas or his birthday.

"Are you all right?" Dan asked.

Connor hadn't even heard him come out of the room. "Yeah, I was just thinking."

"Looked more like grinding your teeth," Dan observed accurately.

"I heard what you said to Jerry and I was trying to remember my parents ever saying such a thing to me. And I can't remember anything like that… ever." Connor sighed and pushed away the memories.

"I can remember my mother telling me she loved me," Dan said. "But just barely. It was so long ago. I knew she did at least at one point, but I always figured that changed when she decided to leave me." Dan stood still and Connor moved into his arms.

"Why do I keep doing this?" Connor asked.

"I'll hold you all day long if that's what you want." That wasn't what Connor meant and he figured Dan knew that, but he wasn't going to argue. "Jerry is so happy right now. But he keeps asking to ride a horse. I've looked into it and I found some places that offer therapy riding, but they're hours away. One that caught my eye was way downstate. I'm tempted to call and see if they'll take Jerry. But I know that once he gets to ride, he'll want to do it again and again, and I can't give him that kind of joy and then take it away from him. I've actually thought of getting him a pony."

"No," Connor said thoughtfully. "I suggest you keep looking. There may be a way."

Dan nodded slowly, and Connor settled against Dan, soaking up his warmth.

"Daddy, is Mr. Connor your boyfriend now?" Lila asked, and Connor felt Dan stiffen.

"We don't know yet," Connor answered for him. "We're still deciding, I think."

She walked over to them. "Okay. But it looks like Daddy's your boyfriend." Then she giggled. Dan released Connor and lifted Lila into his arms.

"Would it be okay if Mr. Connor was my boyfriend?"

Lila scratched her chin and pretended to think about it. Dan poked her belly, and she began to squirm and giggle. "Yes," she said between bouts of laughter. He stopped, and she continued laughing. "But who is going to wear the dress when you get married?" She started giggling again, and Dan put her down.

"You," he said happily. "Go on and get dressed. We're going to have company, so put on your bathing suit and get your cover-up. I'll bring your swim vest. Then see if you can help Wilson, but don't go near the pool without me or Connor with you." Dan went pale all of a sudden, probably remembering Lila's last time in the pool, and then he turned to Connor. "Did you bring your suit? You didn't forget today is the day that your friends are coming over?"

Connor closed his eyes and swore under his breath. He had completely forgotten.

"I have one you can use," Dan said.

Dan got him a suit and a towel. Connor then went back downstairs to clean up his tools and put everything in his truck. He was lucky he hadn't planned anything else that afternoon; otherwise he'd be up a creek.

By the time he went back inside, both kids were in their suits and robes. Wilson was carrying things out to the tables by the pool. Thankfully the sun was shining brightly, and it was one of the few days recently when the wind was relatively calm. In short, it was a beautiful day. Connor used the bathroom to change. He checked his hair and made sure he looked all right. When he came out, he heard familiar voices and found Patrick, Ken, and Hanna in Dan's entrance hall. They were making introductions, and everyone seemed all smiles.

"Connor," Ken said, and they shook hands. Connor hugged Patrick and greeted Hanna, who seemed excited.

"You have a wonderful home," Ken said, looking around. Dan smiled and motioned for them to come inside.

"I thought that while it was nice, we could spend some time out by the pool. Who knows—it could rain in an hour." They all laughed because they knew it was true. The weather could change on a dime. "These are my kids, Lila and Jerry," Dan said as they approached. Connor saw him straighten up proudly.

"I understand you're an artist," Ken said to Jerry. "Connor told me you're very good."

"I like to draw," Jerry said shyly.

"Well, if you want, maybe later you can show me some of your drawings," Ken said.

"Why don't we head out back and enjoy some snacks," Dan said and motioned toward the yard. "There's a restroom right down that hall if you need one, and you can change in there or use the pool house if you like."

Connor led the way out so Dan could help Lila and Jerry, and soon they were all out on the patio by the pool. The kids, of course, wanted to go in, so everyone obliged, and soon all seven of them were enjoying the heated water.

"How long have you lived here?" Ken asked Dan as he stood in the water, helping support Jerry so he could float and stay upright. Connor was right with Lila, who wore her life vest as she played and tried to walk in the water. There was not going to be a repeat of the last time, that was for sure.

"Eighteen months or so, I guess. I bought it as a summer home. After the first winter, I moved in and didn't leave. It was where I wanted to be, even in the dead of winter." Dan held Jerry in his arms and walked around the pool.

Connor had found out that Jerry was not extremely stable in the water. He couldn't use his arms or his legs very well to help him swim, even though he obviously loved the water, judging from his grin. How Dan managed the two of them alone, he wasn't sure, but he suspected Wilson lent a hand.

"How long have you lived here?" Dan asked Ken.

"Patrick was born here and knows just about everyone. I moved here five or six years ago. I needed a picturesque place to paint and work. The city was squeezing the inspiration out of me, and I needed nature in all her glory, both bright and violent. This was certainly the place for that."

They all seemed to converge near the steps, and Patrick joined them. He and Hanna seemed to be having a conversation. "Patrick says he loves your garden," Hanna interpreted, and then she moved around to where Lila was playing. The two girls seemed to hit it off, despite their six year age difference, and soon they were playing together in the shallow water. Connor kept an eye on her as the two girls talked and played. Dan had put a small float vest on Lila to help make sure she stayed above water if her legs went out from under her.

"She's doing very well," Connor told Dan when he saw him looking at the two girls. He knew what he was thinking, but Dan had taken precautions against any more incidents, including the life vests.

"They seem to like each other," Dan said.

Patrick began signing, and Connor waited for Ken to explain what he'd said. "Yes, I'll tell them," Ken said and turned to them. "Patrick wanted me to say that he's having a very nice time and to thank you for the invitation."

"Of course. I'm glad you could come," Dan said.

"Me too," Jerry added with a grin and a slight kick of his legs. "Dad said you made the painting in the family room."

"I did?" Ken asked turning to Dan.

"I bought it a few years ago. A friend from school, his dad is an art dealer in New York, and I bought one of your paintings through him."

"I really like it," Jerry said, and Dan hugged him tight.

"I'm glad," Ken said and then shared a smile with Dan. "I love it that one of my paintings has found its way back here. Even if it was purely by providence."

They talked for a while, and even though the water was warm, the air still held a chill, so after a while, Connor helped Lila out of the pool, and Dan lifted Jerry and set him in a chair after wrapping him in blankets. He pushed him up near the table where the food and drinks had been set out.

"Please help yourself. I have wine if you'd like, or beer, and some sodas for the kids." Dan popped the top on a cooler as Wilson brought out a tray of cheese and crackers as well as some fruit and small sandwiches. Dan asked him to stay, and Wilson reluctantly pulled up a chair as Dan made introductions.

"You have a butler?" Hanna said from the pool.

"That's Wilson. He helps us and takes care of Daddy," Lila corrected her, and Dan smiled.

"So what are you working on?" Dan asked Ken.

"I have an exhibition in Los Angeles in a few months, so I'm working to put that together. I also have a trip planned to London. It seems the British Museum has come into possession of a few of my works, and they have asked me to authenticate them, so the three of us are going to make a vacation out of it."

"We're going to Ant Arbor soon," Jerry said.

"*Ann* Arbor—there are no ants—and it's going to be a lot of fun," Dan said, rubbing Jerry's arm slightly. He smiled at Jerry and then turned back to his guests. The adults talked for a while, and everyone seemed to get along. Patrick kept Ken busy, making his thoughts known through his hands while Ken translated for him. They ate, drank, and laughed together. At one point, Dan excused himself for a few minutes to help the kids get dressed, and then they returned and continued talking.

"Do you wanna see my drawings?" Jerry asked after everyone had had a chance to eat.

"I'd like that," Ken said, and Jerry led him into the house. Dan excused himself and followed. Connor and Patrick talked... of a sort. Connor had learned a few signs, and he'd learned to ask questions that required simple answers. He told Patrick about the piece he was making for Dan's living room, and Patrick pantomimed some of the pieces he was making. Connor knew the signs for wood types and a few furniture types, so they did their best. It was better when they were at one of their shops, but they made it work. Patrick was extremely expressive.

Connor turned when he heard one of the patio doors open and close. Dan came out, strode over to where he was sitting, and placed his hands on his shoulders. Connor leaned into the simple touch. It felt right, and, he was willing to admit, something he'd missed over the last week. Dan holding his hand on the beach had been very nice, and so had Dan holding him when he'd lost it for a while. He should have been embarrassed, but Dan had soothed that away. Connor tensed, and Dan pressed a little tighter, moving slightly just to say he was there and not going anywhere. Connor had no idea how he knew that only from Dan's touch, but he did.

"Are you okay?" Dan whispered into his ear, and Connor had to stop a shiver of delight as Dan's hot breath tickled his skin.

"Yeah, I was just thinking about what I missed this past week," he said softly, and Dan smiled and nuzzled the back of his neck before straightening up again.

Patrick looked toward the door to the house and then back at him. Connor looked up at Dan and tilted his head slightly.

"Ken and Jerry are in the family room," Dan said. "Jerry showed him some of his drawings, and they decided to trade. Ken is drawing Jerry, and Jerry is drawing Ken."

Connor shifted to gaze at Dan, who looked every inch the proud father. It was a sight to behold: tall, proud, eyes shining… the sexiest man Connor had ever seen. Dan smiled at him, and Connor felt the momentary heat in Dan's gaze. It was perfect, just perfect. Patrick touched Connor's hand and then motioned between Connor and Dan before shrugging.

"I think so," Dan said with a grin, since Patrick could hear, just not speak. "It's new between us." He took Connor's hand and squeezed it lightly. It really felt right to Connor, and he hoped to both of them.

Dan sat next to Connor, and they talked with Patrick. Dan seemed to have a real knack for interpreting Patrick's expressions and movements. He even seemed to know sign language. Connor was curious how Dan knew that, but didn't ask, though he intended to later. Dan had shared his past in trust, and he wouldn't betray that. "I had a foster brother who was deaf once," Dan said to Patrick, and Connor realized he'd gotten his answer as well. "I'm a little rusty and haven't read signs in a long time, so if I misinterpret what you're saying, please understand."

Connor took Dan's hand as they shared a very quick smile.

Lila came over, and Dan pulled her onto his lap. She seemed worn out. Hanna sat next to Patrick and nibbled on fruit, joining the conversation for the time being. She seemed to be an intelligent young lady.

After a while, Lila dozed off. They continued talking, with Hanna acting as interpreter when needed. Ken and Jerry came back out of the house, both of them all smiles. "You have a very talented son," Ken said as he sat in the chair next to Patrick. "He understands color and light in a way that some adult artists never do."

"Thank you," Dan said. "I knew he was good, but I thought that might just have been me."

"Absolutely not. His drawings are very mature for his age, and his use of color with simple media is extraordinary. He's also developed his own techniques to deal with his limitations. That's something quite amazing."

"So what do I do?" Dan asked.

"Encourage him and give him what freedom you can to let him explore. The talent is innate inside him. He was born with a gift."

"I will, but I'd like to be able to help him further," Dan said.

"Under normal circumstances, I'd say to find him a good art instructor. They could teach him technique and help bring out his talent." Ken began and then paused. "But Jerry has to develop his own technique. He'll never be able to master the subtleties of a brush, or mix paint to create just the perfect green for a brushstroke that will give luster to a pair of eyes. In fact, they might destroy what he's developed." Ken shook his head. "My advice is to let it develop naturally. Take him to museums so he can see what others have done. Expose him to art—let him experience the wonder for himself." Ken reached over and lightly touched Jerry's hand. "You are very talented."

Connor felt Dan tense and watched him swallow hard, most likely around a lump that felt like the one in Connor's throat. The smile on Jerry's face was as intensely bright as any smile Connor had ever seen, and a realization hit him hard.

His entire life, Connor had been trying to find where he fit in. He figured Dan had as well. Their families hadn't wanted them—the people who should have cared most about them hadn't, and that had sent them each on a long journey to figure out their place in the world. Jerry's smile right then meant that Jerry had already figured it out. He was an artist, and in a way, he already knew his place, at just eight years old. Connor was happy for both the kids. Jerry and Lila would never have to go through what he and Dan had gone through. Dan would absolutely see to that.

"Thank you," Jerry said, his grin forming once again. "I drew a picture for Mr. Brighton and he drew one for me." Jerry rocked back and forth, an unmistakable indication of his delight.

"We left them in the house for now," Ken explained. Dan nodded, and everyone settled in chairs. Unfortunately, a little later the wind began to come up right off the lake and the warmth of the day slipped away. It was one of the perils of living near the lake. Dan invited everyone inside. Everyone grabbed something as the party moved indoors.

Connor helped Dan and Wilson make sure everyone got settled. Dan retrieved some bottles of wine and opened one. Connor was careful this time to only have a single glass. He was hoping for a repeat of the invitation to stay with Dan, and if he received one, he wanted to remember the night.

"I'm sorry about the weather," Dan said as he poured.

"It's perfectly all right. We expect that here, and it was lovely to have the time in the water," Ken said, turning to Hanna, who thanked Dan.

"Dinner should be ready in about an hour," Wilson told him and Dan. It was a bit of a surprise that Wilson had been talking to him as well. Connor guessed that meant he had Wilson's approval.

"How long should the casserole you brought be in the oven?" Wilson asked Ken, who looked to Patrick. He signed.

"About thirty minutes at three fifty," he interpreted.

"Patrick brought some of his special mac-cheese," Hanna said to Lila, who grinned, and then they settled at the table in the corner. Jerry looked like he wanted to join them, but there wasn't enough room. Dan helped him find a place as well, and soon the three of them were talking and playing together like old friends.

"When Hanna wasn't much older than Lila, she was diagnosed with leukemia, and when she was going through her treatments, the only thing that tasted good to her was Patrick's mac-cheese," Ken said, taking the silent man's hand. "That was how we met, actually."

Connor nodded. "I remember helping the town put up the Christmas decorations in August that year. We hadn't met yet, but I remember helping and later heard the story."

Ken nodded. "We weren't sure Hanna was going to survive, so Patrick and his cousin took it upon themselves to make sure Hanna had a Halloween and a Christmas that year, regardless." Ken turned to look at his daughter. "She's been cancer free for nearly four years now, and we're hopeful it's all over." Patrick took Ken's hand, and Connor turned to Dan and took his hand as well when he saw the shock and worry in his expression.

"Sometime after that, I met Patrick at the lumberyard and we hit it off. That was just before it closed down," Connor explained. "Patrick and I sometimes work on projects together now."

Laughter filled the room from the kid's table. They seemed to be having a wonderful time. "Hanna seems very patient."

"She is that," Ken said. Jerry appeared bent over the table, concentrating on a drawing of some sort. He glared at the girls a few times. The light from outside dimmed, and Dan excused himself. He went back outside and Connor followed him. Dan was already pulling the collapsed umbrellas out of their stands and carrying them into the pool house by the time Connor reached him.

"We need to get all this inside. The wind will blow it into the pool or up toward the house," Dan said. Connor stacked the pool chairs and helped him carry them inside. Patrick joined them, and Connor motioned him toward the end of the pool.

"Help me cover it," he said. "We need to keep low so the wind doesn't catch it."

Patrick agreed, and they unrolled the cover over the pool, doing their best to keep it out of the wind. They managed to complete the task without it blowing away, and the cover settled flat on the warm water. Wilson had come out to help as well, gathering towels and other things that had been left behind. Connor grabbed the cooler and put that near the door to the family room.

A flash and a boom rent the air. Wilson hurried inside as Dan got the last items inside the pool house. Connor helped him secure the door, and they ran for the house as it began to rain. "Having a pool here really is useless," Dan commented as he pulled open the sliding doors to let them all inside. The curtains billowed as they hurried inside. They took off their wet shoes, and Dan closed the door as the wind whipped the rain against the glass.

"Welcome to the north," Ken said with a smile.

"I wish we could have stayed outside," Dan said.

"It happens. We're all used to it."

"I've been thinking of enclosing the pool so we could use it more, and I think I should go ahead and do that. We're not going to get much use from it otherwise." Dan watched the rain come down for a few seconds before turning back to his guests.

"We never let the weather stop us," Ken said. "It is what it is, and we do what we've planned, rain or shine. In a few weeks we're having our summer party, and we'd love for you all to come. It's a big backyard cookout, but we've had to move it inside once or twice. It doesn't stop any of the fun, though."

Dan seemed to relax and sat back down. He seemed at a loss for what to do and looked at Connor for help. "So are you all ready?"

"Not yet," Ken said. "Patrick does most of the cooking. He's a lot better at it than I am. But we'll be ready." Ken sat next to Patrick on the sofa, and they moved closer together, lightly touching each other's hands. They were a great couple, and the love they had for each other was visible. They continued talking until Wilson came in and told Dan that dinner was ready. He motioned for them all to go on in and then helped the kids into the dining room, where the table had been set up for a picnic.

Wilson was a miracle worker. They all sat down, including Wilson, at Dan's insistence, and began passing most of the dishes. Wilson and Dan served those that were too hot, and judging by the conversation, everyone had a great time.

Patrick, Ken, and Hanna left an hour after dinner. Connor helped clear the table, over Wilson's protests, and then they settled in for the evening in front of the television. Dan put in a movie, and they watched it with the kids. Wilson brought in popcorn and set it on the coffee table.

"Wilson, watch with us," Lila said, and Wilson sat down for a while, Connor noticed he seemed to be enjoying the time as a family. Once the movie ended, everyone helped clean up, and Dan went to put the kids to bed. Both children said good night with a hug and then they were off.

"Do you need any help?" Connor asked when he wandered into the kitchen.

"I'm almost done, and then I'll be going to bed as well," Wilson said with a yawn that Connor thought was faked. "There's a bottle of wine if you and Dan want one."

"Is this okay with you? Me and Dan?"

Wilson shook his head. "Why wouldn't it be? He's the best employer I've ever had." The rag that Wilson had been using to wipe the counter stilled. "I guess you know as well as I do that he's more than just my employer. Dan is a good man and I dare say a friend. Although in my profession that can make things difficult, it's true nonetheless. He's a good person and he's been lonely for a long time." Wilson began wiping again. "Now please go into the living room so I can finish up in here." Connor heard a smile in Wilson's voice.

Connor did as he was told and took a seat on the family room sofa. He turned on the television and skipped to a weather report that said it was likely to be rainy for much of the night and cool for the next few days. He turned it off again as Dan came into the room.

"Lila and Jerry asked me to tell you good night." Dan smiled and settled next to him. "They're both nearly asleep. They had a great day, and Jerry has been on cloud nine thanks to you."

"Me? I didn't do anything," Connor said.

"Yes, you did. You were thoughtful enough to introduce us to Ken. He's apparently one of the greatest people on earth, if Jerry has it right, and anyone who can put that kind of smile on Jerry's face is special." Dan reached over and threaded their fingers together. "You're pretty special too, by the way." He leaned closer, the leather on the sofa creaking slightly.

"I'm sorry I—"

"Shhh," Dan said softly and leaned closer before kissing him.

"Good night, I'm—" Wilson had the grace to look surprised, but Connor knew he wasn't. "Good night." Wilson turned and left the room. Connor thought he saw the beginnings of a smile before he left.

"I think Wilson is playing matchmaker," Dan said.

"Are you just figuring that out?" Connor quipped.

"I guess not," Dan whispered, moving closer. "But I don't want to talk about him." He captured Connor's lips and kissed him hard, making it difficult for Connor to breathe or think of anything other than Dan's firm, insistent lips. He was on fire and whimpered softly under Dan's onslaught.

"I love that sound," Dan whispered, and Connor shifted closer. He held Dan tightly and slid a hand under Dan's shirt, stroking his warm, bare skin. How anyone could not love or grow to care for this kind man was beyond him. Yes, Dan could be strong and even short-tempered, but he had a good heart, and that was what had captured Connor's.

Connor tugged at the hem of Dan's shirt, pulling it upward. Dan hummed and pulled away. He stood up and extended his hand. Connor took it, accepting the silent invitation.

Dan switched off the lights as they left the room and made their way up the stairs, darkness seeming to follow them through the house. At his bedroom door, he paused. "I've had little to drink tonight, so there can be no misconception of my intention."

Connor smiled. "You sound so formal."

"I just want you to know that tonight there is no mistake. I want you to come with me and spend the night in my bed. I intend to make love to you well into the night, and afterwards I'm going to hold you and not let you go." Dan squeezed his hand and moved closer. "I want you very much, and there is no alcohol at work. This is me telling you this from my heart." Dan opened the door and walked inside, drawing Connor in behind him.

The room was nearly dark. Dan closed the door and then released his hand. Connor heard him move through the room. Dan turned on a small lamp in the far corner, just enough to provide a warm glow. Connor walked toward the bed and heard Dan come up behind him. Dan touched Connor's shoulders and he stilled. Dan's breath made the skin of his neck tingle, and then Connor felt his light kiss. Dan slid his arms around Connor's waist and pressed his chest to Connor's back.

Connor hummed his pleasure and felt Dan's cock pressing against his butt. Up till now it seemed Dan had been circumspect about open displays of his desire, but not now, and Connor liked it.

"You're so handsome," Dan whispered. "I watched you in your bathing suit all afternoon and kept thinking of you like this." Dan tugged at the bottom of Connor's shirt, pulling it up. Connor lifted his arms, and Dan pulled the shirt over his head and then dropped it on the floor.

Connor shivered slightly. The room was a little chilly, but Dan heated him up fast as his hands roamed slowly over Connor's chest. Involuntarily, Connor leaned back and stretched slightly, giving Dan all the access he wanted. "That's so good," Connor mumbled, his eyes drifting closed as Dan made long slow strokes up and down his chest and belly. "I like you touching me."

Dan kissed his neck and didn't stop moving his hands. "There's no one I want to touch more." Dan sucked lightly at his neck and stroked a little faster, his hands traveling a little lower. Connor thought his knees would buckle when Dan slipped a hand under the waistband of his pants. Connor sucked in his breath, encouraging Dan to go farther. At the moment it was all he could think about.

"I've dreamed about being touched like this."

"I hope it was me you were dreaming was doing the touching," Dan said, the words a little mixed up, but Connor got the idea. Dan fanned his fingers over his chest, bumping them one by one over his nipples. Connor groaned deep and long, concentrating on staying upright. His knees threatened to give way more than once, and he ended up leaning more of his weight against Dan, who simply held him tighter.

Dan opened Connor's belt and released the clasp at the top of his pants. The opening of the teeth on his zipper sounded like gunshots in the near silence of the room. All that accompanied the sound was their breathing and the occasional spatter of rain against the window or low moan of the wind. Dan shifted his hips, and Connor's pants slipped to his ankles. He wasn't sure he wanted to move, so he stood still, feeling a little foolish until Dan grazed his hand over the front of his briefs.

"Oh, God," Connor moaned softly as he throbbed inside the confines of the white cotton.

"It's okay," Dan said. "I'm not going to leave you wanting, ever." Dan hugged him tighter, and Connor turned his head. Dan met his lips and they kissed. It was sloppy and inelegant, but Connor didn't care in the least.

"It's not that," Connor said and swallowed hard when Dan stroked his chest. "I'm just not used to being touched." He didn't think he needed to go into that, and from the hum he received in return, Connor knew Dan understood.

"Then I need to get you used to it, because I like touching you," Dan whispered before sucking lightly on his ear. Connor quivered, and Dan gently moved him forward, guiding him toward the bed.

Dan stepped away, and Connor groaned. He turned around somehow without tripping on the pants wound around his ankles. Dan pulled off his shirt and tugged them together, chest to chest, lips to lips. Connor groaned under his breath, and Dan kissed it away, tugging lightly on Connor's lips. Dan used his lips to guide him down onto the bed. Connor kicked off his shoes and his pants went with them, the whole mess thunking to the floor.

Connor watched as Dan stood by the side of the bed. He kicked off his shoes and then slipped off his pants and stepped out of them. Connor held his breath as Dan climbed on the bed and then pressed Connor between his warmth and the mattress. He gripped Dan like a lifeline, holding him tight while Dan kissed him possessively. Connor parted his lips and Dan pressed his tongue deep, devouring him in passionately. Connor ran his fingers through Dan's soft hair, cradling his head as Dan licked and sucked down the side of his neck and then over his shoulder. Connor tried to keep quiet and still, but Dan's lips and hands made that harder and harder.

"Is something wrong?"

"I don't want to make noise. What if we wake the kids?"

"They're both asleep, and my bathroom is between us and Jerry's room. You don't need to be quiet." Dan smiled at him. "Granted, a scream would probably wake them, but those little sounds you've been making…." Dan teased his nipple with his lips. "Like that—those little sounds aren't going to disturb them at all." Dan nipped at his chest again, and Connor dropped his head back against the bedding, arching his spine and thrusting his chest forward, hoping like hell for more.

Dan gave it to him, licking and sucking at his chest and nipples until Connor could barely see or think straight. Everywhere Dan touched, his skin came alive. Tingles ran up and down his body, and Connor shivered and quaked on the bed, hoping like hell that Dan never stopped.

He didn't, and Connor lost track of the amount of time Dan loved on him. That was the only way he could describe it. Dan hadn't actually touched him for real yet, and Connor was so on edge he had to try to cool himself down more than once. Dan rolled them on the bed, and Connor found himself on top, but that didn't matter. Dan was still in charge, and he kissed Connor hard, rubbed his back, and finally slid his hands inside his briefs and cupped his butt. Connor loved every second of it and ground his hips against Dan. When Dan slipped Connor's briefs down, Connor held his breath and lifted his hips. Dan tugged his last bit of clothing down, and Connor kicked off the briefs. Dan felt wonderful against him.

Connor pushed at Dan's underwear until the barriers, at least the physical ones, were gone.

"You're amazing," Dan whispered to him.

Connor doubted that. He was an ordinary guy with ordinary looks. Connor knew he'd never turned heads. Now, Dan was a sight to see, and Connor had difficulty pulling his gaze away from him all the time.

"Don't lie," Connor chided, and Dan rolled them on the bed, staring down at him intently.

"I never lie, and you are incredible," Dan whispered. "I'll prove it." He licked a line down Connor's chest and then sucked lightly on a nipple. Connor's eyes crossed and he gasped loudly at the intense sensation. "See, those sounds are amazing, and that I'm the one who made you make them is even more wonderful. So stop thinking you're not worth it, because you are. We both are."

Connor nodded and tried to let the words sink in. It was hard after years of not being wanted and then simply being mostly by himself. "The bad stuff is easier to believe."

Dan chortled. "Of course it is. The bad stuff was drilled into both of us." He leaned down and kissed Connor, tugging on his lower lip. "But we need to let it go and help each other. I personally intend to tell you how wonderful you are. Thoughtful, kind, caring… you name it, until you start to believe it."

"That may take a while," Connor countered.

"No. See, the kids love you, and they know. Mean people, or ones who aren't worth it—kids always know. It's part of them, and they love you."

Connor stilled. "They do?"

"Oh, yeah. They ask about you all the time. 'Is Mr. Connor coming over? When will we see Mr. Connor?' They adore you."

"That's what scares me," Connor admitted. He realized the mood was slipping away, but he couldn't help it. "What if this… whatever it is between us, doesn't work out? Then they'll get hurt too."

Dan smoothed his hands down Connor's back and then over his butt. "There are no guarantees for any of us. You know that and so do I." Dan kissed him. "A friend of mine, he's a doctor, so he knows this crap. He told me once that unless you take a chance, nothing good ever happens. And I think he's right. So I decided to try to take a chance on you."

"Okay," Connor said.

Dan pressed him closer and kissed him.

The energy between them ramped back up fast. Soon Connor was quivering with excitement. Dan slithered down his body, kissing trails and then blowing on the wet skin until Connor thought his head would explode. His cock throbbed against his belly, begging for attention, but Dan teased him, stroking and loving on him without a touch to his cock until Connor couldn't take any more and begged him.

Dan took pity on him and licked along his length. Connor tried not to fly to pieces from the intensity. "Please," he whispered into the semidarkness.

Connor lifted his head and watched Dan lick his skin and then open his mouth. He shuddered when Dan sucked him into his mouth, wet heat surrounding him. Dan took him deeper, and Connor gave up, flopping back onto the pillow. He gripped the bedding as Dan moved back and forth on his cock, sucking and licking until Connor could hardly breathe.

He gasped, needing a few seconds' reprieve to take in some air, but Dan kept sucking, pushing him high and higher up the mountain of desire that could only lead to his release. God, he hoped that was how it ended, although the top of his head flying off was a real possibility. "Dang," Connor whispered between gasps as Dan took him deep.

He could feel the first tingles of excitement starting to build. Dan paused, and Connor groaned low and deep, needing him to continue. He was too far gone to wait, and Connor began moving his hips slightly. Dan took the hint, and they moved together.

The pressure built and built, getting more and more intense until Connor could hold it back no longer. In a rush, it overwhelmed Connor, and he came in waves that washed over him. Dan took all he had to give, swallowing around him.

Connor couldn't move. He was so wrung out, breathing was difficult. All he could do was lie still and wait for the room to settle back down. He closed his eyes and drifted on puffy clouds of happiness as Dan stretched out next to him, holding him tight.

Slowly he came back down and found Dan resting next to him. He'd already shifted and was leaning close. Connor rolled over to face Dan and kissed him, pressing him back against the mattress. Dan held him close, stroking his back while Connor sucked lightly at the base of Dan's neck until he whimpered softly.

He loved that sound and did it again. Dan groaned for him, and Connor shifted, stroking and sucking lightly at Dan's chest. He was a stunning man, all lines and angles. Dan might have spent much of his recent life behind a desk, but he'd been active and it showed. There was no softness and nothing pudgy. Dan was fit and strong, and that turned Connor on like nothing else. Within a few minutes he was hard again and raring to go.

Connor reached between them and wrapped his fingers around Dan's thick shaft, tugged lightly, and then gripped him tightly.

"Jesus," Dan whispered into his ear, and Connor began stroking a little faster. Dan began moving his hips as Connor stroked. He loved the way Dan responded to his touch and filled the room with soft sounds that Connor knew were because of him. There was nothing sexier as far as he was concerned. "Damn, you're good at that."

"I am?" Connor asked, letting Dan's tongue slip from between his lips. Dan tugged him upward and kissed him. Then Connor crawled down Dan's body and sucked Dan as deep as he could. He loved the feeling of Dan's cock sliding along his tongue. Dan grasped the bedding, and Connor gripped him using both his hands and mouth to drive Dan crazy.

Dan thrust his hips, and Connor did his best to meet them. He sucked and stroked, listening to Dan's breathing and the steady stream of moans and whimpers that quickly filled the room, adding to the percussion of the rain on the windows. He loved all of it and threw himself wantonly into giving Dan as much pleasure as Dan had given him. He pulled back long enough to ask, "Am I doing okay?"

"God, you're amazing," Dan groaned between heaving breaths. Connor sucked Dan again, laving the underside of his fat cock, tickling the ridge as he sucked harder. Dan groaned and throbbed between his lips, his cock jumping and pulsing. Connor sucked hard and continued teasing Dan until he felt him tense. Dan groaned and warned him of what was next. Connor didn't back away and took Dan deep, swallowing again and again as Dan came.

When Dan stilled back on the bedding, Connor let him slip from between his lips and settled next to him on the bed. Dan rolled toward him and they kissed gently. Their passion had been spent, and in Connor's experience, that usually meant it was time for him to go home.

Dan signaled otherwise and held him close, doing what he'd said. Connor kept waiting for Dan to roll over and go to sleep, but that didn't happen. Instead, he continued to hold him. Connor rolled onto his side, and Dan snuggled up to his back, then pressed against him, wrapping him in his strong arms. Connor closed his eyes, stroking Dan absently, wondering when this would be over. Not that he wanted it to, but things like this always came to an end for him.

"Go to sleep," Dan whispered. "I can almost hear you thinking. I'm here and I'm not going anywhere, so close your eyes, and I promise I'll still be here when you wake up."

Connor nodded slowly. "I'm not really used to this."

"Then you need to get used to it. I know I could very easily do this with you for the rest of my life." Dan yawned behind him and shifted slightly. Connor did the same. He got comfortable and closed his eyes, settling in for the night.

He didn't fall asleep right away and spent some time simply listening to Dan breathe softly. He continued stroking his arm lightly and then shifted slightly.

Dan shifted as well, closing the gap between them. "Go to sleep, sweetheart. You don't have anything to worry about."

Connor wasn't sure Dan was even awake, but he did close his eyes and was soon asleep.

CONNOR WOKE to what Dan promised—being held tight. He wondered if either of them had moved in the night. Connor was warm, almost too warm, but he didn't want to move an inch. Dan felt good next to him. "Are you awake?" Connor whispered.

"Yes, I have been for a while."

"What have you been doing?" Connor asked as he shifted slightly.

"Watching you sleep, and being grateful it's Sunday so I can catch up on everything I need to for next week," Dan answered.

"You know, that's the most romantic thing anyone has ever said to me," Connor said. "And that's pathetic."

Dan chuckled and tugged him close. "Sorry. I fell into my usual pattern. I try to get up before the kids so I can work a little before they need my attention, and Sunday is no different. I can usually clear everything and then call my assistant so we're ready for Monday."

"Dan!" Connor said, sitting up. "You expect your assistant to be available on Sunday? What about his life and family?"

"I never call him before nine, and it's only an hour," Dan explained. "He's paid to be there when I need him. It's part of the job."

Connor quieted and settled down, his thoughts racing. "Is that what you expect of your people? To be there whenever you need them? What if I can't do that?" Connor whispered. "I know you built this business of yours and you should be proud of that, but how did you build it? I know you worked all the time, but did you expect everyone around you to do the same? It sounds like it."

Dan cleared his throat. "This was not what I had in mind to talk about this morning. But since you asked, I expect my people to do what they need to do. It's what they're paid for, and I reward them well for it. I spent all my effort for years to build the business, and each of them has asked for more authority and responsibility. But with that responsibility comes more work." Dan pulled him closer. "I'm not asking anyone to do what I haven't done and continue to do." Dan yawned.

"I guess. It just doesn't seem right to me," Connor said softly.

Dan chuckled. "Last month I didn't call Trevor on a Sunday morning because Lila had a cold. Trevor called me all wound up, thinking something was wrong. If I'm not going to call, I tell him, and if he's out of town, he'll tell me. That's why he's a good assistant, and why I can live here instead of being tethered to the office in Ann Arbor. Without him, I'd have to move back there, so he gets paid very well to see to it that I can live here and that I know what's going on and stay on top of things."

"Okay," Connor said. "But if you live here and they are doing the work, what do they need you for?"

Dan chuckled. "Because I'm the one with vision. I know where we're going and I make the deals. The people I've hired are good at what they do. They're managers who make sure we collect the rents that are due and manage the refurbishment or repositioning of the properties in the market. But I do the deals and put together the strategies." Connor could hear the excitement in Dan's voice. "I have a meeting when I'm in Ann Arbor for an apartment building right near the campus. The builders made a fatal planning mistake and didn't build the rooms sized for college students. So they have to rent each one to six college students in order to make the properties pay or find nonstudent renters, which is next to impossible in that area. So the building is half empty, and I can get it for a really good price. Then we'll reconfigure it floor by floor, with some floors maintaining the larger units, because there is demand, just not a whole building's worth. The bigger apartments will be cut down, adding 20 percent more units to the building. I'll be able to actually reduce rents on the smaller units so the students will be able to afford them, and since I'm close to the campus, by the following September, I'll have the building full and making money. That's what I do, but it's all dependent on timing. If I can't get and close on the building in time and don't have plans and everything we need in place, we'd miss the student rental time and it would take us another year to get up to speed, but I still have to pay interest on the money I borrowed." Dan stroked his forehead. "So, yeah, I expect them to work weekends when they're on a project, and they get rewarded for bringing projects in on time and budget. It's the nature of what I do."

"Okay," Connor said. "I agree with you. That isn't what I had in mind for Sunday morning conversation." But it certainly gave Connor a lot to think about. He lived his life by his own schedule and basically the way he wanted. It sounded like Dan did the same, but Connor began to wonder if there was room for him or anyone else in Dan's life. With the business and the kids, it seemed full to the brim. Connor was going to ask more questions, but Dan shifted on the bed and was soon pressing him into the mattress. They looked at each other with longing, and Connor forgot everything else for the next amazing hour or so.

"I think we need to clean up," Dan whispered as he held him afterward. "I hate to bring this up, but the kids will be awake anytime, and then it can get pretty hectic."

"Okay, do you want me to go first?" Connor asked, ready to get up.

Dan held him tighter, nuzzling his neck. "I was thinking we could shower together." Dan pressed against him, and Connor chuckled.

"I like that idea a lot." He'd never showered with anyone before, but he'd done it a lot in his fantasies, sometimes with Dan, who gave him a squeeze and then released him. Dan pushed back the covers, got out of bed, and stood naked next to it. Connor got up as well, and Dan extended his hand, leading him into the bathroom. Once he'd closed the door, Dan turned on the hot water, and then they both stepped into the large stone-tiled enclosure.

It was warm, and Dan guided him beneath the water, smoothing his soapy hands over Connor's skin. Connor held Dan's shoulders to steady his legs at the strongly erotic onslaught. What surprised him wasn't the excitement, but the intimacy. They were alone together in a small space, and the gentle caresses weren't meant to arouse as much as to care for him. That notion was so foreign it almost went over his head. "That's so nice," Connor said, tilting his head back to wet his hair.

"It's supposed to be, I think."

"Have you done this before?" Connor asked.

"Once, in college, but it was more athletic and earnest. This is just… nice." Dan pulled Connor to him and maneuvered them both under the jet of water. Wet skin slid against wet skin, and Dan caressed and held him. Connor did the same, returning the same care that Dan showed him.

"It is," Connor agreed and leaned against Dan, wondering just how long the nice things would last. In his life, they had a tendency to be fleeting, and he knew he should never take something good or wonderful for granted. It could be snatched away in an instant. The only thing or person he could truly rely on was himself, even though he wanted to rely on Dan…. That possibility was yet to be seen.

Dan washed Connor's hair, and then Connor washed Dan's. Then they rinsed off, and Dan turned off the water and stepped out. He grabbed two huge towels and handed one to Connor. They were fluffy and warm. Connor dried himself and went back into Dan's bedroom, where he gathered his clothes from the floor. He didn't have anything fresh, and when Dan came out, he lent him a shirt.

"I want you to be comfortable." Dan kissed him and then picked up his own clothes, tossed them in the hamper, and opened his drawers for a fresh outfit.

Once they were dressed, Dan opened the door, and the sound of Jerry and Lila talking immediately reached his ears. Lila squealed when she saw him and hurried to him as fast as she could with her crutches. "Mr. Connor, did you sleep with Daddy?" she asked and then giggled. Connor hugged her and carefully lifted her into his arms.

"Daddy…."

"That's enough for now," Dan said lightly. "How about going downstairs for breakfast?"

"Pancakes," she squealed happily, and Connor set her back down.

"Watch, Daddy," Lila said, and she dropped her crutches and took first one step and then another. Dan was there immediately, and she fell into his arms. He swung her around and she laughed. "I can walk."

"Yes, you can, honey. But you have to be careful and only do that with someone around until you get stronger." He twirled her again and then set her down and handed Lila her crutches. She put them on and made her way toward the stairs, Dan beaming after her.

"Dad, I'm coming too," Jerry said, happily gliding out of his room.

"Did you get a new chair?" Connor asked. Why he hadn't noticed earlier was beyond him.

"Yes. Dad got it for me a few days ago." He squirmed in it with a smile. "Dad says it's for use in the house, and my old one is for when we go to the pool and stuff." No wonder he hadn't noticed. Jerry had been using the old one. "I really like it and it goes pretty fast." He zoomed down the hall.

"Take it easy. This isn't a race," Dan called after him. "And remember to follow all the steps Connor told you."

Jerry stopped. "I will."

"I'll go watch him," Connor volunteered, and Dan nodded and thanked him.

"I'm going to make my call and then I'll join you for breakfast." Dan followed him down the hall. Dan went down the main stairway, and Connor continued to the second set of stairs just behind Jerry. He helped him go through the process and made sure he was on the platform properly, with both ramps up. Then Jerry activated the lift and slowly descended the stairs. At the bottom, he got off and raised the platform just like he should. Jerry then turned his chair around and headed toward the kitchen almost silently. Connor followed and found Wilson at the counter, mixing up batter.

"Please sit down. I'll have pancakes ready shortly," Wilson said. He paused in what he was doing and put everything on the table. The kids got settled, and Connor took a seat with them. Wilson moved around with efficiency and grace in each movement, nothing wasted. Once he was ready, he began pouring the batter onto a griddle, and soon he was flipping perfect golden-brown pancakes.

"Have you always been able to make pancakes like that?"

Wilson chuckled. "They're Miss Lila's favorite, so I had to learn to make them."

"The firstest ones were yucky, but he makes good ones now," Lila supplied, and Connor smiled. Wilson took off the first pancakes and put one on each of the kids' plates and set them on the table. Jerry and Lila fixed their plates and began to eat. Wilson made additional pancakes and placed a plate in front of Connor. Connor had wanted to wait for Dan, but began buttering the small stack of pancakes.

Dan joined them a few minutes later and sat next to Connor. Wilson put a plate in front of him, and Dan began to eat as well. He talked with the kids, and they made plans for the day. Dan asked if he wanted to join them, but Connor declined.

"I have some work I really have to get done." He knew it could have waited, but he needed time to think and he couldn't do that here. Dan was too close, and he needed distance and a place where Dan wasn't watching him all the time.

They finished their breakfast, and then Connor stood up and said good-bye. Both the kids gave him a hug, and then Dan walked him to the door. "I'm not sure what to say to you right now," Dan told him. "I'm not very good with this sort of thing, but please call me soon."

"I will," Connor agreed. "Maybe you can come over to see my workshop this week."

"That would be great. How about Wednesday afternoon?"

He loved the excitement in Dan's voice. "That's perfect." Connor leaned in close, and they kissed. Dan wrapped his arms around him and kissed him hard and deep.

"I want you to remember that until I see you again," Dan told him. Connor smiled and stepped to the door. He opened it and said good-bye one last time. He closed the door behind him and walked to his truck. It had stopped raining, but everything was still wet, with water dripping off the trees and puddled in depressions. Connor looked back at the house, wondering if he was doing the right thing.

He hadn't wanted to leave, but everything was moving so fast. He needed a chance to figure out what all this meant. He and Dan had slept together, but did it mean to Dan what it meant to him? Dan had said that he only had sex for the sake of having sex. He'd said that last night was more than that, but how could it be? Connor wasn't that special. Connor got in his truck and headed home.

He used the drive time to think. When he pulled into the drive, he came to a stop near the house and went inside to change his clothes. But he didn't stay in the house. Instead, he went out to his workshop and got to work. He needed to do something to help his mind settle. He also had some pieces he needed to make progress on. He turned on the lights and was about to get started when his phone rang. He wouldn't have answered it, but he knew Maggie would give him hell.

"Hello," he said, holding the phone with one hand while he got things ready with the other.

"Are you home? How was the party at Dan's?"

"Yes, I'm home. And good." Connor hoped short answers would get her off the phone. It didn't work.

"Are you just getting home? I tried the house a few hours ago and didn't get an answer." She was leading up to something, and Connor wasn't sure he liked it. "You are, aren't you? Did you and Dan...?"

"Maggie," he growled softly.

"Come on," she said. "Did you two finally get busy? Boom-chicka-wow-mow."

"I hope you aren't at work, where impressionable young minds could be scarred for life," he retorted.

"I didn't say anything wrong," she protested.

"I was talking about your singing."

"Ha-ha," she said. "And no, I'm off today. I'm up to my ears in laundry, if you must know." She paused, but Connor knew she couldn't be derailed. "So did you?"

"Dan and I spent a wonderful evening together," Connor told her. There was no way he was going to go into any details. Many things in his life were private, and this was certainly one of them.

"Fine," she fake huffed. "At least tell me you have plans for another date that doesn't include you going to his house, working on stuff, and then falling into bed together."

"We were together yesterday, you know," he protested.

"Look, I know you've never done this before and you're fumbling in the dark, but think about it. Everyone likes a little romance in their lives. When are you getting together again?"

He blew the air out of his lungs. She wasn't going to leave him alone until he gave her what she wanted, so he gave it up. "Wednesday."

"Will you call him between now and then?"

"If I have questions about the piece I'm working on for him," Connor said, wishing like hell he could get back to work.

"No, no, no," Maggie hummed. "You need to call him, talk to him. Do you like this guy, or are you just using him for sex?"

"Maggie!"

"Good. Then you need to let him know that you like him. You don't have to spend every day together—Lord knows you'd try the patience of a saint if you did that. But talk to him, find out how his day went, tell him about yours, talk about nothing, let him know you care. And on Wednesday, plan something special. Something that will show him that he's special to you." Maggie grew silent for a few seconds.

"Dan has everything. He doesn't need anything from me," Connor whispered.

"That's where you're wrong. Dan has money and can buy things. But only you can show him and give him part of yourself. That's what caring for someone, and maybe even loving them, means. I know it's hard for you, and from what I understand, it's hard for him too."

"Maggie, I...."

"Don't try to bullshit me. I've known you too long," she scolded. "You care for him and you're scared. I know how it works with you. But if you ever want a chance at happiness, if you ever want more than to spend your days working alone in your workshop, then you have to take a chance."

Connor sighed and leaned against the workbench. "But what if it doesn't work out?"

"What's the very worst that could happen? You go your separate ways and you end up alone at your house, working in your shop. Oh, wait, you're doing that now. If it doesn't work out, then your friends will rally around you and be there to listen. It won't change things. But if it does work out, then you'll have the world by the tail. There will be someone in this world who cares for you more than anything. You'll have someone to love, and you'll be loved. There's nothing greater than that."

"You're such a romantic," Connor said.

"Of course I am. Now that I finally have Ethan, I know there's someone for you. Granted, I figured I'd be married and have kids long before you found Mr. Right, but what the hell."

"Are you crying?" Connor asked.

"No," she snapped and then sniffled. "I'm not crying, but if you don't give this a try with him, I'll come over there and beat your butt. None of us gets a bunch of chances at love, so you have to make the most of them."

"All right," Connor said, giving up. "I'll call him and think of something special for Wednesday."

"Good," she said. "I expect a report later in the week."

"Fat chance," he retorted. "Did you call for anything other than to pry into my love life?"

"No, my work is done here." She chuckled and hung up.

Connor put his phone down on the workbench and looked around. He tried to push away what Maggie had said, but it wouldn't budge; it simply kept playing in his head again and again. He picked up his phone again, left the workshop, and headed across the yard to the octagonal barn. Connor unlocked the door, stepped inside, and turned on the overhead lights. He looked over everything and a plan came to mind. He pulled his phone out of his pocket and found the number he wanted.

"Hello."

"Hanna, it's Connor. I need to talk to Patrick if he's around, please." His heart pounded in his chest as excitement took over from trepidation and fear. Maggie was right, as usual—he needed to take charge and see where this could go.

"He's right here. I'll put him on… umm…."

"It's okay; I know how to talk to him over the phone." He waited and then he heard the phone being picked up and a soft hum. "I know it's Sunday, but I need your help." His phone vibrated, so he lifted it away from his ear and looked at the screen.

What do you need?

"Give me a second," he said into the phone and disconnected.

I have a project that I've been working on for a long time, Connor texted.

His phone beeped. *The one in the barn?*

Yes, and I need your help with it. Connor pressed Send and waited.

I'll be right over.

CHAPTER
Eight

"DAD, WHERE are we going?" Jerry asked as Dan helped him into the van.

"Connor invited us out for a picnic," Dan told Jerry. Connor had been excited and mysterious on the phone when they'd talked last night, so something was definitely up. Dan knew Connor was busy on a number of projects. He'd told him all about them when they talked each evening. It had only been a few days since he'd seen him, but Dan had quickly started looking forward to their evening phone calls. Sometimes they were just a few minutes, but last night they had talked for two hours about nothing at all and yet he hadn't wanted to hang up.

"Is that why we took my old chair"

"Yes. He said we would be spending time outside and that Hanna would be there too," Dan explained. He wasn't sure what was going on, but he'd see soon enough. Dan had also packed extra clothes and sweatshirts for all of them, in case it turned cool. He'd told Wilson that though he was welcome to come, the day was his. Wilson had taken him up on the free time and had left a few minutes earlier, taking the vehicle Dan kept for Wilson's use, so he didn't have to worry about transportation. Dan had gotten up extra early to clear his desk. He'd called the office to tell them he was off, but to call him in case of emergency. "Are we all set?"

"Yes," both Lila and Jerry said excitedly from the backseat. Dan backed out of the garage and closed the door before pulling down the drive.

"Is Connor going to be our other dad?" Jerry asked. "I really like him."

Dan swallowed. "I like him too. But why don't we wait to see how things go?" He was a little nervous about how the kids would react if things didn't go well with Connor. Sure, he would be hurt if he and Connor didn't work out, but he thought he could deal with it. He'd survive because he'd survived so much before. But Lila and Jerry were another matter. They both adored Connor, and if he wasn't around, they would be hurt. He figured they would bounce back, but it would still be hard for them.

As they drove, Dan began a chorus of "The Wheels on the Bus" to give the kids something to do. They made it through the song, making up a few of their own verses, and finished as Dan pulled into Connor's driveway. A small canopy had been set up on the front lawn, and Connor came out to meet them. There was also a tractor parked off to the side with a wagon behind it. "What's all this?"

"Part of the fun," Connor answered. Dan got Jerry into his chair, and Connor helped Lila over the uneven ground, guiding everyone toward the tractor. Patrick and Hanna joined them, and Patrick climbed onto the driver's seat while Connor helped them all get in the back. He'd made up a special seat for Jerry so he could be comfortable, and they all settled in, with Hanna joining them.

"Where's Ken?" Dan asked.

"Dad had some work he had to finish for his exhibition, so Patrick and I came," Hanna explained and took a seat next to Jerry.

"Is everybody ready?" Connor asked from his seat next to Dan. Dan smiled, and the kids all yelled that they were. It was a joyful sound. They began moving forward, and Patrick took them along the drive and then around the buildings toward the back of the property. The sun felt wonderful, with just enough wind to rustle the leaves overhead. It was glorious, and as they passed into the thicker woods, the light dappled and danced in the breeze.

"This is pretty," Jerry said, watching overhead as they continued along the track.

"This used to be part of a Christmas-tree farm. See all the pine trees?" Connor pointed out. "They let it go, and now they've gotten too big."

"It would be pretty to light them out here, like they do on TV," Jerry said, watching all around.

"Can we get one for our house?" Lila asked.

"Maybe," Connor told her and looked at Dan with a smile. "The owner doesn't mind. They've let it go for years and are trying to figure out what they want to do with the land. Some people were interested in developing it a few years ago, but that fell through."

Dan nodded, but he was already thinking of possibilities. Not that he'd buy the land next to Connor for development; it was just what he did.

"Is this a hayride?" Lila asked.

Dan lifted her onto his lap so she could see better. "Yes, it is. Are you having fun?"

"Yes," Lila answered, her eyes widening as a deer ran through the brush to the side of them. "Look," she exclaimed and pointed, but the doe was already gone.

They saw squirrels and even smelled a skunk. After a while, they sang songs, with Hanna leading that part. Lila got down and joined the kids on the hay, and Connor moved closer, taking Dan's hand. They didn't talk a lot, but it wasn't necessary.

"Look, Jerry," Lila said, pointing. "Horses." They emerged from under the trees to a wide pasture where a group of horses were grazing.

"Can I ride one?" Jerry asked. "I really wanna ride one."

"Not those, I'm afraid," Dan told him. "I'm trying to find a place where you can ride."

"Just watch them," Connor said and then whistled. The horses lifted their heads and listened. Then one of them began to run, and the others followed, putting on a show that had Jerry entranced.

"Wow," he said softly. "I'd fall off, but it would be fun to go fast."

"Just watch them," Connor said. "Those are wild horses. The man who owns them just lets them run in the paddock. Mustangs," he explained. "Look at them run."

They were gorgeous, free as the wind—well, almost. They watched the horses for a few minutes, and then Patrick turned the tractor around and they started back toward the house. Partway back a straw fight broke out, which left them all laughing and with bits of hay in their hair. When they pulled into the yard, Dan expected Patrick to pull the tractor up near the table, but instead he came to a stop at the red and white octagonal building.

"I'll go get Jerry's chair," Hanna volunteered and she jumped off the wagon, then hurried across the property. Patrick followed and helped her get it out of the van. She brought it over as everyone else got off. Dan transferred Jerry to the chair, and Connor unlocked the building and slid the big doors open.

"It's a merry-go-round," Jerry said delightedly.

"This was part of the reason I bought the property. I've been working to restore it for years, and while it isn't done, Patrick helped me get it ready for today." Connor went inside and then lights flashed on, illuminating the carousel inside. "I thought maybe you could ride one of these horses instead."

Dan's mouth hung open. The carousel took up nearly the entire inside of the building. There were tigers and horses, a lion, swans, even a hippo. All the figures had been painted, and most of them gleamed. A few had raw patches of wood, and Dan figured that was where Connor had been working. He looked up. The top was open to the roof.

"I have the canvas top to put on it, but I didn't have time to get it on and secured. Maybe next time."

Dan reached out and pulled Connor to him. "This is wonderful."

"Patrick helped me get it finished enough so you all could have a ride," Connor said, and Dan stared at him. "You all will be the first to have a proper ride in more than thirty years, as near as I can tell." Lila stepped forward, and Connor helped her up onto the tiger. Hanna got on as well, to ride next to her. Dan gently lifted Jerry into his arms and carried him on. "I have a special horse just for you," Connor said and led them around to a black horse. Dan set Jerry on, and Connor handed him the leather reins. Dan stood on one side and Connor on the other side to steady Jerry. "Are you ready? Patrick, start her up!"

The carousel began to move, and as it did the band in the center began to play. A tingle ran along Dan's spine and goose bumps broke out on his skin. Jerry gripped the reins in his hand, telling the horse to giddyup as it began to lift up and down. Dan held Jerry lightly and watched Connor as they went around and around.

"I get to ride a horse!" Jerry cried.

"I know it's not a real one, but that's your horse," Connor said. "It's a real carousel horse that I did just for you." Jerry grinned, and Connor smiled over at him as they rode.

The carousel began to slow and pulled to a stop. "Let's ride again," Jerry said right away, his smile brighter than the floodlights.

Dan looked back and saw Lila sitting on the tiger, smiling, with Hanna next to her. "Are you okay?"

"I'm good, Daddy. Let's go!"

"I think we're ready for another ride whenever you are, Patrick!" Connor called, and they started to move again.

The music filled the space, adding intensity and merriment to the whimsical animals. Dan loved it and couldn't stop looking at Connor. After a while, the ride pulled to a stop, and Dan lifted Jerry into his arms. "We can ride again later," he promised.

Jerry was reluctant, but went into his arms, holding him tightly until Dan placed him in his chair. "Is the horse really mine?"

"Yes. It has to stay on the carousel, but he'll always be waiting for you when you want to ride," Connor told Jerry. Lila approached, smiling and talking with Hanna. Both kids had obviously had a lot of fun. "Are you hungry? Let's go back and have our picnic." Patrick joined them, and Connor turned off the lights.

"How much more work do you have to do?" Dan asked Connor as he closed the door. Jerry was already rolling across the yard with Lila and Hanna following.

"Some of the figures still need to be finished, and I want to put the top on it. I replaced a lot of the floor and it needs to be repainted, but thanks to Patrick, it's getting a lot closer." Connor closed the door. "There are also panels that enclose the motor and most of the band organ. They need to be restored, but that's beyond my artistic abilities. They have great circus scenes on them. I have to stabilize them and then find someone to do the repainting. They were less important in the short run than getting it running."

"Did you do that for Jerry, so he could ride a horse?" Dan asked. Patrick had joined the kids at the table, so it was just the two of them.

"A little. I've never showed that to anyone, not even Patrick. The carousel was my therapy. I worked on it whenever I needed time alone, sometimes long into the night. Bringing it back to life was how I tried to bring myself back as well." Connor turned toward him. "I figured it was time for me to open up, so I needed to open the carousel as well. I wanted you and the kids to be among the first to get to ride on it."

"What do you plan to do once it's done?" Dan asked.

"I don't know. I thought about opening it up for rides, but it's out here in the middle of nowhere without anything else around it. Besides, it's a century old. She's been used hard for a lot of years and isn't going to take being run for hours on end without constant maintenance."

Dan nodded. He understood what Connor was telling him, and it meant a lot. Connor was giving up his therapy and moving on. It was time for him to finish old things and move on to new. Dan had felt the same way for a while. "Does that mean you're ready?"

Connor looked at the table and then at Dan. "Yeah, I'm ready. I have no idea what will happen next, but I think I'm finally ready for it." He smiled and Dan moved closer. Connor closed the distance between them and kissed him. Until now, it had been Dan who'd initiated the intimacy between them, but that changed with that single kiss. It was Connor who kissed him, and Connor who pulled him closer, deepening the kiss until they heard hooting and hollering from the table. They parted with smiles, and Connor took his hand and led him toward the table.

The rest of the afternoon was amazing. They ate, and after much begging and making the kids wait until their food digested, Connor surrendered and reopened the carousel. The kids had a ball, and Dan enjoyed the ride as well. Lila moved from animal to animal, and Dan swore she was trying her best to ride them all. Jerry insisted on staying on "his" horse. It was a magical afternoon that Dan didn't want to end.

But, of course, it did. The sun got lower in the sky and the kids were tiring when Dan got them into the van and all their things packed and stowed in the back. He thanked both Patrick and Hanna for everything, and then they left with smiles and waves.

"When are you leaving?" Connor asked as Dan was getting ready to get in the van.

"Saturday morning, early. It'll take about eight hours, and I'm hoping they'll sleep for some of the way. I thought about flying, but it'll take almost as long, and on those small planes, Jerry just wouldn't be as comfortable." He'd thought of renting a private jet, but had discarded that idea as well. By driving, the kids would be able to see the sights, and since he wasn't expected in the office until Monday, they could take their time to see things on the way. "You could come with us if you wanted." Dan should have offered earlier. It was very last minute and not a surprise at all when Connor declined.

"You'll only be gone a week?"

"We'll be back no later than a week from Sunday." He was anxious to be in the office for a while, but he knew he would be ready to come home once the trip was over.

"Who will watch Jerry and Lila?"

"There's daycare at the office. I set that up a few years ago because of the number of people with young families. The company provides the space and basically the families pay for the staff. They love it, and it's much less expensive for all of them. Parents can also eat lunch with their kids, and their children are close, with a lot less absenteeism all around."

Connor nodded and kissed him, and then he leaned in the open window and said good-bye to both Lila and Jerry. Dan opened the driver's door and slid into his seat. "I'll call you." Dan stuck his hand out the window, and Connor took it, caressing it for a few seconds before letting go again. Then Dan started the engine, put the van in gear, and pulled out of the drive.

THE REST of the week went by quickly with preparations for the trip. Wilson was going to stay, watch over things, and have a quiet week. Dan had told him he was free to take the week off and travel if he wanted. "I'll get you a plane ticket if you want to see your family," he offered. Wilson shook his head and said he'd stay and enjoy the quiet. Dan had inquired a few times about Wilson's family, but Wilson had always changed the subject, and Dan didn't feel it was his business to press. Wilson was entitled to his privacy.

Friday night, he packed the van with Wilson's help and then called Connor. They talked for a while, and Dan eventually convinced him to come over. It was late and the house was quiet by the time Connor arrived. The kids were in bed, and neither Dan nor Connor seemed in the mood to talk, so they simply went upstairs and let their bodies and hearts do the talking for them. On Saturday morning, Dan and Connor were up early. They said their good-byes in the hall early in the morning. Connor kissed him and then left the house. "I'll see you in a week." Dan was reluctant to see him go and stood in the doorway until Connor's taillights disappeared from view. Then he went upstairs and woke Lila, telling her to get dressed and to brush her teeth. She grumped but got out of the bed. He helped her get ready and then carried her down the stairs and laid her on the sofa in the family room. She fell back to sleep, which was fine.

Dan then got Jerry up and dressed. He'd already packed his good chair, so he carried him down the stairs and right out to the van and got him settled on the seat with a couple of pillows and a blanket. Then he got Lila and did the same. By then Wilson was up and had made coffee. He filled a travel mug for him, and Dan took it and thanked him before getting in the van and starting the drive.

It was still dark when he reached the freeway. He drove for two hours before the kids began to stir. After another hour, they were awake and approaching the bridge. Dan stopped in St. Ignace and they had breakfast at a McDonald's. Lila chose. They also used the facilities. Dan had to help Jerry, but they managed. Then they got back in the van, paid the toll, and crossed one of the world's longest suspension bridges. Lila and Jerry watched out the windows as they passed over, enthralled by the view on both sides of the car.

"Do you want to go to the fort?" Dan asked and pointed off to the side at the stockade next to the lakeshore. Both Jerry and Lila were excited, so he got off the freeway as soon as they crossed, then pulled around and into the parking lot. They were just opening the doors for the day. He got Lila and Jerry out and lifted Lila into his arms. It would be much easier on her if he carried her. He bought tickets at the booth, and they opened one of the gates so Jerry could roll inside.

"This is so cool," Jerry said.

"Just wait here," Dan told him, knowing Jerry was raring to go. "A tour will start in a few minutes." They waited for their guide, who finally walked over to their small group. He was about college age and full of energy.

"We'll just wait for the rest of the group," he said.

"We are the group," Dan explained. He'd paid extra so they could take their time. The kid looked behind them and must have gotten the okay.

"I'm Jason and welcome to Fort Michilimackinac." He smiled and began the tour. They wandered through the various fort buildings, getting explanations of all the numerous functions of the fort as well as a cannon demonstration. The entire time Jerry was enthralled. Lila less so, but it was okay. She put her head on his shoulder, and that was fine with him.

"Mr. Connor would like this," Jerry observed at one point, and Dan agreed that he would.

Once the tour was over, he took the kids into the gift shop and let them pick out something. Jerry, of course, chose one of the horses, and Lila a replica of a settler girl's doll. He paid and they were about to leave when he heard some kids snickering and whispering in the shop. "Look at the retards," he heard one of the kids say.

Dan immediately saw red. He turned to the girl behind the counter and saw that she heard it as well but seemed unsure what to do. Dan was unsure himself, but he wanted to knock both kids' heads together. Instead, he grabbed their purchases and they got out of there.

His heart was pounding by the time he got to the van. He got both kids inside and everything packed in the back before closing the doors and pulling out of the parking lot. Dan was still angry half an hour later, gripping the wheel until his knuckles were ghostly white. A couple hours down the road, he stopped again, this time at a rest area. They needed to stretch their legs, and while the kids were sitting at one of the tables, each drinking from a juice box, Dan called Connor.

"How's the drive?"

"Not bad. We'll stop for lunch in a bit and we should be there about dinnertime."

"What's wrong? You sound all wound up," Connor said. Dan looked toward the kids and then turned away. As quickly as he could, he told Connor what had happened.

"Are you shitting me?" Connor said loudly into his ear. "They're lucky I wasn't there. I would have grabbed them both by the ear and hauled them out of there." Dan knew Connor wouldn't have done that, but his support and righteous indignation made Dan feel better. "Did the kids hear it?"

"I don't know. They haven't said anything, and we left before anything more was said, but I—"

"Sometimes people are assholes," Connor said. "Don't let that upset you. It's their parents who should get a good throttling."

"I know. Thanks," Dan said, finally calming down.

"For what?" Connor asked.

"Listening. It helped a lot," Dan said and looked back at Lila and Jerry. "We need to get back on the road. I'll call you tonight." Dan disconnected, feeling better, and walked the few steps to where Jerry and Lila waited. "Are you ready to go?"

They both said they were. Dan threw away the trash, and soon they were on their way. At lunchtime, he stopped again, and what normally took him a few minutes took much longer. Dan didn't mind. The kids were happy and had a chance to move around without being confined to the car. Once they were done and he'd thrown away the trash, he got them back in the van. Lila fell asleep, and Jerry watched everything as it passed outside the windows.

"Dad, what does retard mean?" Jerry asked.

"It's a naughty word that no one should use. It's a mean term for someone who isn't very smart." He glanced in the mirror. "I don't want you to use it ever, okay?"

"Like shit?" Jerry asked and then put his hand over his mouth.

"Yes, just like that word. Which you also aren't supposed to say." Dan stifled the very real urge to laugh. "Sometimes people are mean and say things that they shouldn't. It means they weren't brought up right, and their parents didn't do a very good job."

"Okay, Dad, I won't say it," Jerry said, and he began looking out the window again. Dan breathed a sigh of relief, and they continued their drive down the freeway.

They ran into rain an hour outside of their destination, and Dan groaned in relief when he pulled into the parking lot of the Marriott. He was thrilled to have arrived, and he helped Jerry and Lila get out of the van while one of the bellmen helped with the bags. They made quite a production as they entered the lobby. Dan went to the desk and got them checked in. He'd stayed there before and they knew what he required. Soon they all piled into one of the elevators and rode to the top floor. He'd booked one of the largest suites they had, and once inside, he helped Lila and Jerry put their things in their small rooms, then put the television on for them. He tipped the bellman and then got situated in his own room. He called Peter and made sure he was ready to see Jerry on Tuesday.

"Yes, I have everything all set. Just come to my office and we'll take everything from there. I promise that, other than a few blood tests, nothing will hurt," Peter told him.

"Good, because Jerry keeps asking. He's a little nervous."

"You tell him that everyone here is anxious to meet him, and Lila as well." Peter sounded happy. "I spoke with Sharon a few days ago, and she's agreed to come up to your place with me for a visit. We've talked a lot in the last week or so, and she wants to work things out. I know it won't be easy, but I think maybe she and I have turned the corner." He definitely sounded more like the Peter that Dan had known in college. "I've decided to take on a partner in my practice. I think you remember

Donald Pepperidge. He was a year behind us. He has a specialty similar to mine, so we're going to work together and hopefully allow each other to have a chance at some time with our families."

Dan glanced out at the living area, where Jerry and Lila sat in front of the television, laughing at some show. "It sounds like you reworked some priorities."

"My patients are important, but so is Sharon," Peter said. "Like you told me, I needed to show her that."

"I'm happy for you," Dan said and clamped his eyes closed as his stomach tightened. The pain came and went, and Dan got up, fished in his kit for an antacid, and took one. "It sounds like you know what you want." Dan sat down and the pain and tightness dissipated. He reminded himself not to eat at McDonald's anymore. "Before the end of the week, let's schedule when you and Sharon want to visit. We should do it before the end of summer or maybe early fall when the colors are at their peak."

"Sounds good. I'll see you Tuesday at nine."

Dan made sure he had everything he needed and hung up. Then he called Connor and talked to him until the kids became restless and required his attention. He hadn't realized he'd been on the phone with him for an hour until he glanced at the clock.

"It's less than a week," Connor told him.

Dan wasn't sure if that was for his benefit or Connor's. Either way, it was nice to be missed.

"I know," Dan agreed and took a deep breath as his stomach rumbled again. He thought about taking another antacid, but decided it was best to let the one he'd already taken work. "What are you working on?" he asked. "I know you're either in your workshop or in the barn with the carousel."

"I'm in the carousel barn. Ken and Patrick will be here in a few minutes. Ken's going to look at the painted panels—he has some ideas for restoration. Patrick and I hope to finish some of the work on the last figure restorations. Once that's done, we're going to replace all the bulbs. Doesn't that sound like fun?"

"It does, actually. I wish I could be there to help you." He didn't have the skills necessary to carve missing pieces of the figures or to paint them, but he could change light bulbs.

"I ordered some special ones that look old-fashioned, but don't take much power. Maybe they'll be waiting for you when you get back." Connor was smiling, Dan could tell. "And tell Jerry that his horse is lonely and so is Lila's tiger."

"I will," Dan told him. "I just got here and I'm all ready to go back home." He'd lived in Ann Arbor longer than he'd lived anywhere else, but it didn't feel like home. Pleasanton was most definitely home for him, and as he thought about it, he realized Connor was beginning to feel like home too. "I need to get Jerry and Lila something to eat."

"Okay," Connor agreed.

"I'll call tomorrow." Dan hung up and thumbed through the room service menu. He picked up the phone and placed an order for all of them. Then he found a movie both kids wanted to watch and started it before sitting at the desk and spending some time catching up on things he would need for Monday morning.

DAN AND the kids spent Sunday seeing the sights in Ann Arbor. Dan took them to bookshops where he'd spent time when he was a student. They had lunch at a little café where Dan used to sit and study. Most of the time he hadn't been able to buy much, and at one point he'd worked there, as a second job, to earn some extra money. It was summer, so places weren't as busy as they would be during the school year, but the town was still busy.

In a used bookstore, Dan found some books for Lila, and Jerry went up and down the aisles of the store, taking in everything. Dan showed him the art books and ended up buying a book of Impressionist art as well as one on Renaissance art. Jerry had been fascinated by the pictures, and Dan wasn't going to deny him what he wanted. After spending over an hour in the bookstore, Dan took them to lunch, where Trevor, his assistant, joined them.

Jerry and Lila loved him. Dan should have known. Trevor was young and vibrant, and he had them all laughing within minutes. Dan and Trevor went over their business, and Dan bought them all lunch. Trevor had made the arrangements for Jerry and Lila to join the daycare for the week, and Dan had brought things both of them would want. So after lunch, they said good-bye to Trevor and spent the rest of the day enjoying the summer warmth.

Monday was a busy day. Dan had back-to-back meetings nearly all day. He stopped in to have lunch with Jerry and Lila, and then went right back to work. It was hard leaving them. At home, they spent so much time together, and here he felt like he was abandoning them. Not that they seemed upset about it. There were other kids and plenty of things to do, so they went right back to playing. By the end of the day, he was exhausted and feeling the pressure. The team he was working with was helping him prepare for his meeting with John McMillan for the purchase of the apartment building. They had to know the details of their plan before Dan could enter into negotiations. He didn't overpay for properties, and he didn't fall in love with the projects. That way he always remained realistic and was able to make money. After his last meeting, Dan gathered the materials he wanted to take with him to review that night and Tuesday morning before picking up the kids and then driving them back to the hotel.

Dan was wiped out by the time he got Jerry and Lila dinner. Thankfully, they had a movie to keep them occupied, and Dan closed his eyes on the sofa. The next thing he knew, they were waking him up, saying it was over. He got them both into bed and then collapsed in his, glad he'd remembered to set up a wake-up call for the morning. Even then, they just made it to Peter's office in time.

Dan provided what he knew of Jerry's medical history to supplement what he'd had sent in ahead of time, and they all went into the consultation room, where he and Peter exchanged embraces, and then Dan introduced both Jerry and Lila. Peter explained everything they were going to do, and Jerry looked at him, a little scared.

"We have to take some blood, but after that nothing should hurt, I promise. We're going to put you in some machines so we can look at your insides, and take some pictures. We'll also measure your range of movement and things like that."

"Will you stay with me, Dad?" Jerry asked.

"I'll be there for as much as I can," Dan said. He felt warm and wiped his forehead.

"This building is attached to the hospital, so the nurse is going to draw your blood, and then we're going to go through the tunnel to the hospital, where we'll get started with the rest."

"Are you going to administer the tests?" Dan asked Peter.

"With help of the technicians, yes. I'll be there with your dad the entire time," Peter told Jerry.

"Don't you have other appointments?" Dan asked.

Peter put his hand on his shoulder. "Not today. I cleared my calendar."

"Thanks," Dan said, and Peter nodded. A knock sounded on the door.

"Come in, Janice," Peter said. The door opened and a pretty young woman with raven hair came in, carrying a plastic kit. "She's going to take the blood we need."

Lila shifted closer to Dan, trying to hide behind him in case the nurse came for her too. Jerry took his hand and held it while she got him ready and then inserted the needle. Jerry flinched but didn't say anything while she took the blood.

"See, that wasn't so bad, was it?" Janice asked with a bright smile once she had removed the needle.

"Nah. But you don't have to do it again, do you?"

"No," she said and put a Superman Band-Aid over the cotton ball she'd used to stop the bleeding. Then she reached into the pocket of her shirt, pulled out a red lollipop, and handed it to Jerry. She handed a yellow one to Lila.

"What do you say?" Dan reminded both of them. They said thank you, and Janice left the room.

"Let's head on over so we can get started," Peter said and turned to Jerry. "I'm going to let your dad help you get changed. We need to put you in a hospital gown. It will make it easier to do the tests. Okay?"

Jerry looked at him and Dan nodded. "Okay," Jerry said. Peter left the room, and Dan helped Jerry out of his clothes and into the gown once he got Lila settled on the chair in the corner.

"It's open in the back," Jerry complained. "My butt is gonna show."

"I'm tying it for you so you don't flash anyone," Dan said. He doubted very much that Jerry was going to flash anyone, but if it made him feel better.... Once Jerry was changed, Dan got him settled back in his chair and stepped out to tell Peter they were ready.

Dan carried Jerry's clothes, and they made quite a procession as they moved slowly out of the office and down the hallway toward the hospital.

"I thought you said this was a tunnel," Jerry said, and Dan smiled as he realized Jerry was probably expecting a rock roof or something. He began to chuckle, but it turned to a grimace.

"Dan, are you all right?" Peter asked.

Dan took a few more steps and the pain intensified.

"Daddy!" Lila called.

"Dad!" he heard Jerry add as he fell to his knees.

Peter was calling for help, and all Dan could do was try not to be sick as waves of nausea and pain washed over him. "Take care of the kids," Dan gasped. Within moments there were people all around him. They got him up and on a gurney. He screamed as pain washed though him.

"Get him to the ER," Peter demanded. "Now!"

Lights flashed above him as he moved. He heard the kids crying with fear and tried to turn to reassure them, but the pain overcame him and that was the last thing he remembered.

"THE KIDS," Dan whispered as soon as he was able.

"Shhh, sir, just relax, you're in Recovery."

"My kids, are they okay? Is someone looking after them?" Dan tried to move, but he was too weak.

"Sir, everything is fine and you need to remain still."

Dan opened his eyes, turned toward the voice, and saw a nurse standing by the bed. "But my kids...."

"Just a minute," she said and walked away. Dan lay still, because damned if it didn't hurt to breathe. "I have a note from Dr. Barry. He said to tell you that Jerry and Lila are with him and are just fine. So please relax." She moved around him, and Dan closed his eyes. "Are you in pain? How is it on a scale of one to ten?"

"Nine," Dan whispered. Not that he really cared. Jerry and Lila were with Peter. At least they were okay. "Am I going to die?" What would happen to them if he wasn't around? "I need to see them."

The pain began to dissipate. "You will," she whispered, and as the pain dissipated, he fell back into blackness. At least this time it felt more like sleep than the inky blackness that had surrounded him before. He hadn't been sure if he was dying or not.

"Sir," the nurse said after a few minutes. Dan didn't open his eyes. "How is the pain now?"

"Three," Dan whispered. His mouth was bone dry, and he tried to wet it. His throat ached when he swallowed, but after doing it a few times, he felt better. The pain continued to decrease, and he sighed and stopped thinking once again. Eventually he felt he was being moved, but he didn't really care. He was tired beyond belief and didn't want to move or open his eyes. "The kids," he whispered.

"Jerry and Lila are fine," Dan heard a familiar voice say. It took him a few seconds to make the connection that it was Peter. "I won't let anything happen to them." Dan took him at his word, and that was the last he remembered for a while.

When he woke again, he was in a dark room. Beeps sounded, and when he turned his head, he saw machines and an IV pole near his bed. He rolled his head to the other side and saw the chair was empty. He was alone, and that made him sad. Dan had built his family so he wouldn't be alone, and yet he was.

"Dan."

He turned slowly as Peter walked into the room. "What happened?"

"Your appendix burst. We were able to get to it just in time and remove it. But some of the infection got into your system. We're handling that now, and it's working."

"So I'm going to live?"

"Yes."

"Where are the kids?"

"They're with Sharon. I couldn't let them go to Child Services, so I called her and she's with them. I got them a room, so they're okay. Worried about you, but they're some kids." Peter walked closer and sat in the chair. "I hope she and I have kids just like them someday."

"Thank you, and thank her for me."

Peter took his hand and squeezed it. "Just get some rest. It's the best thing you can do right now."

Dan thanked him and closed his eyes. Jerry and Lila were okay, and that was what mattered to him. He went back to sleep with a much lighter heart and woke to light shining through the windows.

"You're awake."

Dan looked over and saw Connor sitting in the chair next to the bed, smiling. Dan also realized that Connor was holding his hand. "What are you doing here? When did you get here?"

"Hey. It's okay. I got here late yesterday. The kids told your friend to call me, so he found my number in your phone. I jumped in the truck and drove down here as fast as I could."

"Where are Jerry and Lila?"

"I got in touch with Trevor, and right now they're at your office, in the daycare center. Once the doctor says it's all right, I'll bring them up to see you. I hope it's okay, but I got the key to your hotel room and I'm staying there."

"I can't believe you're here," Dan whispered, his emotions getting the better of him.

"Of course I'm here. Jerry and Lila are worried, but I told them I was going to see you. They both said to give you hugs and to tell you that they love you." Connor's voice broke. "They were both scared. Jerry asked me if he was going to have to go back to the home."

"No. He will never go back there," Dan said firmly and tried to sit up.

"Don't move. It's okay. I spent time with both of them and I'll look after them for the next few days. You just get better, because they need you. I need you." Connor held his hand tighter. "When Peter called and told me you were undergoing emergency surgery, I couldn't think of anything else other than getting to you. The drive was the longest I've ever had in my life."

"So you're staying," Dan said breathlessly. The talking was wearing him out.

"Of course I'm staying," Connor told him. "So you go back to sleep, rest, and get better. I'll be right here when you wake up again."

Dan closed his eyes and went back to sleep. Connor was here. Everything would be all right now.

He had no idea how long he slept, but he was woken by a nurse talking to him. "I'm Linda, your day nurse. Are you in pain?"

"Yes, about five," Dan answered. "It's not too bad."

She injected something into the IV and the pain faded. Dan turned to the chair and saw Connor smiling back at him, still holding his hand.

Linda checked all around Dan, fluffing his pillows and making sure he was comfortable.

"I'm hungry," Dan whispered. "And thirsty."

Connor picked up a cup from his tray and held a straw to his lips. Dan drank slowly, expecting his throat to be raw, but it wasn't too bad. Dan drank a few swallows, and Connor set the cup down.

"If you dial 5555, you can order him something to eat," the nurse said to Connor. "He's on a pretty simple diet for now, but he should eat if he can." The nurse finished up, and Connor turned on the television. Dan watched it for a few minutes and felt his eyes getting heavy. Connor ordered him some food, but Dan paid little attention.

"How are the kids?" he asked a little while later.

"They're fine. I figured my way around town and saw them while you were sleeping. They can't wait to see you. Trevor has your van, and he said he'd bring Jerry and Lila over to see you once he's done with work." Connor squeezed his hand, and Dan yawned. "That young man is a real gem, and he cares a great deal about you."

Dan smiled and closed his eyes. "I just want to see them." He sighed as his strength seemed to give out. "What would have happened to them if...."

"Hey, you're going to be fine," Connor reassured him, and Dan nodded and decided to close his eyes until they brought his lunch or whatever meal they were serving.

His food arrived, and Dan sipped some broth and nibbled on a couple of crackers before he tired. It tasted like nothing. Connor helped him, and Dan ate a little more before closing his eyes and going back to sleep.

"Daddy," he heard at the edge of his dream. He wasn't sure what it was, but the voice was nice. "Daddy, wake up." He opened his eyes and saw Lila standing next to him, her little face scrunched and nervous.

"I'm here, sweetheart," Dan said and gently brushed her hair. He heard the hum of Jerry's chair and turned to the other side of the bed. He reached out and gently held Jerry's hand. "I'm going to be okay now that you guys are here." Dan felt tears well in his eyes. He wasn't alone, and his family was around him, his entire family. Well, almost everyone. Then he saw Wilson standing at the foot of his bed. Now Dan's family was complete. They were all there with him.

"This room is full to bursting," Peter said. "We caught the infection in time. The levels of infection in your blood are on their way down and things are looking better all the time. You'll be weak for a while but should start to gain strength in a day or so."

"How long will I be here?"

"I suspect three or four more days. Then you can go to a quiet place and rest. I wouldn't expect you'll be up for the drive home for a while," Peter told him. "But you have time and you need to take it to make sure you get better."

"What about Jerry's tests?" Dan asked.

"We'll do them in the next day or so, once things settle down."

"But no poking," Jerry said, and Dan heard Peter chuckle.

"Agreed. No needles," Peter said. "For now, rest and spend some time with your family. But they shouldn't stay too long—you need to sleep."

"Thank you, Peter," Dan said. Peter left, and as he passed through the door, Dan saw Trevor. "Thank you for taking care of Jerry and Lila," he said to Trevor. "That was very good of you, and I appreciate it."

"It was no problem. Connor stayed with them last night, and I made arrangements at work so he could spend some time up here with you."

Dan smiled. However it worked out, Jerry and Lila were taken care of, and that was what mattered to him.

"Come on, you two," Wilson said gently. "We need to go back to the hotel and let your dad rest."

They were both reluctant to go. Lila leaned over the bed and kissed his cheek before blowing a raspberry. Dan smiled at her and did his best to give her a hug. He did the same with Jerry. They said good-bye, and he watched as they quietly left the room. Trevor went out as well, and just like that, it was just him and Connor.

"You had me so scared," Connor told him. "They didn't know how bad it was when they first called. I was on the road while you were still in surgery, and thankfully your friend Peter kept me up to date."

"You're here now," Dan said, taking Connor's hand. "You took care of my family for me." Dan blinked his eyes a few times. "You are part of my family now. You know that."

Connor leaned closer, touching their lips together. "Yes, I do. I need you, Dan. When I thought I was going to lose you, I realized just how much I needed you. There was no way I could get here fast enough. My family life has been a steaming pile for most of my life, but you seemed to have brought an end to that in less than a month. Trusting people is hard for me."

"Me too," Dan said and squeezed Connor's hand. "But I trust you with the most precious things I have."

"Jerry and Lila," Connor supplied.

"And my heart," Dan added, taking a chance. It was time he was honest with himself and Connor about his feelings. "You've had my heart for a while, but I was too reluctant to say anything. I know I can be a closed-in pain in the ass sometimes."

"I think we can both be that." Connor leaned over the bed, his face right next to Dan's. "You've been right about some things. It's time we let go of our pasts. I know I've been holding on to mine so tightly that it's prevented me from having a future. I don't want that anymore. I want a future and a family, and I want those things with you." Connor kissed him softly. "When you're better and have a lot more energy, I intend to show you just how much I care for you and what you mean to me. Until then, you'll just have to take my word for it."

"That's good enough for me, as long as you'll take the same from me." Dan took a deep breath and pain flared in his side. He released it and held still again. Obviously moving too much was not a good idea. "I love you, Connor. I haven't said that to anyone other than Jerry and Lila in a very long time."

Connor kissed him again. "I know exactly what those words mean. Neither of us says them lightly, and I love you too. It took me nearly losing you to realize just how much, and I don't want that to happen again." Connor closed his eyes, and Dan held his hand, enjoying the closeness of the two of them alone together. He wasn't sure how long it would last before they were interrupted, but he liked it. Even though he was in the hospital, Dan was content, more than he could remember being at any point in his life.

"When I was sixteen and Mrs. Schaude took me aside and told me that I was smart enough to do anything, I vowed to work hard and make sure I gave myself everything my parents and foster family couldn't. I was going to have it all. So I worked hard in school, saved my money, and started my business. I was determined to get everything I could from life. And I have… or at least I thought I had."

"Oh…," Connor whispered.

"Yeah. But I didn't get it all until today. My business is a success, and I've built my own family with Jerry and Lila, but I wasn't complete— my heart wasn't complete until you." Dan closed his eyes and gripped Connor's hand. He didn't have the energy to do more than that, but it was enough for now. Dan's mind began to wander and then he was asleep, happily. He knew Connor would be there when he woke up, and that was soothing enough that the pain and discomfort fell away. He had everything he needed now, and his life was as perfect as he could ever have hoped.

DAN SLEPT and rested for almost two days more. Wilson and Connor brought Jerry and Lila up to see him every day. Peter had sought permission for the tests he wanted to run with Jerry, and Dan had given it, as long as Wilson and Connor accompanied Jerry. Once he realized his condition was improving, Dan wanted to make sure Jerry was getting all the help and support he needed, and to do that, Dan knew they needed a good handle on his condition.

By the fourth day after his surgery, Dan was starting to feel better and getting restless. He was tired of sitting in the hospital doing nothing but watching television. He'd asked Trevor to bring him in some papers from the office, but Trevor had told him no. "I rescheduled the final meeting with McMillan so you can go over the deal directly before signing it."

Dan sat up. "What deal?" he asked.

"Well," Trevor said, "McMillan needs to sell, you know that. So I got everyone together and we worked through a tentative deal for the building with him. It's just a framework and you can review it when you get out."

"Trevor…," Dan said, more than a little worried.

"I worked with all the senior people who've worked on all your deals before. They said we got it at dang near fire sale prices."

"How low did you get him?" Dan asked, intrigued. Trevor looked toward the doorway and then turned back to him.

"He was asking fifteen million, and I told him he could dream on."

"You better have. I will not pay any more than ten for that building and...." Dan shifted nervously.

"Good, because I got him down to eight-five. Like I said, the deal isn't done until you and McMillan review and finalize it, but...." Trevor was smiling, and Dan grabbed his hand and pulled him toward the bed.

"Don't you ever do that again!" Dan said firmly. Then he smiled. "When I get out of here, I think you and I need to talk about some additional responsibility for you. It seems you have a knack, and we need to make sure it's properly fostered." Dan settled back on the bed. He might have to go looking for another assistant if he wanted to keep Trevor with the company.

"You mean it? You're not going to fire me or kick my ass or something?"

Dan smiled. "Not today," he told him with a wink. "I should be released tomorrow, so maybe you can come to the hotel in the afternoon and we can go over what I've missed and review anything that's urgent, and we'll also talk about a raise."

"Everyone helped," Trevor said.

"I know, so make a list and we'll see about some appropriate rewards. You've all earned it." Dan sighed.

"I should be going," Trevor said with a smile. "Call me when you're released, and I'll come over and help you get back up to speed." He smiled, and Dan watched him leave the room, walking on air.

"Someone is happy," Peter said as he entered the room. "I just passed your assistant. He had a huge smile."

"He just hit one out of the park," Dan said, glad he was still sitting up. "Are you here to talk about me or Jerry?"

"Well, since I'm not your doctor, I'll let him talk to you when he makes his rounds." Peter pulled the chair up to the bed. "This is probably the most unusual consultation of this type I've ever done. I got the results of the tests we performed with Jerry, and overall he's doing remarkably well given the condition he has and the fact that he's had very limited treatment." Peter touched his arm. "I'm not telling you anything you don't already know. Jerry is terminal. Eventually the condition that has attacked his legs, arms, and hands will begin to affect other parts of his body. However, there are treatments that we can put him on that will help delay that onset. Ten or fifteen years ago, kids with his condition rarely lived beyond ten."

"Jerry's eight," Dan said. He'd truly been hoping that the original diagnosis was wrong.

"Don't panic. Overall Jerry is healthy, and with some medication, we can hope to slow down the progression. In some cases, we've been able to add a few years. In others, up to a decade or more."

"What about his dexterity?" Dan asked.

"Initially there might be some improvement. It's hard to get back what's been lost, but there could be improvement. The thing is, the rate of loss will slow. How much, I don't know. It varies by patient, but Jerry is extraordinary in a lot of ways. He's done very well, has minimal speech impairment, and seems to be able to cope with his limitations so he can do what he wants to do. That is amazing for someone eight years old. You know that."

"I do. So where do we go from here?" Dan asked.

"When you're feeling better, I want to sit down with both you and Jerry. I really believe these kids need to have a say in their treatment. He's the one who will be taking pills and then going to the doctor on a regular basis to make sure the medication isn't affecting his other systems. There are potential side effects and we'll watch for those, but both of you need to know the consequences and make a decision together. From where I sit, it's a no-brainer. He could have years more and live a better life. But nothing is ever cut-and-dried."

"So you think you can help him?" Dan asked.

Peter smiled. "Yes, I really do. Many times I work with children where I'm trying to give the parents some sort of hope to cling to. Jerry is extraordinary, and I firmly believe we can help. I'd need to see him on a regular basis, but I'm sure we can arrange that for your trips down here. But I need to caution you like I do everyone—this is a therapy. There is no cure. We've made a lot of strides and learned a lot in the last ten to twenty years, but the hardest thing you learn is that there isn't a cure for everything."

"I know." Dan had been holding out hope, regardless of what he'd been told. Connor came in the room with the kids, and Dan brightened immediately. Jerry was grinning, and Lila was smiling as they came in the room.

"I'll talk to you in a few days," Peter said and stood up. "I'm going to give your family room." Peter lightly patted his shoulder. "It's all good, believe me."

Dan put his hand on Peter's and nodded. It was all good. It was just that he'd been hoping for a miracle, and those had already been used up. He had his miracles—he was surrounded by them already.

"When do you get out?" Lila asked as though he were in prison.

"I think tomorrow. Then I have to rest for a while before we can go home."

"Do you have more yucky meetings?" Jerry asked, making a face that made Dan laugh.

"Yes, I'll have some meetings, and Trevor is going to come over to help me. We're going to have to stay here a little longer than I originally expected." He needed to contact the hotel and extend their stay.

"No, you won't," Connor said. "Wilson came down with me, so he's going to drive the van back, and I'm taking my truck. You'll be more comfortable at home than a hotel, so we're going to drive you. You can rest a few days in the hotel, and then we're taking you home where you belong on Saturday."

"Yay," Lila said. "I wanna play with my dollies, and they're not here."

"I wanna ride my horse," Jerry said.

There was no way Dan could fight them in the face of such a united front. "I do still have some business to conduct, and some of it is time sensitive."

"Then work that out with Trevor, because for the next little while, you're not going to burn the candle at both ends and try to be everything to everyone," Connor told him. "You take care of the kids and work hard, both early in the morning and well into the night. You need to take better care of yourself." Connor leaned close. "We all need you, and we all want you to be around for a very long time."

"Well…," Dan demurred.

"The compromise is that you can ask Trevor if he'd like to come with us and stay for a week to help you and arrange to move your meetings to Pleasanton if necessary. But that's it." Connor's voice held a note of finality. "It's been decided, because we all love you."

Dan didn't know what to say. "All right. You win. I just have a meeting I have to do to finalize a deal and you can take me home." As soon as he said it, Dan was ready to be out of the hospital, go home, and be with his family. He'd almost lost them, or they'd almost lost him. To Dan, it was the same thing. He had what he'd wanted most in life and it had nearly been taken away. He reached out to Lila and hugged her, kissing her hair. "I love you so much, sweetheart." She hugged him back, and it felt like she wasn't going to let him go. Soon he realized that Lila was crying and he soothed her, rubbing her back. "You're my best girl."

Connor took her and lifted her up. Lila rested her head on Connor's shoulder. Dan then hugged Jerry, scooting to the other edge of the bed. "I love you too, and I always will." Jerry didn't move at first. "I know I scared you. But you'll never have to go back to the home. I'll make sure of that."

"But what if something happens to you?"

"I'm fine now and nothing will. You're my son and you'll always be my son. I promise, no matter what." He hugged him tight. Wilson had already agreed to act as guardian should anything happen to him, but that detail wasn't important at the moment—comforting his son was. Dan's side hurt as he did it, but he ignored the pain. Jerry needed him more, and a little discomfort wasn't going to get in his way. "I'm your dad and you're my son. You always will be," he repeated.

"But they said I was…."

Dan held him tighter. "They were wrong. Dr. Peter talked to me, and when this is over he has some ideas that he thinks will help you. Whoever said you weren't going to live much longer was full of *that word* we don't say." Jerry giggled. "You'll always be my son, no matter if it's for five years or fifty." Dan couldn't talk any longer. He was simply too choked up.

When Jerry released him, Dan settled back on the bed, wrung out for the moment. Connor took his hand and squeezed it gently, and then he helped get the kids settled off to the side. Dan didn't want them to leave, and Connor used the tray table to give them a place to color. Dan was more than willing to give it up, even if the nurse wasn't so sure about it when she came in. It didn't matter to Dan.

CHAPTER
Nine

DAN CAME back to the hotel on Saturday morning, and they spent the weekend quietly. Connor helped Wilson entertain the kids, and Dan spent most of the time either in bed or walking up and down the halls. Trevor came over, and he and Dan worked a little, but Connor limited the time because Dan still needed to rest. The best part of those two days was sleeping next to Dan each night. They didn't do anything other than sleep, but it felt so right that Connor knew he was going to miss it once they got back to real life.

On Monday, Connor and Wilson packed the vehicles. Jerry and Dan rode with Wilson in the van, while Lila rode with Connor. Connor was looking forward to it. Of course she slept a good portion of the way. Not that it mattered. They stopped often enough that he was able to stretch his legs, but by the end of the day, Connor was thrilled to see the "Welcome to Pleasanton" sign at the edge of town. They drove right to Dan's and got him and the kids unloaded.

Connor got Dan settled on the family room sofa, but Lila and Jerry were wired. They had spent much of the day in the car, so once the car was unloaded, Connor played games with them while Dan rested. Wilson seemed happy to be home and immediately began cooking. Connor allowed the illusion that he belonged there to last for as long as he could, but as evening came on, he prepared to go home. Dan said he didn't have to leave, but Connor knew he did. It was time for him to go back to real life. While Dan was in the hospital, he'd been playing house, but that was over now. Connor said good-bye to Dan and the kids before heading quickly to the door. This was Dan's family and Dan's home. As much as he wanted them to be his, they hadn't known each other long enough for him to assume he belonged.

When he'd gotten that call from Dan's friend Peter explaining that he was going into emergency surgery, Connor had dropped everything, rushed over to Dan's to get Wilson, and then they'd driven like bats out of hell. Dan, Mr. Organized, had at some point designated Wilson as the person who could receive information about his medical condition if the need arose, so he was able to get a status of Dan's condition and relate it to the rest of them.

And those kids. When he'd first arrived, they were with Sharon and Trevor, but both of them were frantic with worry and cried when they saw him, worried about their dad.

Connor drove home, parked, and went inside. He was too tired to do what he normally would when unsettled, which was work, so he went right into the house. He liked the house, but it felt empty and quiet after almost a week with the kids and spending time at the hospital. He dumped his bag in the bedroom and flopped down on his old sofa.

He should be happy. Dan was okay, and he'd said that he loved him. The kids loved him, but like always, he was on the outside. It was how he'd felt for so long, though he'd hoped that would change—and it still might. He'd simply done what he'd known he shouldn't: he'd let himself get carried away with all the people around him. They were Dan's family, not his, and that was the way it was. Connor turned on the television, lay down, and eventually fell asleep.

In the middle of the night Connor got up. He felt grungy, so at two in the morning, he stripped down and took a hot shower before falling into bed and not being conscious of anything until he heard banging on the back door. Connor wondered who in the hell was here at this hour. Somehow he remembered to pull on pants and a shirt before padding through the house. He pulled open the door and saw Dan standing on his step with flowers. "What are you doing here? You're supposed to be home in bed. Should you even be driving?"

"Well, I would be if you hadn't run out on us last night," Dan said, thrusting the flowers in his direction.

"What are these for?" Connor asked as he took them.

"I'm not a really romantic guy, and I'm a moron when it comes to gestures and stuff like that, but after you left I got to thinking and I realized that maybe you needed one."

Connor stepped back and Dan went inside. "Why would you think that?"

"Because of the way you left." Dan shifted from foot to foot. "If you want the truth, I was a little confused and wasn't sure what to do, so I called Maggie. I don't know a lot of women, but I needed advice, and she told me that I had better be on your doorstep first thing in the morning with flowers. So here I am."

"Is that all she said?" Connor asked.

"She said that unless I was completely dense, I'd figure out the rest on my own."

"That sounds like her," Connor said. "So what do you need to figure out?"

Dan sighed. "Damned if I know." He shrugged and seemed to sway a little. "I do know that as soon as you left, I missed you. We've spent the better part of the last week together. You hardly ever left the hospital unless it was for the kids, and once I got out, you were always there."

"You needed me," Connor said.

"And I don't now, just because we're back home? I need you in a lot of ways. And not only because the kids love you and because you're so great with them. I need you because I love you. I think I said that back in the hospital, but I don't really remember it. They had me on too many drugs, so I'm saying it now. I love you and I want you to be with me."

"But Dan, you have everything: your business, the kids...."

"I also need you. You make my heart do flips just by walking into a room, and when you're around I feel settled and at home. Hell, you made that hotel room feel comfortable and warm just because you were there with me." Dan smiled. "Maybe that was what I was supposed to figure out. Dang, Maggie is really good."

"For not being good at romantic stuff, you did pretty well," Connor said with a smile. "And just so you know, Maggie is brilliant."

"So why did you leave?" Dan asked.

Connor sighed. "You were with your family, and...."

Dan stepped closer and pulled Connor to him before he could continue. "Sometimes you sound just like Jerry. You *are* part of my family, and just like him, you're a part I don't want to be without. I know everything is really new between us, but you are family."

Connor held Dan back and tried to get his thoughts together. "I don't know how to be a part of a family."

"And you think I do? I've tried to build my own, but it was incomplete until I met you. I knew it as soon as I let myself believe it, and I really knew the night we were both drunk and you stayed over that first time. I wanted to hold you forever, but I was scared to admit it. Hell, I've been living my life in fear of getting hurt for so long I didn't know how to stop, and I didn't want too, until…." Dan began to laugh, and Connor wondered if he was okay. He set the flowers he was still holding on the table and helped Dan into the living room.

"What's gotten into you?" Connor asked as he helped Dan to the sofa.

"You've brought new meaning to home improvement. Because you didn't just add the lift and help make things accessible for Jerry—you helped make a home." Dan sat down, and Connor settled next to him. "Do you understand?" he asked earnestly.

"I think I'm starting to," Connor admitted.

"I don't talk about my feelings. I learned to keep things to myself a long time ago. But I love you and I want you around, and I want you to be part of our family." Dan sighed and settled back on the sofa. "If that isn't what you want, then say so now. Because I'll go home and that will be that."

Dan started to get up, and Connor touched his arm. "I have a hard time believing that anyone would want me to be part of their life. I always have," Connor said. "And you come in here offering me everything I've ever wanted—a family, love, a home. It's too good for me to believe. I know you're for real. If I didn't, I wouldn't have raced all the way down there when you were hurt. There's something wrong with me." Connor didn't know how else to explain it.

"No, there isn't. You're scared, just like I used to be, and until you give it up and accept that people can love you and, in fact, do love you, you'll never have what you want." Dan turned toward him. "You need to figure out what you really want, and then all you need to do is ask for it." Dan closed his eyes, and Connor stared at him. Could it be that simple? "Normally I'd get up and walk toward the door, waiting for you to stop me once you realized I was right. But I'm tired already and neither of us needs the drama." Dan reached over and without opening his eyes pulled Connor closer.

"Sometimes you're so sure you're right," Connor quipped.

"I am right, and you know it," Dan said.

"Okay," Connor said as he scooted closer to Dan and stroked his cheeks.

"I know it isn't that easy. It isn't for me. Some things take time, but we have that. Trust needs to be built and nurtured. But I want to ask you one question. If you were sick the way I was, do you believe I would move heaven and earth to get to you?"

"Yes," Connor answered without hesitation and then stopped dead still. The answer had come so quickly because he knew it was true. Dan would be there for him. He *was* there for him.

"Then what more is there to say?" Dan asked him quietly, and Connor moved closer until he could feel Dan's breath on his lips.

Dan kissed him, not hard the way he had sometimes in the past, but gently, ghosting his lips over Connor's. He knew Dan was tired and needed more rest, but he'd come over anyway, with flowers. "I love you, Dan."

"I know. I love you too." Dan held him close without moving. "I know this is going to sound strange, but I like sitting and doing nothing with you."

Connor wasn't sure what that meant. He looked at Dan with one raised eyebrow.

"See, I knew it would be strange. But people fall in love and do all kinds of things together. They go places and make memories, see sights, take trips—all that stuff. But I think real love is sitting on the sofa in a quiet room and being happy simply because the other person is there. That's what I feel with you. I'm happy to sit here and do nothing with you. Now I suppose doing nothing in bed is better, and…." Dan chuckled. "Well, let's face it, doing stuff in bed is pretty awesome too."

"Now you're just being silly," Connor said.

"Now? I want to show you how I feel, but I'm too tired." Dan kissed him again. "So will you take a rain check?" He sighed and slowly stood up. "I need to get back home before I can't get up again. It's supposed to be a nice day, and I promised the kids ice cream." Dan slowly leaned close enough that Connor could smell the scent of his soap. "I know you have work to do, but please come over to the house when you're done." Dan kissed him and then slowly turned and walked toward the back door. "I'll be looking forward to it."

"Okay," Connor agreed.

Dan reached the back door and stopped. "After you left, the kids asked if it would be okay to call you Uncle Connor. I told them no," Dan said. Connor stared at him and felt his mouth drop open. All that stuff about family, and then he said that.

"I...."

"I'm holding out for Pop," Dan told him, and then he pulled the door open and left.

Connor stared after him, unable to move as he digested what Dan had just said. Pop. The thought brought a smile to his face. Dan was serious. He never joked about the kids. They were the center of his life... and maybe now Connor was too.

He hurried to the window and watched as Dan pulled out of the drive. Then he went to the kitchen and put the flowers in water before he brushed his teeth and shaved. Dan was right—he did have work to get done. So he rushed out to his workshop and got to it. Connor had always escaped into his projects, but now he simply wanted them complete. He didn't skimp, but the escapism he'd always felt when working with the wood was gone.

Connor worked and over time his rampaging thoughts settled into happiness as he rubbed a warm final finish on a coffee table. The matching end tables were completed, and this was the last step before letting it cure. Once he was done, he cut out the final pieces for Dan's cabinet and stared at the blocks of fine wood he'd set aside for carving. They'd talked about four figures, but Connor thought that would be too busy. His mind was already conjuring the flowing shapes he wanted to use. They would be perfect.

Connor picked up the first piece and drew on the figure, making a few changes before he was satisfied. Then he did the second one, and it was perfect. He thought about starting the carving work, but knew if he got into it, he'd get lost in it, and he wanted to see Dan. So he put everything away and locked up the workshop before he went back to the house, cleaned up, and drove over to Dan's.

The front door opened before he could knock. "Daddy said he was lying down and we were to entertain you awhile," Lila told him as she invited him in and carefully closed the door.

"Where are your crutches?" Connor asked, concerned.

Lila pointed to where she'd left them against the wall. Then she turned and slowly walked over to them. "I'm getting better," she said proudly before picking up the crutches and leading him back toward the kitchen.

"I knew you would, so did your daddy," Connor said. Dan had told him she was astounding her doctors. It was amazing what love and care could do for a child.

"It's good to see you," Wilson said when he entered. "Would you like tea? I was going to take some up to Dan. I can pour you a cup."

"Thank you," Connor said.

"Please come into the living room. Dan asked me to alert him when you arrived." Wilson smiled and left the kitchen with a tray. Connor followed him, and Wilson set their tea on the table in the living room before leaving again with a pleased expression.

Dan joined him a while later, looking better and with more color than he'd had that morning. Connor patted the sofa next to him, and Dan sat down. "Are you feeling better?" Connor asked,

"Yes. I needed to rest. The doctors told me that because of the infection from before the surgery, I might get tired and should rest when I felt like it." Dan leaned closer to him. "I'm glad you're here." Dan kissed him as laughter drifted into the room. "I take it they're busy."

Connor smiled. "I think Wilson capitulated. They're doing Play-Doh on the kitchen table."

Dan rolled his eyes. "Wilson hates that stuff, so they must have really worked on him." More laughter drifted in, and Connor swore Wilson's was included. He had to see what was up, so he quietly left the room and peered into the kitchen. Then he went back to sit with Dan.

"Apparently he doesn't hate it that much. He's sitting at the table with the kids, and they're having a ball. It seems Wilson likes bunnies, because he just got done making one for Lila."

Dan nodded. "Maybe we should join them."

Connor shook his head and shifted closer, taking Dan's hand and leaning against his shoulder. "I got done what I needed to today and have cut out all the pieces for your cabinet. I also have an idea for the figures, but I think it should be only two so it doesn't get too busy." Dan nodded, but didn't say anything. "Is that okay?"

"Of course," Dan said. "I trust you to make the piece perfect." Dan smiled at him, and Connor's heart skipped a beat. That smile, the one that was just for him, always seemed to do that. Connor leaned in and kissed him. Dan returned it, and for a few minutes they both seemed to forget where they were as they got carried away. Little moans reached Connor's ears—Dan's and his—and he kissed Dan harder, sampling the rich warmth of his lips.

More laughter broke through the passionate haze, and Connor pulled back, sheepishly glancing toward the kitchen to make sure they were still alone. "I feel like a teenager. Well, at least what I thought a teenager might feel." He didn't have a real frame of reference. His teenage years were best left forgotten.

"I know what you mean," Dan told him. Connor poured more tea, and they sat quietly for a while, content just to be together. Eventually, once they'd finished their tea, they joined Wilson and the kids in the kitchen. They had a nice afternoon, and after cleaning up and having dinner, the house quieted. Dan was wearing down, so they sat in the family room and watched movies until it was time for Jerry and Lila to go to bed.

Then he and Dan went upstairs to Dan's room, closed the door, got undressed, and climbed into bed together. Dan's heat filled the bed, and Connor thrummed with energy, but Dan almost immediately fell asleep. Once Connor's body settled down, he rolled onto his side and gently put his arm around Dan. He wasn't sure if Dan was fully asleep, but Connor still smiled when Dan slowly caressed his arm before placing his hand on Connor's.

WHEN CONNOR woke the following morning, Dan was holding him, and something hot and hard was pressed against his butt. Connor smiled and pressed back. Dan groaned, and Connor rolled over. "I know we have to be careful, but…."

"I want you too," Dan whispered.

Connor pulled him close and wondered exactly how they were going to do this. He knew Dan couldn't take his weight. So Connor rolled them and made sure Dan was on top of him. Then he tugged him down into a kiss that Connor felt to his soul.

"I love you," Dan whispered against his lips, and Connor shivered at the intensity conveyed in those few words.

"Just lie still," Connor whispered. "I want to show you how I feel." Connor pushed the covers off them both and carefully maneuvered until Dan was on his back. Then he straddled him, being very careful to avoid the bandage at his side. "You're beautiful, Dan."

"Not so much now," Dan said, indicating the bandage, but Connor ignored him.

"Close your eyes," Connor whispered and grabbed the lotion Dan kept by the bed. He rubbed some on his hand and then placed his palms flat on Dan's chest and slowly massaged up and down his chest and belly. He kept the touch light to be soothing, and watched as Dan's eyes drifted closed. "See? Just relax and float on a sea of calm." Connor leaned forward, stroking all the way up the base of Dan's neck and then over his broad shoulders before returning to his chest. He slid his hands down his belly and then along his hips. As soon as he got close, Dan's cock perked up. Connor stroked along the length, one hand right behind the other. Dan gasped, but held still.

"If you want me to relax, that isn't the way to go about it," Dan hissed.

"I know what I'm doing," Connor whispered as his own body reacted to the way Dan felt in his hands. Connor pulled open the drawer of the nightstand and found what he was hoping would be inside.

"I was hopeful that someday we'd—" Dan began, and Connor lightly touched his lips with a finger.

"I had the same hope," Connor admitted. Next to the condoms, he found a small bottle of lube. Connor squeezed some on his fingers and reached around behind him, preparing himself. It had been a very long time since he'd allowed anyone inside him. Connor stroked Dan and waited for his body to loosen up. Then he rolled the condom down Dan's length and straddled his hips before slowly lowering himself onto Dan.

The heat and stretch threatened to short-circuit his brain. Connor breathed deeply and willed his body to relax. Then, slowly, Dan pressed up, and he swallowed hard.

"Connor," Dan said breathlessly, almost like a prayer.

"I know," he returned, locking gazes with Dan and not looking away no matter how intense the sensation became. He was so full, and Dan throbbed and jumped inside him. It felt like they were joined more than physically. Once he'd adjusted, Connor began to move. He watched Dan's face for any signs of pain, but saw only pleasure that mirrored his own. "I love you and I trust you."

Dan gasped and held his hips. At first Connor thought it might be pain, but it wasn't. Connor knew what it was, because he felt the last of barriers between them crash to the floor all around them. He wanted to be with Dan and he wanted him to see him for who he was—all of him. He wasn't going to hide any longer. Connor had done plenty of that. Dan already had his heart and he'd been gentle with it, just like Connor would be with Dan's.

Connor leaned forward and kissed Dan softly, but it quickly grew into a kiss that rivaled the intensity with which Dan began thrusting upward into him. He hoped like hell Dan wasn't in pain, but he couldn't think about anything when Dan's cock brushed and rubbed a spot deep inside him that sent Connor rocketing to the moon.

"Does this hurt?" Connor gasped.

"Nothing hurts."

Openmouthed and breathless, Connor straightened up and met each of Dan's thrusts. He was careful of how much weight he put on Dan, and yet he was having trouble controlling his own body. Eventually he ended up giving himself over to Dan and releasing the last of his control.

Connor threw his head back and moaned softly while Dan slowly and deliberately took him to heights he'd only imagined could exist. His heart raced and his chest heaved as pressure built deep inside him. He'd had sex before, but never sex combined with love, and that was a whole new experience that he knew he would never forget and didn't want to be without ever again.

Connor stroked himself to Dan's soul-touching thrusts and soon he was rolling his head, gripping the base of his cock in his fist to keep from coming. He was determined to wait for Dan, though from the sound of his breathing, he was right behind him. Connor held off as long as he could. Dan pressed up into him and stilled, his cock throbbing as he whimpered softly. That sensation was the last Connor could take, and he stroked once and tumbled over the edge, coming onto his hand and Dan's stomach as his mind soared with passionate happiness that filled the emptiness inside.

Connor stilled and let the wonder wash over him. He was careful not to hurt Dan, but that was all he was aware of. The world beyond the bed ceased to exist. Slowly, the world returned, and Connor gently lifted himself off Dan, groaning when their bodies separated. He carefully stood up and then leaned over the bed to kiss a smiling Dan before heading to the bathroom.

When he returned, Dan had taken care of the condom. Connor used the cloth he'd brought to wipe Dan's chest and then returned it to the bathroom. When he came back a second time, Dan's eyes were closed, his lips curled upward in a smile. Connor stood at the end of the bed and watched. The lines that sometime graced Dan's face were gone. There was no worry or concern, just Dan, his Dan, the man he'd quickly grown to love and need almost as intensely as air. The concept both thrilled and scared him. *He needed Dan.*

"Come back to bed," Dan murmured without opening his eyes. "You won't be able to solve the problems of the world in the next hour."

"I thought you were asleep," Connor whispered, slowly moving around the huge bed.

"I can't sleep—you aren't here," Dan told him, and just like that, the last of Connor's reservations was gone. He climbed into the bed and pulled up the light covers. Dan shifted closer, holding him, sliding his soft, warm hands over Connor's chest and then stopping. Dan was asleep; Connor was sure of it. Connor, of course, was wide awake and staring at the ceiling.

Over the next hour, the room lightened. Connor shifted slightly to get more comfortable and started looking at the various drawings on the walls. He saw the ones Lila had done, the same ones he'd seen the first time he'd been in this room. There were newer, fresher ones, with more clearly recognizable shapes. Next to them were some of Jerry's drawings, detailed pages from coloring books along with freehand pieces, each beautiful. As he shifted where he looked, Connor's gaze fell on the only photograph on the wall. It was a carousel… his carousel. Connor hadn't even realized Dan had taken the photograph. Connor, Lila, and Jerry stood in front of it, looking at it, their backs to the camera. Somehow Connor didn't think for that picture that they were as important as the carousel, which filled the entire frame.

"When did you take that?" Connor asked out loud.

Dan shifted next to him. "What?"

"That picture?" Connor asked, pointing.

"That day when you first showed it to us," Dan answered.

"Why? Why did you take it and why is it on the wall with the kids' drawings?"

Dan rolled onto his side. "Each of those drawings was a gift from Jerry or Lila. They're each a masterpiece because they were done with love and care. I put them on the wall because I want family things around me. Before Lila and Jerry, my walls were blank because I had nothing I wanted to put on them. Now they're full of things from the people I love."

"Okay… but…."

Dan pointed toward the picture. "That's your masterpiece, and it's just as important to me as theirs are. So I took the picture of all three of you looking at it and had it blown up and framed." Dan tugged him closer and kissed his shoulder. "Now go back to sleep. The kids will be up soon and that will be the last of the quiet we get for much of the day." Dan stilled, and Connor figured he was dozing again. He, of course, couldn't sleep, and just looked at the picture that hung on the wall as his eyes filled with tears.

AS DAN predicted, they didn't have much time alone after that. The kids were already up, and Dan got dressed and helped them with their morning routines. Connor used the time to shower and then he had to leave again. He had work to do, and so did Dan. Apparently a business contact was traveling up to meet with Dan, so Connor said good-bye to everyone and left, hurried out to his truck, and drove home. He went right into his workshop and set about the day's tasks. He assembled much of Dan's cabinet, consulting his detailed measurements again and again to make sure each section was exactly right. Once the sections of the base cabinet were glued and clamped to dry, he turned his attention to the figures and began carving them. The few times his phone rang, he let it go to voice mail and kept on working. Things had clicked and he knew exactly what he wanted. It would take hours, days, to carve, smooth, and finish each one, but they would be perfect. He'd decided not to do full figures like on some Victorian furniture, but ones that were more stylized and flowed right into the piece.

He worked through the day and only stopped when he realized the light coming into his workshop had shifted from one set of windows to the other and that the color was changing. Then he put everything aside, returned the calls he needed to, and went into the house. He was about to begin making dinner when his phone rang again. It was Dan.

"Where are you?" Dan asked as soon as he answered.

"At home, just making some dinner. Why? Did I forget something?"

"Yes. We're having dinner and there's a place set that's currently empty."

"Don't you have a guest?"

"Yes, I do, and I'd like to introduce him to my partner. That is, if you aren't still too busy."

Connor stopped dead, staring at his empty kitchen. "I'll be over as soon as I clean up." He hung up and grinned as he hurried to the bathroom. He showered and changed clothes in record time and drove to Dan's, arriving at the end of appetizers. Dan introduced him to John McMillan, and they all sat down to eat. They had just completed the details of a deal that made them both happy.

John seemed like an amiable man, and the conversation at dinner was lively and surprisingly fun. Dan's guest left soon after the meal, and Connor and Dan spent time with Jerry and Lila until their bedtime. Then the house was quiet, and Dan settled them in the living room in front of the fireplace. "Thank you for coming."

"I would have come sooner, but I didn't realize I was expected."

"Expected, maybe not," Dan told him. "But wanted… all the time. I don't have a right to expect you to do things, but I do very much want you to be here with us. You're a very important part of our lives."

Connor heard the words, but their meaning wasn't quite clear to him. "Dan, you need to speak plainly. I'm a country kid. If you want to ask or tell me something, please just say it."

"I want you here with us. I know it's probably too soon, but I miss you when you're gone."

"I miss you too, but I don't want to rush into things. I know you've made up your mind, and the businessman inside you runs full speed ahead once you've made a decision. I need a little more time. I'm not saying I don't want to be with you, and I'll admit my house seems too quiet and empty whenever I'm there, but I need to move a little slower," Connor explained gently.

"Okay, but will you at least come over for family dinner?"

Connor smiled. "So what you're saying is that I'd work in my workshop and join you and the kids here for dinner? Then you'll spend the evenings doing what you're doing now."

"What's that?" Dan said innocently, without pausing the little circles he was making on Connor's thigh.

"I don't know. Sitting so close I can feel your heat and smell your desire." Connor put his hand on Dan's to stop him. Dan tugged him closer, and their lips met in a kiss that took away the words and the last of his argument. There wasn't much of one, really. He wanted to be here with Dan as well, but didn't want to seem too eager.

"Let's go on up to bed."

"You're going to make this a routine, aren't you?" Connor asked, and Dan hummed before kissing him again. Not that Connor was about to complain. He had people who cared about him, loved him, and smiled when he entered a room. This had been his dream, and it was being offered to him in the gentlest and kindest way possible. All he had to do was say yes. When they broke their kiss, he took Dan's hand, helping him to his feet. They turned out the lights as they went and together checked in on Jerry and Lila before walking quietly to Dan's bedroom. Dan closed the door and darkness enveloped them.

"I love you," Dan whispered, stroking Connor's cheeks before kissing him breathless. This was definitely a routine Connor could get used to, and one he hoped lasted for the rest of his life.

Epilogue

DAN KNEW Connor was upset as soon as he closed the front door. The hard-footed, almost marching stomp down the hallway told him plenty. "What's got you upset?" Dan asked innocently when Connor appeared in his office doorway.

"Some developer bought the property next to mine. No one in town knows what they have planned, but the last thing I want is some housing development springing up around my place." Connor sat in the chair across from Dan's desk and crossed his arms over his chest. "Maybe I should sell the place to the developers as well. I could dismantle the carousel and...."

"But that would ruin all my plans," Dan said with a smile and passed a sheet of paper over to Connor. "I bought the land next to you, and not for development. I just used the company name so no one would mess with me. And I have no plans to build anything on the property."

"Then why?" Connor asked. "After a year I know you well enough that you don't do things like this without a plan." Some of the tension drained from Connor's posture.

"I wanted this to be a surprise. But the gossips in town beat me to it. The land I bought was a Christmas-tree farm, and I thought we could return it to that. There are plenty of trees that are salvageable and could be cut either full-size or topped if necessary. In the spring we could plant a few sections of the property with new trees."

"You want to own a Christmas-tree farm?"

"Look at that paper more closely," Dan said and waited for Connor to see just what he'd done.

"You want *us* to own a Christmas-tree farm?"

"Yeah, and I thought we could make it a destination. Decorate the place up when the time comes, and open it to people who want to tag and cut their own trees in the fall. Give hayrides, open the carousel for riders who pay extra—make it a family destination." Dan stood up and walked around his desk. "You only work there these days. The house could be an office for the farm and the development office I've decided to start in the area."

"So you want us to become farmers?"

Dan shrugged. "We don't have to. We could simply let the land sit, if that's what you want. I thought it would be nice to put it to use."

"No, it's a good idea," Connor said. "I don't know much about growing trees, but I can learn. I always thought it was a shame that the farm had been let go like that." Connor paused. "You don't expect me to plant a thousand trees, do you?"

Dan laughed. "Goodness, no. I figured we'd hire some people to do the planting, and when I develop the property on the other side of the tree farm, we'll use the arborist to help us there. See, I figure I can kill two birds with one stone. Create a nice development, with the tree farm next door. The trees will be great neighbors, and you can keep your domain private."

"Okay, you win," Connor said. "You always think of everything."

"I really try, but it was you who gave me the idea last fall, when we brought the kids out on that hayride. You said how great this place would be all decked out for Christmas, and you were right, so I thought, why not?" Dan walked back behind his desk and shut down his computer.

"Are you going somewhere?" Connor asked, already getting out of the chair.

"Actually, we are," Dan said.

"Where are Jerry and Lila?" Connor asked, and as if on cue, laughter drifted into the office. "Watching a movie?"

Dan nodded. "Margaret is upstairs cleaning, so we figured it best to keep them out of her way for a while. Wilson is watching them, and we have an appointment in town."

Connor checked his watch. "Isn't it a little late?"

"Maybe for some things. Come on," Dan said, and he left the office. Connor followed him through the house, where they met Wilson on his way to the kitchen. Dan told him they would be back in an hour or so. Then they stopped in the family room and said good-bye to Lila. Her crutches were pretty much a thing of the past. She didn't run, but Dan figured that was simply a matter of time. Both of them hugged her, and Dan explained that they would be back in time for dinner.

"Where are you going?" Jerry asked as he glided his chair toward them. Dan stroked Jerry's hair. He was growing now. The medications really did seem to be helping. He had more dexterity and was able to move his fingers somewhat. Mostly he was a happy kid who added sunshine to all their lives.

Dan sat down on the sofa and motioned the others to join him. He was about to run off and do things the way he'd always done them. But he couldn't now. He had the entire family to think about, not just what he wanted. This was better. He needed to explain things to everyone because it affected their lives too. "Do you remember the little girl you visited at the children's home the last time you were there?"

"You mean Janey?" Jerry asked in a crystal-clear tone. The slight slur in his speech only came out now when he was tired. "She's going to be adopted, right?"

"Well, the family backed out," Dan said, looking up at Connor. "Maggie called me an hour ago. So I thought she could come here and live with us. Be a part of our family." Connor's eyes widened, and after a few seconds he nodded and smiled. Dan then shifted his attention to Lila and Jerry. "What do you think? Would you like another sister?"

Jerry nodded and then began to sway back and forth in his chair. "Yes." Dan looked to Lila, who hugged him.

"I know it will be a change for all of us, and I won't do it if you don't want me to."

"Will you and Pop still love us?" Lila asked.

"Always. Me and Pop will never stop loving you." Dan hugged her tightly. "Either of you. You know that." Lila nodded against him and then backed away. "We'll be back in a while."

"Can we go too?" Jerry asked, and Lila nodded.

"Yes. Go get your jackets. If we're going to welcome someone new into our family then we should all go," Dan said, and he stepped out of the way as the kids hurried to do what he'd told them.

"You can't help yourself, can you?" Connor asked as soon as the kids were out of the room.

"I guess not. Are you mad? Maggie honestly thought Janey was going to be adopted, but the family backed out. I suppose the idea of raising a deaf child was too much for them. And she needs care and attention."

"No, I'm not mad. But I do have to ask: Does that mean I need to carve another figure for the living room cabinet?" Connor had carved the two flowing figures, one with Jerry's face and the other with Lila's. It was a stunning piece of work, and Dan loved it and thought of it as a representation of their family expressed in wood.

"We'll see. You might need to make our room bigger so we have more wall space for masterpieces." Dan said. There was hardly an inch that wasn't covered at the moment. And Dan had covered the walls of his office as well with the kids' artworks, and he loved each and every one of them. He heard the lift operate on the stairs, and a minute later both Jerry and Lila returned.

"Wilson," Dan said. "The kids are going with Connor and me."

"Very good," Wilson said, coming in from the kitchen. "I'll have another room ready before you get back." He smiled. "I always figured you wouldn't be happy until they were all filled."

Dan smiled and put his arm around Connor's waist. Connor leaned closer and kissed him. The kids headed out toward the car, but Dan lingered back with Connor. "Do you think I'm crazy?"

"No. I learned a long time ago that you have the biggest heart of anyone I've ever met. You rescued Lila, Jerry… and me. You realize you have quite a collection of throwaways."

"No, *we* collect treasures… some of them happen to be ones no one else recognizes." Dan leaned close to Connor and kissed him hard. He had everything he could possibly want at the moment. Connor returned the kiss, and they stood quietly together before going out to the car and starting a new journey as a family.

ANDREW GREY grew up in western Michigan with a father who loved to tell stories and a mother who loved to read them. Since then he has lived all over the country and traveled throughout the world. He has a master's degree from the University of Wisconsin-Milwaukee and now works full time on his writing. Andrew's hobbies include collecting antiques, gardening, and leaving his dirty dishes anywhere but in the sink (particularly when writing). He considers himself blessed with an accepting family, fantastic friends, and the world's most supportive and loving partner. Andrew currently lives in beautiful historic Carlisle, Pennsylvania.

Visit Andrew's website at http://www.andrewgreybooks.com and blog at http://andrewgreybooks.livejournal.com/.

E-mail him at andrewgrey@comcast.net.

Andrew was the featured author at Two Lips Reviews in Feb. 2010.

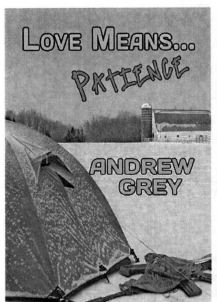

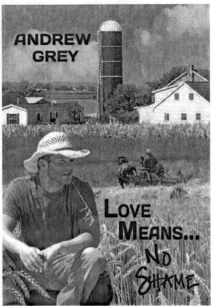

http://www.dreamspinnerpress.com

http://www.dreamspinnerpress.com

http://www.dreamspinnerpress.com

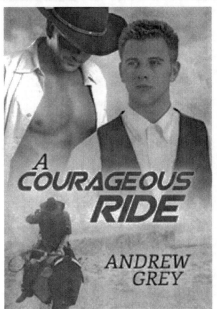

http://www.dreamspinnerpress.com

http://www.dreamspinnerpress.com

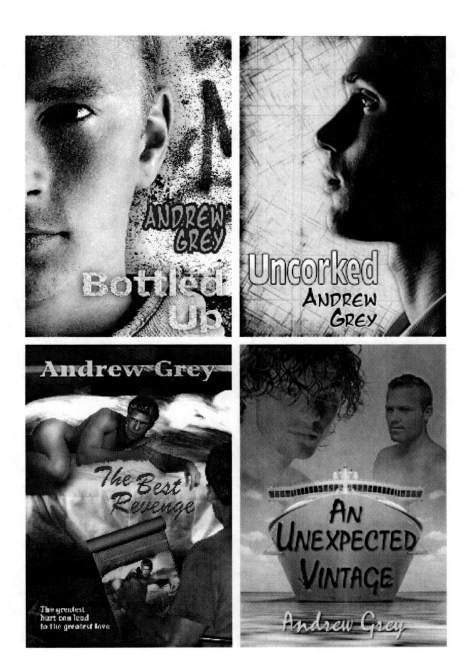

http://www.dreamspinnerpress.com

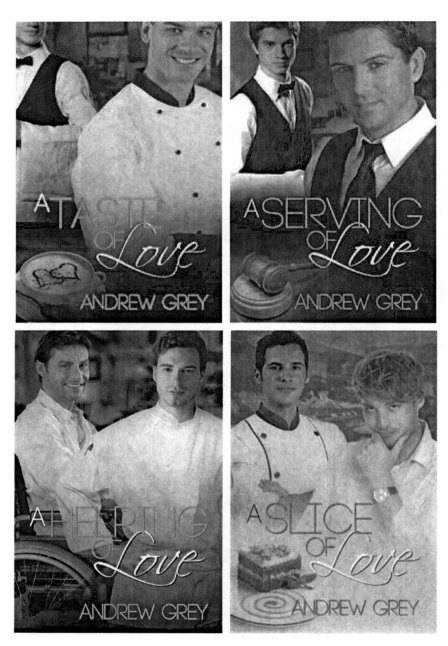

http://www.dreamspinnerpress.com

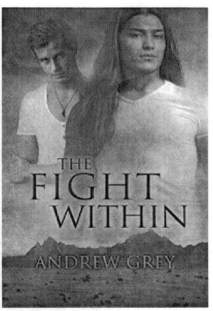

http://www.dreamspinnerpress.com

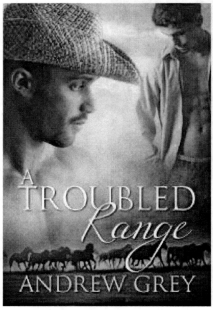

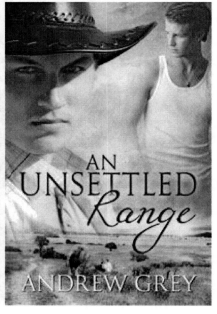

http://www.dreamspinnerpress.com

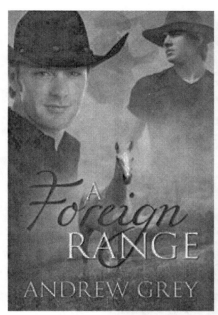

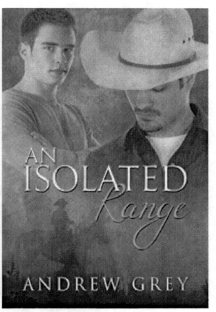

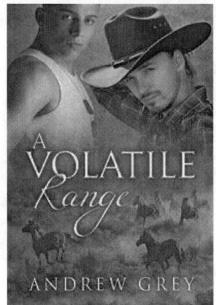

http://www.dreamspinnerpress.com

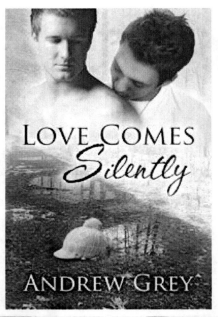

LOVE COMES
Silently

ANDREW GREY

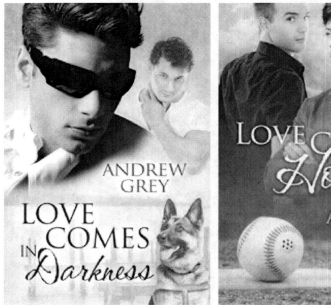

ANDREW
GREY

LOVE
COMES
IN *Darkness*

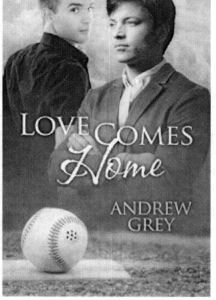

LOVE COMES
Home

ANDREW
GREY

http://www.dreamspinnerpress.com

http://www.dreamspinnerpress.com

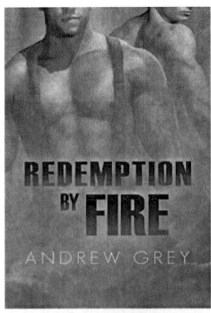

REDEMPTION BY FIRE

ANDREW GREY

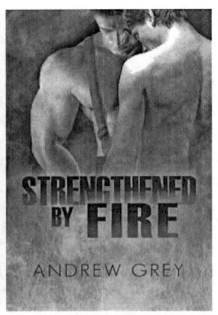

STRENGTHENED BY FIRE

ANDREW GREY

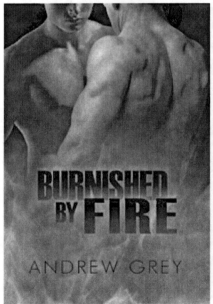

BURNISHED BY FIRE

ANDREW GREY

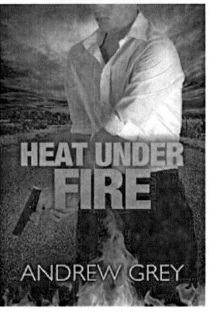

HEAT UNDER FIRE

ANDREW GREY

http://www.dreamspinnerpress.com

http://www.dreamspinnerpress.com

CPSIA information can be obtained at www.ICGtesting.com
Printed in the USA
LVOW07s1054250315

431964LV00003B/246/P